Crysxer —

Enjoy the love and
adventure

Pinka Poranya

She'd warned him, but the stubborn man wouldn't listen, and now look what he had done...

Sedna did not want to venture nearer, fearful the beast must feel their presence.

Rolv concentrated on his goal so that he no longer spared a glance downward at his footing. Aku skimmed the ground behind him, her belly touching the snow.

The huge walrus looked up from his sleep. Rolv hesitated, stepped backward in his same tracks, and twisted his body sharply, as if trying to stave off sinking into the icy water when the ice cracked beneath him. Only the end of his lance showed as he slowly descended into the sea.

Aku snapped and growled at the walrus, lunging toward the large creature until it slipped off the side of the ice and floated away.

Sedna dropped her bola and ran, leaping from ice pack to ice pack, secure in her slight weight and propelled by the heart-smashing fear of his sinking into the cold, black water—to be forever lost in Sednah's grasp.

When she arrived at the edge, his head bobbed to the surface. She grabbed hold of his hair and began pulling him toward the shore, skirting around the ice. Once she had to drag him over a shelf of ice and she made a new grab onto the fur collar of his coat. Aku pranced and howled, circling around her until she had to shout at the wolf to be silent. She did not know if Rolv was dead or alive. All she could think to do was haul him to the house and warmth of the fire. Once she pulled him onto the shore, she knew dragging him was impossible. He was too big, too heavy, weighed down with frozen water. Only her Raven power and her terror had helped her get him this far.

When Sedna, Raven Woman, and her clan of Inuit people discover a Viking ship wrecked on the shores of their Arctic island in the spring of 975 AD, Sedna is warned by the Raven Mother not to let her people kill the lone Norseman aboard. Heeding the warning, she stands between him and her angry tribe, causing her people to shun and distrust her. Thanks to her intervention, the Viking, Rolv, lives to repair his ship and sail to his home on a nearby island, where he has been banished for a year by his father, Eric the Red, in Greenland. When Rolv leaves Sedna's island, he kidnaps her, certain that her own people will slay her as punishment for defending an outsider. But he knows nothing of how to survive in the harsh environment and, without Sedna, would surely perish during the coming winter. But even if she can keep this strong, stubborn Norseman fed, clothed, and warm, despite the dangers of her icy home, how can she keep him safe from her people who continually stalk them and what will she do with her heart, when he leaves her world to return to his father in Greenland once the spring has come again?

KUDOS for *Sedna, North Star, Raven Woman*

In *Sedna North Star Raven Woman* by Pinkie Paranya, Sedna and her tribe of Inuit people discover a Viking whose ship has run aground on the shores of their Arctic island in 975 A.D. Sedna, who is a shaman of her people and a Raven Woman, is warned by the Raven Mother not to let her tribe kill the Viking, Rolv. If they do, it will go very bad for them. So Sedna warns her people, who accuse her of taking his side against them. When the Rolv's injuries have healed and he is able to repair his ship and leave the island, he kidnaps Sedna, fearing that her people will kill her for protecting him. He and Sedna fall in love, combining their two worlds and customs and changing both of their lives forever. Like the first two books in the series, this one is well written and makes you feel like you are right there in the Inuit village with Sedna and Rolv or on his strange Viking ship. The story has a strong plot, filled with twists and turns, and takes you back to a time long ago when life hung on by a thin precarious thread. ~ Taylor Jones, Reviewer

Sedna, North Star, Raven Woman by Pinkie Paranya is the third in the *Women of the Northlands* trilogy. This one revolves around Sedna, the Raven Woman and shaman of her Inuit clan. In the spring of 975 AD, Sedna finds an injured Viking and his damaged ship on the shores of her island in the Arctic. Her people want to kill him, as he is an outsider, but Sedna gets a warning from the Raven Mother, the first in the long line of Raven Women, that this man is very important to the Raven Women line and she must not let him die. So she and her wolf Aku stand between her people and the stranger, Rolv. She tells her people what the Raven Mother has said. Out of respect for, and fear of, her powers, the people back off and allow the man to live. Sedna takes him back to her summer dwelling, which she shares with her elderly mother and father, and nurses him back to health. But the tribe is unhappy with the situation and is only holding off until the old shaman, the more powerful one, and the hunters return from the hunt, including Sedna's betrothed. But Rolv fears for her life when the men return so he coaxes her onto the ship and sails away before she can get off. It is a move that will bring them both happiness and tragedy, but neither will ever be the same again. *Sedna, North Star, Raven Woman* is, in my opinion, the best of the trilogy. As well written as the others, with vivid descriptions and the author's deep knowledge of both ancient history and the Inuit people, this story weaves in a sweet romance, among the suspense of the plot and the dangers of life in that time, that pulls you in and warms your heart. Bravo, Paranya!

ACKNOWLEDGEMENTS

Faith, my editor at Black Opal Books, has worked her usual excellent editorial magic. Thank you.

Jack from Black Opal's Art Department, is a master at insightful, vibrant covers. I appreciate all the covers you have made for me.

Many thanks to my loyal readers who have impatiently awaited the arrival of the third book in the *Women of the Northland* trilogy.

SEDNA
NORTH STAR
RAVEN WOMAN

PINKIE PARANYA

A Black Opal Books Publication

GENRE: HISTORICAL ROMANCE/ADVENTURE

This is a work of fiction. Names, places, characters and incidents are either the product of the author's imagination or are used fictitiously, and any resemblance to any actual persons, living or dead, businesses, organizations, events or locales is entirely coincidental. All trademarks, service marks, registered trademarks, and registered service marks are the property of their respective owners and are used herein for identification purposes only. The publisher does not have any control over or assume any responsibility for author or third-party websites or their contents.

DEDICATION

Much love to kindred authors, R. L. George, Ramona Forrest, Jannifer Hoffman, Ellynore Seybold-Smith, Joanne Taylor Moore, and Debbie Lee and June Agur, author and photographer.

CHAPTER 1

A.D. 975:

Sedna heard the high pitched, excited voices rising in hysterical anger, tinged with fear. "Kill him! Kill him!"
Children shrieked and screamed, the sounds merging with the people's shouts, ripping the smooth arctic evening apart in shreds.

She stood aside from the crowd rushing in one body toward a beach. The sky was no longer sunny, but a dull gray and she smelled snow in the air. Squat huts scattered over the tundra and, behind the huts, fish dryers fashioned of odd pieces of driftwood. The chill wind off the water seared her flesh like a burn, even under the heavy furs she wore.

As a shaman, she had just returned from a mind-journey to speak with Tulunixiraq, the Raven Mother. Now the pandemonium surrounding her crawled beneath her skin and became a part of her aching head as she struggled to normalize her thoughts.

"Sedna! Come and see the stranger. We need you to intercede for us," one of the men called to her, just barely interrupting his headlong rush to follow the others.

People hurried by, shouting excitedly. "Come! Come!"

Others in the crowd slowed to shout at her on their dash to the beach. "The people need your counsel. Sedna, come!"

She looked down into the yellow, feral eyes of a snarling wolf and touched her hand to the animal's head to calm her.

Sedna's father hurried from behind, limping along with a crutch made of a gnarled piece of driftwood, while her mother passed him and clutched her arm. "Daughter, now is not a good time to stand dreaming." The older woman pulled Sedna along, without waiting for the old man.

Sedna bumped into a person ahead of her who wore a bulky sealskin coat. That person gave way respectfully. "Hiyah, hiyah," she murmured, pushing away her parka to feel the ivory belt she wore as the next Raven Woman.

The crowd parted, making way for her until she stood in the forefront of the group. At her feet was a large, dark shape of a man lying face up on the beach.

She cried out in remembrance of the thoughts that had come to her in her trance. She recognized the body at her feet as that of a Viking. The ship beached in front of her was a Norse sailing vessel. Shock and fright warred with fascinated surprise as she wondered how she knew the strange words that had come into her head.

Sedna murmured a chant to protect the villagers. This man was one of *them*. A *kablunaet*, a giant white man. She moved closer. The man's head was wet and dirty from the sand, but she could see his hair was not black, like everyone she had ever known. His hair came to his shoulders while the men in her village wore theirs cropped to reach their chins. She swallowed hard, seeing for the first time, the bottom of his face and the area under his nose covered with a curly mass of red hair that caught fire from the sun which momentarily split apart the clouds.

She closed her eyes and murmured a brief chant to the Raven Mother and also to Sednah, her namesake and goddess of the sea. Why would a wondrous creature such as Sednah show her disrespect to the people by casting this stranger on their shores?

Men prodded the sprawled body stretched in awesome length upon the sand, but carefully, with their spears. The children poked at his legs with long sticks.

A force within Sedna caused her to pause, considering the unfamiliar memories whirling through her mind. Anything was possible with shaman, especially in such a grave situation, but how did she come to know who this man was? What he was? Why did she name him Viking when the people's name for these giant white men was *kablunaet*? The man was from the other side of the island, the place-of-giants-who-walked-with-heads-touching-the-sun.

The stranger bled profusely from a cut on his forehead. A harpoon might have gone into his arm. Blood also seeped from a large rent in the shaggy fur he wore over his back. She bent to look more closely, to determine if he was safely dead in spite of the bleeding. When he opened his eyes to stare up at her, she almost fell over backward, a very bad sign for a shaman.

His eyes were as gray as the sky above them, as gray as plumed smoke rising from a fireplace. She had never seen any color of eyes but black. He raised his hand and she jumped away, unwilling to be touched by the stranger. Who knew what damaged a shaman's powers?

Instantly the surrounding Inuit jabbed lances at him, none too gently, and he subsided with a shuddering sigh. As though gaining strength from their pitiless hostility, he

glared at them and began to speak in their tongue. He
used halting small words incorrectly, such as a child
might utter, but understandable.

Did Sednah the Goddess of the Sea, in her mysterious
wisdom, thrust this creature up to them for a purpose?
Was this a sign? Was he a *wiivaksaat,* one of those who
left their body behind and came around again?

The people surged forward, striving to hear. A barrage
of black eyes focused first on Sedna, then on the stranger,
then on Sedna again. She knew their thoughts. They
might have spoken out loud. They wished for the old
shaman, Analusha, but since he was out hunting, she
must ward off the demon.

Analusha would have had one of his writhing fits by
now. His dramatic display of ferocity was a favorite with
the little band of Inuit. He usually whirled around and
around in one place, dancing his weird dance until blood
seeped from the corners of his mouth. At the end of his
ritual he collapsed in a heap and the crowd waited in awe
until he awoke to tell them where he had journeyed and
what his decision would be.

Sedna did not wish for this power. It was not her way.
Perhaps that was the reason the people would never fear
her as they did Analusha. Without fear, there was not as
much respect.

The stranger struggled to his feet. She could tell the
pain made him dizzy and weak and she felt his concern,
surrounded by a circle of people who looked like small,
angry bears.

He stared down at them. "Are you trolls then? You resemble dwarfs—unfinished people. *Skraelings*, that is
what we call you," he concluded with contempt.

Sedna felt amazed that she understood many of his
words. Her visit inside the glacier with the Raven Mother
had changed everything.

He brushed away the weapons poking him. In spite of his weakness, he glared at his captors without fear. Unlike the milder brown bear, he was like one of the giant polar bears, *naanuk*, a force that even the bravest hunter hesitated to face.

Apparently sensing movement at his back, he turned "Leave my ship! Do not touch it!" His words carried authority. His deep voice sliced through the cold, dry air, startling those who had gained enough courage to touch mittens to his sailing craft. Women who had begun to gather the broken boards scattered on the beach, stopped. The ferocity in his thundering voice frightened them so they dropped their burdens and ran back away from him.

Sedna remembered two summers ago, when she had only fourteen sticks on her mother's floor to show her age. Strangers, much like this one, arrived at their summer hunting area across the woodland on the other side of the island.

She recalled huge ships as big as glaciers, ships with fierce, ugly faces carved in front to split aside the water. Her people had watched, hidden, when the strangers entered the mouth of the valley.

Unlike their own small skin boats, which could hide nothing, those giant ships disgorged amazing quantities from their bellies. Giant men, women, and children appeared—faces pale like snow and hair the color of fresh blood or like the sun. They were strange beings that should not exist on the Earth.

An ancient crone echoed Sedna's thoughts. "We had to move from our own shores, leave our good summer underground dwellings because of these men, do you not remember?"

"Yah! Yah!" voices mournfully intoned, with anger seeping around the edges.

"Last season of the sun, four brave seal hunters ventured close to look again upon these strangers. The hunters were captured, only two at last returned to us, two have never again been seen."

As if on a signal, the families of the two missing men began the death chant.

In the rear, a man shouted and the cry was taken up by the crowd. "We seek revenge for our dead!"

Sedna frowned. With a simple gesture she could have the man punctured by a handful of harpoons and lances and the incident would be ended. Perhaps that was the best decision. She looked up into the stranger's face, her own body experiencing the pain of his wounds. He swayed, but remained upright. The icy wind off the water had chilled his skin, and the bleeding ceased. His face beneath the hair looked as white as the snow against the side of the nearby hill.

She still detected no sign of fear from him.

Their stares met, locking in place so that she might never be able to look away. She sensed his surprise at their bonding and his eyes held a message she could not fathom. She knew this person from somewhere in time. Chills ran up her arms beneath the heavy fur as she studied the stranger.

'*He is the one. He must not die.*' The Raven Mother spoke again inside her head. Sedna slipped off her belt and turned to the crowd, holding the belt high. "We will not slay him. Wait and see what this person has to tell us. He is a sign from the sea. We must not permit anger and a thirst for vengeance to interfere."

"Analusha will be angry when he returns," shouted one of the men.

"Aya, aya," many voices intoned.

A woman's voice rang out. "Who then will be responsible for admitting a killer whale into the midst of seals?"

Sedna's parents moved close beside her, showing their

support. She thanked them with a look of affection. "The Raven will be responsible," she said, turning from her beloved parents to face the animosity in the villagers' stares. She met each individual's glare with her own calm one and fastened the Raven Belt around her waist again.

The villagers turned and headed back toward their dwellings. She and the two old people were left to face the stranger. A noise made her whirl in time to see the big man crumple to the beach. Before she gave it too much thought, she ran to his side and knelt, needing to touch him, to impart some of her strength until he regained his. Those strange gray eyes were closed, he was breathing deeply as if in sleep. She stood and faced her mother and father.

"Do you truly wish to be here?" She feathered her fingers gently over her mother's wrinkled brown cheek in the Inuit's age-old gesture of love. "The people may become even more angry after thinking overlong on this. They could leap upon us—slay us all."

"We believe you are a more powerful *angokok* than even the old shaman," her mother said with a calm that did not agree with the unrest in her eyes.

Her father, always the practical one, asked the question. "Must we build a shelter over him?"

It hurt to see a once-proud man ask a mere woman, a daughter, such a question. Because Suutak had been wounded by the tusks of a fierce walrus on a hunt long ago, the village had to provide them with food. The people gave them meat mostly because Sedna was shaman and they were afraid not to. Suutak deferred to her as one would a provider.

"A daughter thinks it would be well to drag him by his feet if we have to," Sedna said. "The people may return and slay him."

"You mean we must *touch him*?" Her mother's expression registered horror. She stood on her toes as she often did to peer up into Sedna's face, cocking her head sideways so that she resembled the little summer squirrel, *siksik*. "You are different since you came back from speaking with the Raven Mother and looked upon this man. My daughter the shaman would have had this man thrown back into the water to die and leave us in peace."

Sedna understood her agitation. Her mother, Kuliit, sensed the transformation that happened within her just before the arrival of the Viking on their shores.

The man on the beach stirred and groaned.

The three waited anxiously until he opened his eyes.

"What curious eyes, the color of seal's skin," her father said.

"I can walk, if you only support me a little," the man said as he struggled to his feet again. In spite of the below-freezing wind, his face broke out in beads of sweat.

Sedna took his arm. She had understood most of his speech, though he mixed the broken Inuit language with his own.

"Daughter, do not touch him. Take my walking stick."

Sedna stared at her father in surprise. That stick was his totem, he never went anywhere without it. If the stranger defiled it, he would have to burn it or leave it out on the ice.

Her mother and father stood apart, their fear of the stranger even stronger than their concern for their daughter.

"Stay away," Sedna commanded them. "I am shaman. He cannot harm me." She was not sure of this. Sometimes through trickery, a shaman's power could be diminished or destroyed for short periods, or forever. She didn't know why she was willing to risk it for this man, except that his presence called to something deep within her. To him she said, "It is not far to our home. Lean on me if you must." Sedna was not certain if he understood her words, but he knew by gestures what she wanted him to do. The feel of his long body against her, his arm held within her own nearly made her stumble. Beneath the furs both of them wore she imagined she could feel his hot skin. A peculiar, thick sense of uneasy pleasure threaded through her body. Her husband-to-be, Nagatok, had mated with her two times, yet she had never felt this pleasurable sense of anticipation before. Was this man some kind of a shaman in his world? Had he enchanted her? She did not want to look up into the stranger's face, nor stare into his eyes, else her feet would not move.

They hobbled along, the old people trailing a safe distance behind. All the while, Sedna's whirling thoughts dizzied her. The knowledge that this was what her Raven belt commanded caused a soft warmth to emanate from the ivory links encircling her middle. When the man clamped his big hand on her shoulder for support, she touched the Raven belt with her sealskin mitten to give her courage. No one spoke as they made way through the swirling mists of the incoming fog.

When they neared their hut, people gathered to watch, standing away to avoid being harmed by strange magic. "When Nagatok returns, he will be angry," an old woman muttered.

The union between Nagatok and Sedna had been arranged since her birth by their parents. With circumstances changed since Suutak's injury and loss of hunting ability, Nagatok's father would have liked to cancel the promise but could not, with honor.

"I am glad Nagatok has gone hunting with the shaman," Sedna's mother said in a low voice. "He hates strangers more than any of us since his brother was one of the hunters slain by these terrible people."

"We do not know they were slain, do we?" Sedna

asked the question in what she thought a reasonable way.
"They could be prisoners."

She had seen visions of the two men, captives in a
dark place below the water on a boat like the Viking's,
only much larger. She saw the waves sloshing alongside
the ship and a long journey for the two Inuit men to a
land far across the water. They were kept alive, fed well,
and cared for like caged bears. Now was not the time to
share her vision.

"To be captured as slaves of the white men is worse
than death," her mother said, as if guessing some of
Sedna's thoughts.

Kuliit hobbled ahead to lift the flap of caribou skin
over the doorway for her daughter. Sedna hesitated per-
ceptibly at the entrance of the skin and whale rib dwelling
and then bent down to enter. The man crawled in behind
her, dropped, and lay panting like a spent animal from his
exertion. His long legs stretched out to fill most of the
interior.

"We can sleep outside," her father said dryly.

Sedna hid her giggle behind her hand. He was known
for his joking and the song-stories from his memory. Perhaps that was another reason the people were willing to
share their food supply with the little family.

The stranger seemed to understand their discussion.
He pushed himself up against one wall and sat, with
knees drawn close to his chest to make room for them.
"My vessel—will they carry it away piece by piece?" He
sounded more worried about his ship than his injuries.

Sedna only understood him after he repeated his words
slowly, mixed with some of her own language. "No. They
will leave it alone until Analusha returns from the hunt to
advise them."

"Who is Analusha? Is he your chieftain?"

"Analusha is the old shaman. His name means 'excrement of wolves' because when he was young, before even my mother came upon this Earth, he slept with wolves and foxes, in preference to human companionship. He wears his name with pride. He will return soon. Do not worry over matters you cannot control."

He made a wry face. "Wise words coming from a child."

Sedna leaped to her feet, her head almost brushed the low ceiling. "I am not a child."

"Shush, daughter, you act as one," her mother said. "Tend to his wounds. You have touched him already. What is done is settled."

Blood had begun to seep out again with the warmth inside the close confines of the hut. The hollowed-out stones of the lamps shed a ghostly light with the burning oil flickering and dancing over the walls and the ceiling of the dome-shaped dwelling.

"Remove your tunic so I may see where you are wounded," Sedna ordered with a firmness to her voice she was far from feeling. This man filled her with strange emotions she could not quite tie together with her thoughts.

He shrugged wide shoulders, the gesture divesting himself of the bloodied and torn cloth. Kuliit picked up the material between callused fingers, her expression filled with wonder and curiosity that outweighed her fear of the stranger. "What manner of skin is this?"

"It is no skin." He winced and moved to sit upright. Sedna placed a clump of clean moss on his arm to staunch the flow of blood. "It is a woven cloth from the sheep in our pasture." He struggled with the mixing of two languages.

Sedna laid another clump of dampened moss against his feverish forehead. Only great resolution allowed her to take his hand and place it against the moss, indicating he was to hold it in place. Where their hands touched, she felt a burning sensation, as though her fingers had dipped into the hot, melted-blubber lamp. She should have been disgusted, but instead wanted to touch him even more.

Kuliit stirred the bubbling, gurgling pot of seal meat and busied herself preparing the meal. Her brow puckered with worry, which saddened Sedna. Her parents had already been very old when she was born. Everyone in the village and even in faraway villages had been shocked when old Kuliit became big with child after being barren the whole of her life. Instead of choosing a name from a departed ancestor to help bring a soul back to life, as was the custom, Kuliit named her child Sedna. Thus she was born a shaman and the next Raven Woman.

As shaman, she must use her strongest powers to cure this stranger and remove him from their tent before Nagatok and the old shaman returned, or they would all suffer. The thought of the shaman returning and working magic on the helpless Viking was almost more than she could stand. She must call the people together for the ceremony of summoning the spirits, to see into the future and how much time she had to cure him so that he could leave without harm coming to him. The shaman would surely inflict vengeance on her family for what she had done without his permission, but he would be less angry if he came home and found no intruder to heighten his wrath.

Sedna studied the stranger. In spite of his wounds and loss of blood, she believed he would be a good match for Analusha—an Analusha without his magic to be sure. It would be a fight to the death.

Her fingers itched to reach up and touch the stranger's face, touch the curious sun-locked hair on his chin and under his nose. Sedna willed away the treacherous thoughts. It mattered not that she was shaman. She was a woman and belonged to Nagatok. She was lucky to have such a brave hunter and good provider. Even so, she acknowledged an innermost place within her body that wanted to be touched, to be loved, and Nagatok had never come close to it. At that moment she sadly realized he never would.

Sedna stood and moved toward the doorway from the little room. "I must go outside. I must be alone." Leaving the distress behind her, aware her parents were afraid to be alone with this man, she had to withdraw from his presence. He had somehow cast a magic spell she must fight to break. Sedna walked down to the shore and sat on a large boulder upthrust from the sea.

For a long moment she stared out on the black water, watching the lap-lap of the rivulets coming into shore. Her life had been determined in advance, long before her birth, and could not be changed. Yet something had changed, within her with the appearance of the Viking.

Out in the dark sea, she imagined she saw a form watching her, Sednah, *she down there*, was close. She closed her eyes and turned back to her meeting with the Raven Mother, reliving it all over again.

When she approached the glacier, the home of the Raven Mother, the ice had screeched and shivered beneath her feet. Recessed within a large crack that formed an entrance, she saw billowing fog and the outline of a woman.

Sedna recognized the tall, stately form of the Raven Mother, Tulunixiraq, just as her mother and grandmother had described her according to the legends from the beginning of time. Without knowing why, Sedna's heart sang out a greeting.

A welcoming look mirrored in the Raven Mother's expression when the mist gradually cleared. Tulunixiraq beckoned and Sedna had followed without hesitation, not glancing down as her boots trod a high precarious path skirting on the slippery ice. Her legs felt as if they floated forward, and her feet barely touched the surface. When she came closer to the large crack in the ice, the sun faded away, unable to compete with the brightness of the mound of crystal.

Sedna expected to keep floating off the face of the glacier. Without fear, she crossed the slippery ice and bent to enter the crack. She thought she heard the people cry a warning chorus: "Come back! The *wiivaksaat* are inside! They will take you away with them!"

She was not afraid. The mournful wails of the people faded and she entered darkness as blue as midnight.

Ahead, a pale green light whispered from the bowels of the glacier. A surprising, dream-like lethargy gripped her, but she was wide awake and alert—her senses sharpened to exquisite heights. The only sound intruding on the dream-state was the continuous creak and groan of the shifting ice. No wonder the Inuit believed such strange noises came from demons.

Sedna moved toward a fur covered object lying on the floor of the glacier in the center of the pale light. The texture of the thick fur surrounding the Raven Mother was unknown to Sedna, though she knew all the fur bearing animals of the area. Once her eyes became more accustomed to the ethereal green light, she could see huge tusks piled against the wall. She recalled childhood stories almost forgotten, stories her father and grandfather told of the ancient animals, the *kilivaciaq*, that roamed the ice when the Raven first created the Earth. Sedna began to feel more sure of herself. Her hand barely trembled when she pulled away the rest of the furs to reveal the entire length of Tulunixiraq. The Raven Mother lay wrapped in a soft mantle of animal skin, tawny in color with slashes of black against the gold. An identical ivory belt such as Sedna wore, carved also with intricate designs, encircled the Raven Mother's waist and she wore a headband of woven raven feathers.

The story handed down from generations was that the first women put on Earth by the Raven were very powerful Amazons, with men created to serve as their slaves. When one Raven Woman refused to give up her male child, as tradition demanded, all women were punished by the creator, lost their exalted place and became subservient to man. Sedna had heard the story many times during the first winters of her lifetime. It was one of the people's favorite legends. She thought she had forgotten it until the moment she saw Tulunixiraq on the furs.

"Why am I here?" The sound of her own voice echoed up and down the narrow chamber and into the depths beyond, startling her. She waited for the Raven Mother to respond, but Tulunixiraq lay still, looking frozen.

The creaking sound from the constantly changing pressure of the ice no longer alarmed her. The cavern was so peaceful, Sedna began to relax and her eyes turned upward beneath closed lids. She did not open them, even when something soft brushed against her cheek and fanned the hair on her neck.

"Tulunixiraq?" she asked softly.

'*Daughter of the Raven. I am Raven Mother. Do not fear, no harm will come to you here.*'

Sedna had no thought of fear. She didn't even know if the voice was audible or in her head. It didn't matter. She understood perfectly.

'*I have waited long for you.*'

"I listened to stories of you as a child. I carry the name Raven Woman proudly."

The Raven Mother continued. '*You have been told the story. Our people came in great numbers, following the kilivaciaq across a narrow bridge of ice. At first we saw only ice. Then we came to deep valleys with green forests and more animals than we had ever seen in one place. Not only did we find the hairy beasts, but also giant bison with horns as wide as I am tall, and huge sloths that fed us well, for they were the easiest to slay. Women were the hunters of the tribe. Our men did the work and took care of our children.'*

Sedna listened, her eyes tightly closed, not moving for fear of breaking the spell. She saw the tall, graceful huntress, standing in a long green valley. Her shoulders were thrown back, her lance poised and she looked magnificent. She chose her prey from the multitude of bison and mammoths grazing peacefully close by. Her spear found its mark.

'We pursued the giant beasts and they moved farther into the valley. We awoke one morning and they had disappeared.'

With eyes still closed, Sedna saw the Raven Mother's body rise up out of the furs and stand looking down on her. Sedna was afraid to open her eyes. The Raven Mother was two places, standing near her and still lying on the furs.

'We thought to return to our land, but the narrow bridge had gone. There was no crossing back, so we continued forward.'

Sedna tried to imagine how it must have been to come to a strange place and then not be able to return. She saw the icy whiteness surrounding the lush green valley, the huge animals threading through a pass into the next frozen expanse of land beyond.

Tulunixiraq's lips parted in a slight smile and she nodded with approval. *'Your vision is good. It happened just so. We followed the animals and they led us toward beautiful, treacherous glaciers, over mountains of ice and into more green valleys.'*

The story fascinated Sedna. Huddled on a scrap of fur,

she hugged her knees to her chest, unmindful of the bone-snapping, frigid air in the center of the glacier.

'*We crossed treeless, rolling tundra and saw animals as far as the eye could see. We made our camp, staying for the time it takes a small child to grow to the age of mating, but again the way was blocked for us. When we wanted to return, the mountain pass had closed with ice. When the animals moved, we followed, staying in one place until, one terrible night, a giant wave of water came across the tundra, and Sednah claimed many of the people. That was the beginning of the salt ocean and the ice pack as you see it now.*'

The apparition folded her hands across her breast and stared down at Sedna as if seeing inside her mind and soul. Her expression was one of satisfaction.

'*You have much to learn of life, but you have inner strength and courage which will serve you well. Put trust only in yourself, I cannot come to your aid. You must not expect it, for I am not of your world. If you fail in this task, the Raven Woman line will disappear forever as if it had never been.*'

This time Sedna did not offer a protest. She had a sudden desire to discover what it was the Raven Mother wished her to learn.

Tulunixiraq floated close to her own body and blended with it briefly. When she rose into the air again she held her exquisitely woven headband made of raven feathers which she extended toward Sedna.

'*Your mother has given you the Raven belt. She was not a Raven Woman. You are the first after many descendants. The belt will become a part of you, as much as your own skin or heartbeat. The ivory belt is to make certain that the last Raven Woman does not perish. The headband is my gift to you.*'

Sedna accepted the headband, warm in her mittenless

hands. She turned the band of feathers and stones over, examining it. Sewn between and among the raven feathers were delicate slices of jade and ivory and rare quartz crystals shot with gold.

"I have never seen anything like this." Sedna placed it on her head, and immediately felt comforted.

The Raven Mother smiled a secret, sad smile. *'You must never be without the belt, nor allow anyone else to touch it—until you give it to your own daughter. I learned to make the belt from the priests and shaman in our land across the ice bridge. Each Raven Woman who wears the belt must carve one of its ivory pieces before giving it to the next. Soon a stranger comes to your shore. You must protect him, for he is of the future.'*

Sedna fingered the flexible belt. Most of the oval pieces of ivory were carved with delicate lines—and the rest plain, as if waiting to be finished. The pieces were attached by strong swivels also carved of ivory. She wondered how many Raven Women had worn this belt down through the centuries.

'I am a part of this belt always, as has been and will be every Raven Woman who possessed it. The belt serves each of you at that time you need it most. The belt will give you additional courage when you need it most, and it will serve as a constant reminder that even though I am not of your time and cannot offer aid, you are never alone. Not every generation puts forth a Raven Woman. Only the most devoted, the strongest, the most intelligent, of the succeeding generations will be a Raven Woman.

'Now you must go!' Tulunixiraq's voice became charged with urgent intensity. *'When my spirit returns to my body, nothing remains to protect you.'*

Sedna opened her eyes and saw the Raven Mother fading, settling down into her furs to sleep again, the soft green mist around her growing more dense. Unmindful of the cold, which had swept in like some live being after the green haze faded, Sedna knelt at the side of Tulunixiraq's body and touched her hand. It was as if another person spoke from inside her own body. "Do not fear, Raven Mother. I will treasure the belt and guard it with my life."

She leaned over, touching the band on her forehead to the cold, hard hand of the Raven Mother a long moment. When she arose, the green light had diminished to a dull glow hovering just over the body. Sedna gently restored the furs around her, and over her face as before.

'*Go! Now!*' The voice whispered in her ear, compelling her forward. A compulsive urgency made Sedna rush toward the crack and the faint light of day beyond.

By now, the voice of warning filled the inside of the glacier; the eerie whisper echoed and bounced off the walls and the dark ceiling. '*Go! Hurry!*'

Sedna ran forward, panic pressing her heart up against her throat. The glacier boomed and cracked and groaned—loud noises that terrified her, and chilled her from inside out.

As she fled across the slippery floor toward the crack of light, her feet slid from beneath her and she fell.

The remembrance of falling shook Sedna from her dreaming and she looked once more out into the darkness. Over the sea, an iridescent spray of foam lifted from a place out on the near horizon, bringing a comforting warmth to caress her face.

Sedna turned to go back into the hut and face her parents and the Viking.

CHAPTER 2

The temporary summer quarters of the little tribe of Thule Eskimos strung out in a long row, on the level above the beach. The tent-like structures made of furs and whalebone would be taken down at the end of the summer hunting season. Behind these quarters, not a distance of more than five huts standing end to end, their permanent mud, stone, and whale rib huts waited. Semi underground, the winter quarters harbored the people during the cold months, away from the frigid winds that swept unceasingly across the sea. Sedna's family's summer abode stood apart from the others, due to her shaman status, but close enough so that everyone knew what everyone else was doing at all times.

Many sleeps had passed since the Viking washed up on their beach. But it was too soon for him to walk about. Spying eyes watched every move he made. While he stayed ill and helpless, the people could pretend he did not exist.

When the Viking tried to work on his broken ship the people watched him from a safe distance far back on the beach. He moved his shoulders and arms about in relentless abandon. His movements were extravagant, and he muttered to himself in a loud whisper that carried far

across the ice. Even the smallest child of the Thule Eskimos knew one must learn to conserve energy, not move
so quickly about, striding back and forth across the floor
of the ship as if he could not finish his task quickly
enough.

The people spoke of his outlandish movements in
hushed whispers. He would not survive in the wintertime,
when the temperature froze even the fast running water to
the depths of a person standing upright.

The clan had no fresh wood, only pieces of driftwood,
worm-holed and fragile. He sliced some of the driftwood
with his sharp knife of a strange shiny substance, piecing
them together over the hole in the side of his vessel that
had smashed into the ice.

Away from her mother and father, the Viking's rich-
timbered voice coaxed Sedna to forget her reserve. Sometimes she brought out mending to sit on the beach and
watch him. He stopped working long enough to join her.
"My people are called Norsemen. Why do they call you
Raven Woman?" he asked.

"It is not a subject for discussion with a *kablunaet,*"
Sedna replied.

"I need you to call me by my name," he said. "No one
has done that in a long time. My name is Rolv."

Sedna stopped sewing a moment to consider the idea.
He was a stranger, a wild Norseman with a name that was
hard for her to listen to, much less pronounce. But the
Raven Mother had bid her to keep him safe. That had to
be enough for her.

"I will try to call you—Rolv," she pronounced carefully, rewarded by his wide smile.

She sewed on trousers or leggings she and her mother
would use for winter. A woman could take pride in wearing them for they were made of the finest polar bear fur,
which Nagatok had brought to her as his share of a kill.

The plop-plop of her little bone needle going in and out of the skin had a lulling effect while she and Rolv sat for a moment on the fringes of sunshine and shadow.

Children sidled up, eyes darkly slanted, mouths open in fear and wonder. Rolv smiled at them and tried to speak in their tongue. They did not laugh. That would have been impolite, even to an uninvited guest.

"They look like giant winter rabbits in their furs," Rolv commented.

Sedna laughed and beckoned them to come closer. Little by little they did.

"I wish I had something to give them," he said.

"They would not accept," she answered.

He smiled once more in their direction and they scattered like round bits of fur across the beach. "Why do they fear me?"

She laughed at his outrageous question. "I could not begin tell you why, there are so many reasons."

He leaned back and regarded her beneath sun-tipped lashes. Sedna knew he was studying her in his mind while he appeared to look out across the narrow opening of the inlet, toward the large water beyond.

∽∾∽

What a curious person this dark-haired beauty turned out to be. Taller and more slender than the inhabitants of her village, by the standards of his Norse people, she was small and delicate.

She watched him with the sidelong glimpses from beneath her lashes.

The wolf stayed close to her side, never ceasing to watch him.

"I never knew anyone to tame a wolf."

"Her name is Aku. I did not tame her. She is my

tunaraq, my helping spirit. She came to me one winter night when I sat out on the ice to speak to Brother Moon and try to absorb the ways of a shaman for the first time."

The wolf moved closer. The creature seemed to listen, chilling Rolv to the bone.

"We would have slain it," he said. "These animals have wondrous fur that keeps away the cold."

"We are not permitted to slay these creatures. Each clan has its own spirit. Sometimes within a clan, each shaman has a different helping spirit. Analusha's is a bear."

She carefully put away the sharp needle in a tubular case of bone and tucked it in her jacket pocket. Taking up a knife of chipped stone, slotted into the side of an ivory handle, she began opening shellfish her father had brought earlier and dumped onto the beach.

Rolv thought she owned an odd charm. Delicate, small and finely made as she was, he sensed her to be sturdy and strong. Her black hair, straight and thick, shone like a crow's wing in the sunlight. Looking into her eyes, fathomless and black as her hair, was like staring into the darkest, deepest sea. They tilted up at the corners, giving her an exotic, foreign look he found very intriguing. He wondered what it would be like to bed her.

"What is a subject we might discuss?" he asked formally, lapsing for a moment into his native Norse.

Sedna cocked her head sideways. He knew she listened to his voice, trying to understand. It never stopped amazing him that most times she did understand.

"You look like a little winter magpie with your head tilted like that and those bright black eyes." He struggled to speak in her tongue.

She stared down at the ground for a long time.

He didn't say anything, only waited.

She turned her face up to stare into his eyes. "I cannot

say how, but I understand some of what you say. It is not our language, yet I know."

It wasn't imagination that told him she understood his Norse speech. He sensed it in her eyes. How could she know?

"We honor the Sun and the Moon and Sednah, goddess of the sea. There are others. Do you have Gods and Goddesses in your land?" she asked.

"Yes. But I have no words to tell of them in your tongue."

"Then I will tell you about the Raven Woman." She folded her arms across her chest. "I have never spoken of the powers to a stranger."

"I am listening."

"Before time began, our people believe the Raven created the skies and our Earth. He made the Raven Mother first. She had dominion over everything. One of our ancestors did the unforgivable. She gave birth to a male child and refused to give him up. Raven Women are permitted to keep only female children. Otherwise our powers diminish." Sedna glanced at him and seemed gratified to observe his intense interest.

"After that Raven Woman disobeyed the authority of the Raven, the male became supreme. But we have our own power passed down through the ages with this." She pulled aside her fur parka and touched the belt. "Each mother in the Raven line offers the belt to her daughter. Not every daughter will wear it. My mother did not."

"How do you know who is chosen?"

"We know. My mother was not a Raven Woman but she knew when she gave me life that I would be."

"Does being a Raven Woman mean being a shaman?"

"Legend tells of some who were not. Most are. It is a separate power entrusted to those Raven Women who become shaman."

"That is very complicated. Our Gods do not demand so much."

"We have a duty set aside for us, but we do not always know what our purpose is. We are set on the Earth to alter the lives of our people. We must change what we can, to help them survive."

"Your father is a hunter who is afraid. Every man dreads that happening to him. You will seek to dispel his loss of manhood?"

Sedna's expression reflected surprise and pleasure that he had perceived this in her father. She continued to watch him politely, her wide-spaced, delicately slanted dark eyes expressed none of the curiosity she must have felt. He had a hard time guessing her thoughts.

"In a small way, helping him will change our lives. It is like a rock thrown in a still water. Each circle coming from the rock and the water touch each other. When Aku came into our village—a wolf that had never been with people—that was also something of importance for the future."

"Would it also help to tame a wild Viking, making him your *thrall*, your slave?" His voice was husky, his gaze steady.

Although she could not know each word he spoke, he knew she did not misunderstand his meaning.

Sedna touched her palm to her chest, as if frightened at his expression of bold desire. She changed the subject. "Where do you come from? You are not from our land."

He thumped his chest with a fist. "I am Rolv, bastard son of Eric the Red. We come from Norway first, then Iceland."

She said his name slowly again, trying it out on her tongue.

He liked the way her small mouth twisted with the effort to say the name so strange to her. "The Norsemen also revere the raven. Sometimes we call them crows, but I believe the raven is a larger bird," he said.

He had ceased working in order to talk to her, something he rarely did since he became well enough to go back to his ship. By now, he knew he had to leave before the snow fell and the shaman returned.

"Our warships carry three crows on every journey." He waited for her to ask why.

She looked away, for a moment, her hand touching the wolf's head.

When she did not ask, he continued, wanting to hold her interest. He should work on his ship, but this was the first time she had ever sat still long enough to talk.

"When we think land is near, a crow is released. He flies high above us, around and around in ever widening circles. If he returns to the ship, we know no land is near. If he takes a direction, land is certain to be there and we follow."

"What if he flies back toward the journey's beginning?" she asked.

He laughed at her quick perception. "Then we are in trouble," he said, still laughing.

"And so will you be, if you and your boat are not well before the *angokok* returns."

"You mean the shaman? I hear someone say he is old. You are shaman. You have as much power as he, do you not?"

Shocked at his stupidity, she said, "Of course not. When I am as old as he is, perhaps I will have such power. My power comes from the raven, his from the white bear. There is a difference."

"What will he do if I am still here?"

"He can slay you. That is his decision. You must prepare to do battle with him if he demands it."

"I do not fear old men."

"You should fear Analusha. He is smaller and older, that is true, but he has magic, many potions to call on for help."

"Are you afraid of him?"

She did not answer immediately. "He has the face of a wise grandfather, teaching me what he knows while I grew into a woman. He also has another face, merciless and cruel. He is unforgiving with those who break our rules."

"He would harm you?"

"He may put a lance through me," she touched her chest with her hand. "Or he could banish me so that I may never return to our village, our people, or my family."

Her voice was resigned, her expression passive. He had trouble understanding that peaceful resignation to fate. It was an entirely different attitude that made trouble for both himself and his quarrelsome father. Their fighting back at people who proved untruthful and corrupt had brought nothing but trouble. His father had been banished first from Norway and then from Iceland. He too, had been cast out for fighting.

"I cannot leave without my ship!" Rolv exploded in fury.

"Take my father's kayak," she urged. "Go—with or without your ship—before the hunters return."

"I live alone—on the tip of an island. I must use my vessel to return home to Ericksfjord when the time of my exile is over. Soon I could be ready to sail if these patches hold."

Sedna made a noise deep in her throat. Aku leaped to her feet, growling low until Sedna put a hand out to calm her. Rolv moved away, to a safer distance. He noticed that Aku tolerated few people, but seemed not to mind him if he did not intrude too close into their territory.

"We have dogs at Ericksfjord. Sensible, well-bred intelligent dogs—who know to obey us, not wolves."

"What are dogs?"

He did not think their command of each other's language was enough for him to explain.

"You beat upon the sides of your ship in such a fierce manner. We would call that *wittiko*—senseless. How can one repair a boat while beating it to death?"

He laughed. "That makes a curious kind of sense. You would have to come aboard to see the results."

"No, I cannot do that. What are those peculiar hard black things you hold in your fingers and pound into the boards?"

The little vixen had been watching longer than he supposed. "Nails. Iron nails." He handed over a handful for her to examine.

She moved them in her palm. "I have never seen anything like this. The pieces of hard rock that fall out of the sky look and feel something like these nails, as you call them. The men make knives from the sky rocks."

"I hear you have been promised to someone."

"Nagatok. He is a mighty hunter."

"You need someone to provide for you and the old people?" He didn't know why that thought disturbed him, but it did.

"My father was also a great hunter." She tilted her chin and looked at him directly, challenging. "He was wounded in a walrus hunt. Then when he went out one day to hunt on his own—to prove he still could hunt—he came back changed. He suffers from the kayak sickness, but I will cure him of that one day, when the time is proper."

"Is this the sickness we spoke of before?"

She touched her hand to the she-wolf and it rolled over on its side to be rubbed. "Many hunters get *makraaq*, kayak sickness. Alone in a small boat with only the white cliffs, white ice in the water, and the stillness of death…it brings…" She struggled for words to finish. "Reality is lost. Perspective diminishes. I am told by survivors it is a terrible void with no way out. Some hunters never return. We do not know where they go. Perhaps they fall off the end of the land and water. My father came back, but was never the same."

"It is not our custom to hunt or fish alone. Perhaps that is why I have never heard of this sickness of your father's."

"You came here alone. Were you not hunting or fishing?"

How could she manage to get to the heart of every secret he ever owned? His mouth worked and he said the words without wanting to, as if not saying them out loud made them untrue. "It is the law we live by. I have to hunt alone. I am cast out—exiled." He could see she understood this concept.

"We too cast out troublemakers from our village. They soon die, afraid to live alone. You did not die."

"I may tell you of that later. I must now work on my ship." Rolv arose from his place next to her and moved toward his ship, long legs eating up the ground.

の気の

He removed his shirt. Soon the ping-ping of his hammer striking against the nails rang through the still, cold air. The reddish hair on his beard caught colors from the moving clouds in the same manner of a glistening chunk of ice.

His hair, the color of the sun, curled in a remarkable way around his ears and neck while everyone in her world had hair as straight as a lance. Sometimes he gathered his hair back with a leather thong, other times he wore some sort of band around his forehead.

His chest had fur, like an animal. A mother, and later a wife, always saw to it a man's hair on his chest and face was plucked off when it first appeared. A man wanted his body kept clean and smooth.

From Sedna's vantage point she could see beads of sweat on his muscular upper arms and chest in spite of the icy blasts of wind that twisted off the water. His chest was broad, his legs thick and muscular beneath the torn leggings he wore. What sort of creature had descended upon them? Why did she feel this strange, sad ache in her breast that never seemed to go away since he arrived on their shore?

She forced herself to stop her foolish gaping. Soon Nagatok and the shaman would return. Old Analusha's fury would be terrible. He would surely slay her along with this stranger, or worse, banish her. She had to prepare her father to hunt—to take care of himself and her mother. In the past, she'd had visions, urging her to help her father. Soon it might be too late to help him. It had happened that old men sat down and died when they were no longer of use to the family.

Rolv's voice rent the stillness with an explosion of sound and the hammering stopped abruptly. She was certain his bellow of pain and anger could be heard across the water to where the sound fell off the Earth. He was angry. What would make a man working alone angry? She saw him shake one of his hands and hold the tips of his fingers inside his mouth.

Sedna wrinkled her forehead in stern disapproval. The people never made a display in such an unrestrained, impolite manner if they harmed themselves in a mishap. She had seen her father and some of the older men work on an *umiak,* patiently stretching the hides over the frame until the boat was watertight, only to have it tip over on one of the men and knock him to the ground so that he was a long time rising. She had seen women cut themselves using their knives on tanned hides. No one shouted and raised a voice in useless anger. The others laughed and made fun of the unfortunate person until that person felt ashamed of the injury and laughed also.

Rolv looked down at the watching crowd, gave one last fling of his hand, and went back to pounding, although he seemed to work a little slower and more measured this time. Sedna and the wolf turned away from the ship. It was time to go inside, to talk to her parents. She knew they were worried.

In the small lodging, Sedna still felt the Norseman's presence, from the days he stayed with them while he was too weak to move. "Father, it would be well to find eider ducks before the cold comes. You need a new tunic."

Kuliit served their meal from a communal pot in the center of the room. It benefitted them that their home was away from others. They did not have to abide by all the rules.

Usually, the man of the family ate first and the women and then children consumed what was left. In Sedna's family dwelling everyone ate together.

Suutak stabbed a piece of floating seal meat with his knife, popped it into his mouth, and sliced off the meat at the edge of his lips. Then he passed the knife to his wife. They both drank broth from little baskets made with baleen from the whale's mouth. He determinedly chewed the stringy meat. The tenderest, softest parts of a kill went to the hunters. The rest was shared by members of the tribe who needed the meat.

"I remember hunting journeys when your sleds dragged home the fattest, juiciest seals," Sedna said.

"I wish I had gone in search of the giant fish before the spirits cursed me," Suutak mourned.

"Very few hunters capture one of them. Most are never even in on a kill," Kuliit reminded her husband.

The whale's body provided the camp with food for an entire cold season and the ribs and bones made their shelters. Sometimes their special spirit in the form of a killer whale forced a giant gray whale to beach. No hunter ever put a lance to a killer whale. They were feared and respected and never ill-treated. Noise from outside their cozy room intruded. Sedna leaped to her feet and ran to the doorway.

"We wish your permission to slay the intruder. My son, Analusha, would have done so himself."

"Ogiak!" Kuliit and Suutak came up behind Sedna. The three faced the crowd in front of their hut. None of the others spoke, their respect for Sedna's shaman status too great. Their frowns, their angry glares, their turned down mouths, said enough.

Ogiak carried a lance, as did the others in the group. They were not sure of themselves, or they would have rushed the ship and dispatched the Norseman without calling her out.

"You are forbidden to slay a man without leave from a shaman," Sedna reminded the crowd. She tried to stay calm, but the mental picture of the Viking with lances driven into his body turned her throat dry. She swallowed and stood as tall as she could, shoulders back, eyes looking into each man's face.

It was time she showed them strength and boldness. If she did not, they would kill the Viking at night while he slept. "I will call a meeting this night in the *karigi*, and visit Brother Moon. He will tell me what we must do." All shaman worked their best magic in the meeting hall.

The sound of satisfaction spread through the gathering. During the long winter, the meeting place was a source of their main excitement. The men held sham fights, gambled, or exchanged songs. The women sat sewing in a corner, while the children played quietly, underfoot of everyone. But the best time of all was when the shaman called for a seeing.

When the crowd dispersed and Sedna went back inside the hut, Suutak's face wrinkled with concern. "Daughter, you take a chance. If you are not received by Brother Moon, the people will turn on you. You have never held a meeting without Analusha to guide you."

Sedna leaned forward and touched her nose to her mother's cheek. She knew her mother worried in spite of trusting her daughter to be strong. She would have made the same gesture with her father, but a daughter could never be that familiar. "I must do it. Leave me so that I may prepare myself."

The couple went about their business in the little hut, as if the young woman sitting in a corner did not exist. They did not look at her, nor speak, to avoid breaking her concentration.

She would ask Brother Moon to give her words to save the stranger's life until he could leave their shores. She also needed to ask Sednah, Goddess of the Sea, how she might help her father regain his hunting prowess. He would soon die of shame if he did not get it back.

When Sedna was ready, she entered the meeting hall alone, as befitted her stature in the village. She held herself with a taut grace, knowing she must appear self-assured and confident to make up for the flamboyant belligerence the old shaman would have imparted.

The tented structure of the meeting hall contained a large fireplace in the center circled with sacred stones loaned from the hearths of everyone in the village.

The villagers had spread furs on the ground and made

themselves comfortable. Sedna surveyed the crowd. She sensed the antagonism, the questioning of her judgment. She took off her Raven belt and held it high above her head. "You see before you a daughter of the Raven Mother. Tonight I will speak with Brother Moon to ask his advice." She would speak to Sednah, the sea goddess too, but that was a personal matter and no one would hear it. Her voice lowered and she spoke in a monotone that carried to the farthest corner of the tent. The old shaman had taught her well. After the first hesitation, she felt the fear and unease depart.

The older people's heads nodded after some time had passed, but the children were still restive. Most of the people had just finished a large meal and usually dozed afterward, anyway. Sedna reached for her drum, touched her fingers over the flatness of the taut skin before taking up the ivory tusk beater. She had carved it with Raven heads up and down the length of it.

"Aya ya, aya ya..." she intoned softly. At first, she spoke directly to her father, trying to fit her voice between his dreams so as not to waken him. The sound of the drum continued with monotonous regularity. Her chin tilted up and her head leaned backward on her neck. Only the crisp crackle of the fire intruded on the Raven Chant.

Outside, the wind blew against the walls, pushing the skins in and out with a gentle, steady whooshing sound. In the distance, she heard wolves howl and Aku answer back.

"Sednah—powerful mother of the sea—one who
provides the people with life...
You see before you a man who would again be
called a hunter. Take me into his soul so that
I can see what torments him.
Were you offended by his strength and prowess?

Can one who owns the creatures of the
water suffer jealousy as we poor humans?
Rise up from the sea and touch this man—
Touch his heart, his great hunter's heart
making it one with his soul."

Inside Sedna's closed eyelids, a scene came forth. The
day shone brilliant with icy freshness. The sun slanted off
the still water in a rainbowed array of sharply bursting
colors. Sheer cliffs of white towered along the shoreline.
In the sea, huge shards of ice floes hung suspended in
space between the blue sky and black water. They shim-
mered in the soft tracing of light. The Sea Goddess had
answered by letting Sedna go inside her father's head
where he relived that most terrible time of his life.

The old man in the small kayak knew he was the sole
human remaining on Earth. He stared down into the still,
fathomless water where nothing moved and no sound is-
sued. There was no dimension to this strange world, only
flatness.

He did not move even a finger, for fear of frightening
the seals he knew must wait down there. His family hungered, he hungered. Hunger gnawed in his empty belly
like starving wolves attacking a fox. The weak sun sank
lower and lower in the horizon, sending a stark red glare
into his eyes, like the blood in his veins that thrummed
through his body. Still, he did not move. The silence
turned sinister. The towering cliffs loomed closer. Their
shadows fell across his knees. The tall white pieces of ice
turned to horrible creatures, stalking him.

The bottomless void of dark water sucked him down.
Sinking—he was sinking. His eyes whirled in their sockets; his head twisted around and around. The kayak he sat
in also began turning, spinning around, tip for tip, in a
fury of circular motion without pause. The whirling sen-

sation left and a cold sweat replaced it all over his body. The whirling stilled—like death. He tried to move, but couldn't. Unreasoning terror struck him. A moving fingertip, a blink of an eye would break the spell, but he could not move. He had turned to stone, frozen into eternity. He stared at the water, time immeasurable until, just as the sun made its upward journey again, the water rippled slightly, breaking the trance.

Sedna stopped drumming, her own body sweating from the ordeal. She saw her father with new respect, not just as an *ituk*, an old broken man. In his lifetime, he had been to the other side—to the world peopled with those who had gone far away. No wonder he refused to go close to the water or a kayak again. The Sea Goddess released her from the dream.

Immediately, Sedna invoked another trance, which took her in the opposite direction, upward, toward the stars and the moon. Up into the night sky, she felt herself floating through space and, looking down, saw the village spread out upon the land and the Norseman's ship at the beach that would otherwise be empty. She flew forward, over a rise of mountains, and saw a scene that froze her heart so that she almost came out of her trance. She did not know what would happen to a shaman, interrupted on a flight to Brother Moon, but she did not wish to ever know, either.

On the ground, a tight little group of tents clustered in the midst of large green trees. In one tent she spied a lamp burning. Was it the shaman's or Nagatok's dwelling? They were but a full moon's rising from the village. They need only cross the trail in the mountain. Had they finished their hunting? Something strong told her yes and that they were on their way back to the people. She spoke out loud to Brother Moon who watched her with half his face gone. The songs and stories called it a reindeer moon when they told of the animals pouring out of the tipped moon and racing downward to Earth to provide food and clothing for the people.

From where she floated in the sky, she felt stirrings among the crowd below in the meeting hall. She closed her eyes and floated downward to enter through the opening in the roof. Her father awoke first. He stared at Sedna, aware that something of importance had been shared. The terrible fear had been taken from him, shaken and discarded in the bone pile behind the shelters. He would hunt again without dread.

As the crowd gradually awoke, began whispering and wriggling on their numb bottoms, she said, "A shaman has been to speak with Brother Moon. At the next full moon, our hunters will return. They have brought much meat for the village. We will have a good winter. Brother Moon commanded that we not harm the stranger. We must permit him to leave with his ship."

Sedna saw a grudging acceptance on the fierce visage of Ogiak. Now he would counsel the villagers to wait and watch—until the old shaman returned.

She had purchased time to ready herself to meet the shaman head on. Even if it meant her death, she was determined to save the Viking.

CHAPTER 3

Sedna walked toward the Viking vessel with a stone bowl of chopped seal. She'd made up her mind to step upon the boat for the first time. Rolv seemed intelligent, powerful, and disciplined, yet none of her people would have permitted anyone to sneak up on them as she was doing. He had much to learn if he planned to survive alone on the ice.

"A woman is bringing you food," she called out, at the same instant the terrible weapon he always fastened to his side nearly decapitated her. She dropped the bowl and stood trembling.

"By Odin's beard!" Rolv threw down the weapon, a look of pure terror replacing the fierce protectiveness for his ship. "I could have slain you where you stood, woman." His voice was harsh with unexpressed fear. He encircled her in his arms in a hug, and she could hear his heart tripping in his chest under her ear.

He leaned back, holding her at arm's length, lifting her feet off the plank floor, but not releasing her. "Never slip onto the ship again without warning me."

Sedna was engulfed in the concern filling his eyes. She wanted to stay close, to share his warmth. His eyes reminded her of the sky and water the day she journeyed inside her father's mind, to the land of the shadows. That day the sky had been gray, as had the water. There would have been no color on the Earth had it not been for the glaciers that reflected upward with the sheer force of their brightness to create a radiance just beyond the gray.

When Rolv continued to hold her, Aku snarled from shore. Sedna should protest, draw back with dignity at his touch, but she could not. That might mean the stranger—Rolv—had magical power over her. She closed her eyes and concentrated, then pushed his hands away and stepped backward off the boarding plank toward solid ground. "I—I can bring you more food," she managed, still pulled to him by their gaze that never broke—until she turned and fled back to her dwelling. Hurrying in order to reach him before he started to work again, she brought out another bowl.

Rolv was waiting. He leaped down to the beach and towered above her. She tilted her head and looked up at him, moving back to keep a cautious distance between them.

He reached out to steady her. "There now, I am sorry that I nearly killed you."

When she flinched, he dropped his hand and turned his palm up for the bowl of food she held out.

She wanted to put her hand in his, curious to see how much their hands differed in size. His fist looked as big as three fists the size of one of hers. Sedna handed over the bowl and they sat on nearby rocks.

The sun was pale in the autumn sky. Clouds formed and skidded away, re-formed and again disappeared, creating a ghostly effect below. Rolv pulled a strange device from his pocket and began to eat with it, instead of with fingers. After several mouthfuls, he stopped, and noticed her stare. "This is rare good and refreshing. Thank you."

She nodded. "I have never seen an object such as you use to put the stew in your mouth."

He smiled, wiped it off with beach sand, and handed it to her. "It is called a spoon. I carved it from wood. We use knives too, like I have seen you and your family use to eat."

She handed the spoon back, her curiosity satisfied. It didn't seem nearly as practical as using fingers. "I am worried about Nagatok and Analusha returning. Are you soon finished with your work?"

He shrugged and answered. "Do not worry about your hunters. I have faced worse. I have faced Eric the Red in a rage."

"Eric the Red?" Her tongue faltered over the words.

"Eric Raude is my father. A powerful, brave leader, with a fearsome temper. He loves to fight, but no man is his equal."

Sedna waited, hoping he would tell about his family.

Rolv didn't speak for so long, she feared he wouldn't continue. "You have a father. Do you also have a mother?" she prodded, as politely as she knew how.

His dark golden brows drew together, his long, shapely lips twisted. "I have a mother. I've had two mothers. What makes you ask?"

"You said you lived alone. I thought you might have always lived alone."

He laughed, the sound of it harsh to her ears. "I wish to Odin I was home now. I would gladly suffer the crow's cawing of Thornhild, my father's wife. By Odin's sweat breath, I would! Have you any idea what it means to be banished?"

Sedna wrinkled her brow. It was the most dreaded punishment of all. She only knew of one instance of banishment, in her grandfather's lifetime, yet the people still spoke of it.

A brother killed a brother over a woman and the people took him far out onto the ice and left him. When the people saw him in the distance, they avoided him if they could, or passed by as if he did not exist. The man howled all night like a wolf in death throes, just beyond the village. When daylight came, he disappeared, forever, no one knew where. She shivered and waited for his story.

"When people get together and make a ruling against a man, they do it in the *Althing*, the judgment assembly. I fought fairly. Olaf's father had no right to call the men to judge me. I did not wish to kill Olaf, but if I had not killed him, he would have killed me." Rolv looked down at his powerful hands, as if they offended him, then dropped them to his sides in a gesture of despair that went straight to her heart. "A man has nothing if he does not have his good name so he is remembered after death as a brave man."

She did not entirely understand his meaning.

"Freyda put Olaf up to it, I know it!" He leaped aboard his ship and paced across the deck in long strides, his deer skin wrap-around boots making whispering echoes in the quiet morning.

A premonition of destructive violence swept through Sedna's body as she mouthed the name. "Freyda?"

"Aye. My sister, damn her eyes. She has caused more trouble than the lot of us men in the village, but never is punished."

"You were punished?"

"Even Eric could not gainsay the *Althing* judgment, for he suffered the same punishment when he was banished from Iceland. His own father before that was driven from Norway for killing a man in a feud. They sent me away to live alone for two years. I must not see my family or friends, or set foot in Ericksfjord for two long years from the judgment. Come spring the exile will be over and I can go home again."

Though she did not understand every word, his strong emotions hid nothing. Her people did not believe in expressing emotions so openly. It invited censure from watching spirits.

"I blame Freyda more than anyone." He raked long fingers through his curly beard. "You see, both of us are bastards with the same father and different mothers. When the family lived in Norway, before I was born, Eric captured her mother from an outland and made her a *thrall*—a slave. She died after birthing my half-sister, Freyda. Freyda should have died then too. She is depraved. An evil person from the beginning." Rolv smacked his fist again into his palm in a way that made Sedna jump and edge away.

Sedna wanted to take this man away from the terrible reddish haze she saw surround him when he mentioned his half-sister. "And your mother?"

"My mother was a princess of royal blood. From the Westmen, she came, Irishers some called them. Eric and his men captured all her kin and her valuables. He kept her by his side for many years, even if old Thornhild, his wife, hated her. My mother died and I was so young, I remember little about her but eyes like mine, and her gentleness. Some say she was beautiful, a tall slender woman with hair like yours, only curly, not straight." He touched the thick curve of hair on her forehead.

"And who is your mother now?" All this talk of mothers was confusing, although understandable. In her clan, if a child lost its parents, the tribe took over raising him unless someone special wanted to keep him. Therefore, that child would indeed have many mothers.

Rolv smiled at her puzzled expression, his eyes crinkled at the corners. She never tired of looking at this

strange new custom of his. Her lips pulled back tentatively to match his, in an effort to show her politeness. The
people did not show their teeth in greeting. Showing teeth
was used to intimidate. A wolf or bear growled and
showed teeth.

"Thornhild is a mother. Not a bad one, although un-
generous with affection. She is a stern, strong woman.
She would have to be to keep up with Eric. My own dear
mother died before Eric was banished from Iceland.
Thornhild dotes on her oldest son, Leiv. But what mother
would not? He is perfect in every way."

Sedna listened for jealousy to underline his words, but
heard none. He too loved this brother Leiv.

"Thornhild has taken my side above Freyda many
times. Thornhild and Freyda despise each other, but
would not dare show it in front of Eric."

"Tell me more about your mother." Sedna wanted to
hear what made him happy, not what angered him.

"My mother loved to sing and compose songs. I do not
sing, but have made poems or *kvads*. That too makes
Freyda jealous. There has never been anyone in Eric's
family who could compose sagas. I am the first. But the
old man, he favors his only daughter."

"Are there other sons?"

"Eric has three sons by Thornhild—real sons."

She didn't understand "real sons," but let it pass when
she felt the sorrow beneath the words.

"There's Torstein, Torvwald, and Leiv. Leiv is the finest of the lot, an explorer. But sometimes he goes off for
years on journeys."

"Are they all as big as you?"

His harsh laugh echoed across the empty beach. "I am
the runt of the litter."

Sedna didn't understand the word runt, but knew what
he meant and thought he must be lying. How could peo-

ple be taller and larger than him? They would have to stand as high as the great white bear. She shivered, hoping she never saw any of this.

"Do you have any idea of what a runt is? No, you wouldn't. You are taller than the men in your tribe."

She squirmed. Her difference was not something she liked to think about. It set her apart, helping with her shamanism but distanced her from day-by-day relationships with others in her village. She had never had a friend except for her parents. Her mother said her ancestors came from the woodland people who were not Thule Eskimos.

"Probably your people would set runts out on the ice to die. Maybe that is what my mother should have done with me."

Sedna heard the bitter note in his voice. "It is true," she answered quietly. "In times of starvation, we must set the old ones and babies out on the ice to die. They will return to life in another's body, though, so they are not afraid."

"Another's body? I do not understand."

"What happens when you die?" she asked.

"If we die in battle, we go to Valhalla. I do not know about the women. Perhaps they go there too. I never thought of it."

"We believe when one of us leaves our body to journey to *tununirn*, the 'land beyond the back of something,' we return in another body, perhaps that of a newborn. That is why we give our children names of those who are gone—to encourage the person to return."

"I will have to think on something so strange. But now, I must go back to work. Thank you for the stew."

"Will you be ready to leave soon? I fear for your safety."

"As I fear for yours. I know you dread the shaman and

your lover returning before I leave, but I am not afraid of any man alive. Only the weather." Rolv looked out over the water, which was hardening into white foamy ice here and there in the middle. "If I do not leave here soon, my ship will be land-locked until spring." His voice had a hard edge of desperation.

"You are right about the time of the cold coming, but you have more to fear from Nagatok and Analusha. I feel this very strong in here." She hit her chest with her fist.

"Why should I fear them? Do your people lay claim to all of this land?"

She was surprised. "Claim the land? What a foolish thought. We claim nothing we cannot pack away on our sleds or on our backs. The Earth—the sea—the animals in it—who can make a claim for any of that? But you have come *uninvited* among us."

His eyes reflected his lack of comprehension, and anger flared in his expression. "I did not come to your shore on purpose," he reminded her. "The wind blew me here when I became lost after my ship ran aground on boulders."

"It matters not how you arrived here or why. When the hunters go out onto the ice to search for *naanuk*, the great white bear, they slay him with dignity and honor, using only the lance and a knife, as is befitting. When they finish, they offer him a drink of fresh water. Then they cut off his head and return it to the sea so that he may tell his brothers and sisters he was treated with respect by the people."

"What does slaying the white bear have to do with the people killing me?"

Sedna pushed back the hair that escaped from her braid and blew around her face. When she married, she would be allowed to wear her hair up in a knot on top of her head, but for now it had to be in a braid or loose, in the proper way for a maiden. He waited patiently for her to complete her story, even if he might not understand.

"When a bear enters our village, the people, even women and children rush in with knives and harpoons. They cut him to bits, then dance and sing over his body. He has no claim to respect. He invaded our village, his presence was not asked for."

Rolv considered her story a long moment. "You think I am like a bear entering your village? But I am human!" he protested. "By the sword of the great Thor—I am no animal!"

Surprised at his fervor, Sedna looked at the ground, unable to find the words needed to make him understand his great danger. "*Naanuk* also has feelings. Every living thing has feelings, else how could they be alive? The animal wishes to give us his body to nourish ourselves. All he asks in return is that we respect him. If he *intrudes*, it is not the same. He deserves no respect."

Sedna wondered how a man, even from another people, did not understand about *inua*. Everyone knew that even the rocks, the bent scrubby willow trees, the sea, the snow—everything held a spirit within. For that reason, everything deserved respect. She reached for words, anxious to have this man know the truth of what she was saying.

She could tell he had become uncomfortable. No man, with the exception of a shaman, liked to discuss thoughts of life and of death.

He persisted. "A Viking does not fear death, only dying outside of battle. When we die in battle, we live forever with Thor and Odin." He stood and faced the field of ice and water. He raised his arm that held the heavy sword, the sun glancing off the polished blade. His great rumbling voice addressed the sky over the silent water. "O great Thor—Odin the magnificent—be with me as thou are in battle—so that I might live to sail the mighty seas. To fight by the side of my father and brothers and not be set upon by this village of trolls."

The echo of his voice died away. Sedna stood close beside him, looking over the water. Together, blending with his mind and thoughts, she saw the sea filled with graceful, curved Viking ships splitting through the water, their great sails flapping against the wind. Ships so huge they made the sea look small. Men were fighting, bleeding, dying, and still she sensed their joyous exultation. For to die in warfare was the supreme honor and every man's desire.

He looked down at her, his fierce countenance softening. "Have no fear, winsome little troll. I will not permit any of your people to do me harm. I am meant to die in battle as is my father, Eric."

"You are a Viking."

He showed no surprise at her use of the word. "Viking means king of the sea. We *are* kings of the sea. Every country we sail to in the *langskibe*, our warship, the populace shakes in their boots, they fear us so."

She wondered why that was a good thing, but did not ask.

∾∾

Activity increased in the little village. The women worked long hours, slicing cod fish to put out to dry for the winter. Colder weather would bring seals to hunt and the great white bear's hiding places to dig out. Later, the people could walk out on the frozen sea as if it had been a beach. Sedna expected her father to join in the hunts to come.

She lay awake, listening to the wolves running in night packs across the ice, chasing rabbits or fox, and worried about Aku going with them. But the wolf was free to go where she desired. A wolf could not be contained against its will, any more than the ice, or the wind. It took the passing of many full moons before Aku ventured inside their hut. Now the wolf came to Sedna in the night and stayed near her side, except for the times when the pack called and she had to go.

Sedna shivered, even in her warm robes, and muttered a chant to ward off the spiritual forces of the wolves. The old shaman had a bear as his *tunarak*, his helping power, yet he could have sent the wolves to look into the village and make a report back to him.

The next day was overcast, when Sedna looked out. The village lay quiet. No children shouted; even the constant pounding from the Norseman's ship was absent. She hurried back inside. "It will be a morning of glowing lights. We must stay inside and work until it passes."

Kuliit looked at her daughter with fond approval in her eyes before turning away and changing her expression. If the spirits saw someone too happy they became envious and made trouble.

Sedna knew what the sky looked like without being outdoors. Magical lights flung themselves across the sky, humming and snapping, undulating in a continuous wave of color. Brother Moon and Sister Sun were fighting again for supremacy of the sky.

Suutak chewed on a morsel of dried caribou. "Daughter, a hunter feels strong. The force of your power is good."

"A father might go on a seal hunt in this coming time of the cold," Sedna suggested.

He nodded without comment. Her mother stopped stirring the contents of a hollowed-out stone pot over the fire. Her round face folded into wrinkles of concern.

"Perhaps not," Kuliit disagreed quietly. "It could be

some men were not made to hunt when they become old."

Sedna knew her mother worried for fear her husband would do something foolish again to prove his manhood. "Wait and see, little mother. Do not steal trouble away from its hiding place."

They had no need to steal trouble away. Sedna feared it would find them all soon enough.

CHAPTER 4

The Viking worked on his ship. Others watched with Sedna, but from discreet distances up and down the beach. The dying sun of late afternoon lingered on his naked, sweating chest which at first she had thought as barbaric. Often the men in her clan went without tops in the summer but their bodies were clean of hair.

Rolv noticed her staring and leaped down off the ship, disdaining the plank put from ship to shore to walk on. "I thought you would not come today," he complained. "I missed you."

Sedna smiled, matching his mouth in her earnest intensity to get it right. After one became used to this spreading of lips, it was a pleasant thing to see matched in another's expression. A person could learn much from watching another's mouth. "Someone left you food, no?"

"I thank you for that. But it is not the same as when you bring it and stay to talk."

"Why is it—" she began.

He laughed at her. "Oh, another question, always questions. You are a curious creature."

Not put off by his teasing anymore, she continued, ignoring his interruption. "Why is it your hair is the color of—" She took the headband from her head and pointed to the quartz stones shot with gold. "There. That is the color. Yet the hair beneath your nose is different."

"I do not know the answer to that, sweeting. My father and all my family have hair the same as mine, only my mustache and beard are different. My mother had hair like yours. Freyda's is dark red, the color of copper. It can be very confusing."

"Have you a woman?" She had not intended to ask such a question and wondered what made her do it.

Startled, he looked at her in an unsettling manner and cleared his throat. "I have no woman. Some of your people visit me on the island. I have...I have coupled with some of their women."

Her eyes widened. "None of my people—none of them ever—have gone to your island nor lain with a *kablunaet*!"

He laughed. "Well...perhaps not your clan," he conceded. "But they looked the same."

She snorted with derision. "A man who calls himself by the foolish name of Rolv can have no idea of what people look like. The people resemble only ourselves. We are *The People*—that is what Inuit means. We were created by the Raven to keep her company." Sedna's voice was haughty, her chin tilted in anger at his impropriety. Imagine comparing her tribe to another clan, probably those who came from the far away forests to trade. "Are these the people who taught you to speak in such a ridiculous manner?"

He gave her shoulder a light touch to turn her toward him. "How can it be so ridiculous? You understand me, do you not?"

She did and dared not explain to him how that was. None of the others in her village knew anything of what he said. Even her parents declared they did not understand his tongue. Yet from the first, she did and it came easier with time.

He stood in one easy motion and walked up the boarding plank. "I must finish. Soon the ice will come." His arm was better. He could move it freely. The wound on his forehead left only a thin, white scar.

She left before he turned back again.

ⲉⳝⲉⳝ

Each day he worked ceaselessly on the ship, fitting piece after piece in place with painstaking care. He worried more than he cared to admit that the girl's suitor and the old shaman would return before he could leave. He knew how merciless Eskimos could be. He had witnessed the fierce fights between the hunters and his own people. They fought to the end and dispatched many stout Vikings until they were slain. He wished his father had not taken the two Eskimo prisoners and shipped them back to Norway, to be kept as prize pets in the king's court.

Not only was he concerned about the return of the hunters and the shaman, there was the ever-encroaching ice. He did not want to be land-locked—trapped within this mouth of the sea where he knew he would die. A Viking must not allow a group of trolls to slay him. He imagined the great god Thor laughing at him as he waited outside the gates of Valhalla, praying to enter.

Rolv stood at the helm of his scaled-down Viking craft originally made for three or four men to sail. His father and brothers had helped him modify it before his banishment. They outfitted it in ways that enabled him to travel alone in all but the worst weather.

Fortunately, most of the damage from the rocks and ice was done to the hull above the water line. He hoped to patch it enough to make it to Nordrsetur, the name given his solitary home at the tip of the island. While Rolv hammered the stout iron nails into the patches, the curious Eskimos came to watch, standing well back and ready to run.

Sedna brought a meal. He knew it was she walking across the frozen tundra, her wolf close to her side. She moved with grace and dignity. Her exotic beauty came from within as well as lying easily on her face and body for all to see. Sorrow rose in him at the idea of leaving her behind.

When this feeling had first come to him, he thought it was a fear for her life. She said the shaman could have her killed or banished. This new awareness was disturbing. He did not want to think about how much he would miss her questions, her soft spoken rebukes when he blustered too close to her private thoughts. He loved her inscrutable expression in repose. She was so calm, so soothing to be with.

He grimaced when he thought of her in the middle of his family. They would overpower her with their size and exhilaration. But that was a foolish thought. He would never take anyone like her home when he was free to go.

∾✺∾

From behind Sedna came Ogiak's voice. "This *kablunaet*, the stranger you have accepted as a friend, he is *wittiko*, is he not?"

Sedna looked around to see Nagatok's father, Ogiak, glaring at Rolv who had stopped work to watch her approach.

"Why do you say he is crazy?" she asked mildly, with the respect due the most powerful hunter of their tribe.

Ogiak snorted and spat upon the ground. "Are you blind? He claims to repair his boat, yet he beats upon it,

plainly wishing to break it to pieces. This is not something a reasonable man does."

Sedna bent her head to hide her smile. She, too, had
thought in this same manner until the Viking explained to
her how he worked with the pointed objects that he
pounded into the wood to make it stay in place as tightly
as if he'd lashed it with a strip of leather. She decided not
to tell. Let Ogiak think the Norseman owned powerful
magic. It would stay the hunter's hand against Rolv until
he could leave.

When the people moved away, Rolv came down the
plank and sat by her side on the fur she spread over the
soft sand.

"What is that stick you put marks on?" she asked.

"There is that curiosity again. This is a tally stick.
See? Each line is what you call a sleep. By this I know
how long I am here."

"But of what importance is it to know how many
sleeps you stay somewhere?"

He laughed, his teeth a slash of white against the
leathery tan of his face. The color had returned since he
had been fed and cared for. The hollows of his cheeks
had filled out, and his eyes lost that haunted look which
troubled Sedna so much at first.

"What is it you are doing?" he asked to turn her attention to the project she had brought with her—to allow her
time to ponder her confusion of the word "time." He had
tried hard to explain "time" to her, but she had once told
him time was like the wind, smoke, fire, and the sea, a
living thing with a soul or *inua*, as she called it. That
seemed to explain everything for her, although he did not
understand the word and shied away from it as he did
from anything not of this Earth. He said his people
marked time in sensible measure. Many Norse believed
in witches and terrible beings deep in the sea, but most

did not speak of it. What was sensible to him did not make sense to her.

She spread her work out on her lap. "This is a cape, made of Raven feathers." She touched it with tender pride. She had woven shiny black feathers in with the paler gray of down and backed it all with the thinnest of baby seal skins.

"When Nagatok comes to live in our tent, I will wear this and make an identical one for my daughter, who will be a Raven Woman after me. Then I will be a complete shaman, for I will be a woman, not a girl."

"Must you have Nagatok, to become a woman?" he asked, half teasing, half serious.

She nodded. "It is our way. I have more freedom than most girls, but we do not look kindly upon those who prefer to live alone. Every man needs a woman to bring children to his fireplace, sew his clothing, prepare his meals."

"And women? What do they need?"

She tilted her chin and looked up at him, her black eyes innocent of the coquettishness of the women he had known.

"We wish for a strong provider, any fool knows this. Women are not permitted to hunt large animals, although we may fish and trap. A babe wishes for a mother, as well as a father, when it leaves the world of our ancestors to come into this one."

He looked deep into the depth of her black eyes, drawn to the child-like wisdom and purity he saw there. "Do you love this man—this Nagatok who is your betrothed?" He had grown to hate that thought. He didn't stop to wonder why.

"Love? I do not understand love." Her delicately rounded face reflected her puzzlement. "Nagatok's father, Ogiak, saved my life. I was promised to his son when I suckled at my mother's breast."

"I understand that. In some countries women are promised like that, although in my mother's land and also in my father's, they do not do this. A woman is equal, except during battle. How did Ogiak save your life? I do not understand."

"I was born of my parents late in their lives. They had hoped for a son to help them in their old age. Since a mother suckles a child for five summers, they would have been too old to have another. The shaman advised I be put out on the ice so she could conceive again. He promised my mother and father the next would be a boy."

"You would not be here then." The thought made him angry.

"In times of famine, we eat the soles of our boots and chew on the sinews of our weapons because we have no food. We remember always that everyone who passes through the death darkness returns later in the form of another person or an animal. I would have returned."

"You said your mother knew you were destined to be a Raven Woman. Perhaps the shaman feared that."

She wrinkled her forehead with thought. Obviously this had never occurred to her. "Ogiak said if they kept me, he would promise his second son to be my husband. Perhaps the Raven Woman wanted to protect me and chose his mouth to speak from."

Rolv grunted and turned away to begin working again. She had never answered him about her feeling for Nagatok.

൜൜

The warm days just above freezing passed too fast for Sedna. She still had to finish the trousers of the white bear for her mother and herself. Suutak needed a new parka for his hunt. The family had saved up three fox skins, but it took five to make an outfit. They were not permitted to trap more than five of any one animal at a time or the animals would become offended and not return. Perhaps she could trade some of her carvings for furs. The piece she had just finished, of a loon's head carved from driftwood, would bring good magic to whoever owned it.

She heard the pounding of the ship repair and thoughts of the giant man came unbidden to her. Why was she so drawn to Rolv when there were so many things about him that distressed her? His fierce lack of fear when they found him on the beach, his violent temper when he hit his fingers with the strange instrument to put the iron bits in his ship, his extravagant motions and movements, all so unlike anyone she had ever known. Yet he always spoke gently to the curious children who clustered at the edge of the beach to stare at him and who no longer feared him. His eyes, the color of Aku's coat, had never looked at her in anger.

She pushed past the skins on her doorway and moved down the beach, drawn by him. Once she was there, she knew not why, she looked up at him working. He must have sensed her presence. He stopped working and leaped over the rail to the ground.

They stood together, looking out over the water.

Sedna asked when he would finish, fearful it would not be soon and more fearful to hear that it would.

"Soon, little one. My ship is nearly ready. I could leave tomorrow."

"Then you must go! I had a dream last night. The shaman is close. He is not many sleeps away. Their hunt was successful. He is filled with importance, which is a very bad sign for you."

"And you? What will he do to you, for helping me, for feeding me?"

Sedna looked away, but Rolv touched her chin with his thumb, forcing her to look at him.

"Perhaps he will slay us both if you are not gone. I am shaman, but not of his significance. I cannot fight against him. It would not be fitting. The people would turn against me."

"Then come with me!"

She stared up at him, startled. His eyes told her he was serious. She took a backward step. "My home is here. I do not belong in your life."

"Think of it. At least promise you will think of it." His voice held steady, but she felt the trembling beneath his words and didn't understand why this should be.

Her mother called. It was time to help her with the evening meal. Sedna ran away, up the hill toward her hut.

The next daybreak, she was awakened from a troubled sleep by yelling and shrieks. Had the hunters returned? She and her parents bounded from their furs and ran outside, pausing only for Sedna to grab up her Raven Belt by her bedside, and her father his lance.

When they arrived at the beach, the direction of all the noise, half the village was already standing there, in a semi-circle facing the Norseman's ship, but at a respectful distance.

Rolv paced back and forth on the beach, unmindful of the cold foam of the sea splashing up on his boots and the cloth which he wore bound around his legs. When he spied Sedna, he ran toward her. The people gave way in the face of his savage countenance. Kuliit and Suutak came closer to her, offering their mute support, though they trembled.

She held her belt tightly in her fist and stepped forward, motioning the others back. "What is it? What has happened? Why are you angry?"

He stopped bellowing for a moment and shook his

mane of hair from around his face. "They—" He pointed toward the crowd of villagers. "They came in the night and stole Gramr."

"Gramr?"

"My sword!" he exclaimed impatiently, as if she should have known this. "Eric gave it to me after my first battle. He named it 'the fierce one' and had it fashioned just for me. I was ready to leave today. I cannot leave without it."

Sedna understood the importance of a talisman. She turned to face her people, looking each one in the eyes in turn. Many refused to meet her gaze, but that signified nothing.

Some were embarrassed by the white man's strange actions, which they didn't understand. When her stare collided with that of Ogiak, she knew he was the one who had taken the talisman.

"Do nothing hasty in your anger," she cautioned the glowering Rolv.

"*Skraelings*! Barbarians! I should have known to stay on guard tonight, but a man has to sleep." He touched Sedna on the shoulder, lightly so as not to frighten her. "You will bring back my sword? It is very important. Like your belt is to you." He pointed toward the belt she still clutched in her closed fist.

He looked up at the sky and then across the water. There was little difference in the flat grayness between them. The appearance of the dull gray colors bespoke a storm, the first of the winter. The wind had picked up, teasing the sea into choppy little breakers that slapped against the hull of the ship, breaking the heavy silence of the crowded beach.

Sedna took in the same omens and felt his uneasiness. He had to leave. Now.

"I will talk to them, if you will return to your ship."

She didn't have to look behind to sense the crowd dispersing. Never mind, she knew who to talk to.

"Nagatok will be very angry if you confront his father," Kuliit cautioned.

"Yes, Mother."

"Stealing from an outsider is not the same as stealing from our own people," Suutak put in. "There is no punishment demanded for such a thing."

"I know," Sedna said. "Go back to our dwelling. The Norseman needs his sword, just as I need the Raven Belt. He said so. I believe him. I must return it to him so he can leave."

Sedna regarded the two old people with affection. Her insides crumbled, torn apart when she looked into their dear faces. She also felt a splintering between them, as when a shard of glacier breaks away from the ice and becomes separate. Heavy loss seeped through her blood, coursed through her with every heartbeat. Without considering her odd action, she took both of their hands in hers and brought them to her cheeks. The tears from her eyes rolled across their palms.

She felt their surprise at her conspicuous showing of feelings. She let go of their hands and turned, walking toward the center of the compound without looking back. Her wolf stayed close by her side and she felt grateful for Aku's presence.

The huts sat close together, with boneyards of eaten animals in the rear of every abode and small rock fireplaces in front of the doorways.

When she reached the hut of Ogiak, she paused and cleared her throat. "A woman wishes to enter a great hunter's dwelling."

Ogiak's wife had died many winters past and he never replaced her with another. Perhaps that was why Nagatok liked to visit with them so often. He liked her mother and father, and they liked him. Ogiak was very stern and harsh.

"Enter," Ogiak said gruffly. He did not challenge the wolf as she entered close by Sedna's leg.

When she pushed back the opening, he sat by the fire bowl, Rolv's sword in prominent display.

As was proper, he motioned for her to sit. After a moment of polite silence between them, she said, "You must give this weapon back to the Norseman so he can leave. It is his talisman."

"No." He ground his teeth together, an Inuit's polite way of showing irritation with a guest. "I will give it to my son when he returns."

When he returns. The words sent chills down Sedna's back instead of the anticipation it should have brought. In her dream before the commotion awoke her, she had seen wolves coming into the village. Great black wolves roaming the camp, silently sniffing and searching. In the background, she heard the shaman's drum thrumming through the night. Analusha had sent his spirit to the village ahead of his body.

The lolling red-tongued wolves searched through every tent, looking into the sleeping faces of the people. She could hear the panting, the beats of their wolf hearts as they neared her own tent.

Analusha knew what was happening here. By this time, both Nagatok and Analusha were surely outraged at the intrusion. Outraged at the people for permitting it, and mostly at her, for she was the keeper of the village while he was away.

"I must have the weapon." She stared at Ogiak. Their stares locked, unblinking until, at last he looked away.

"You are shaman," he said. "I cannot disobey you. Take the weapon. When my son returns, he will seize it from the stranger and split him apart with it." Ogiak made the sign of the fist upon an open palm, a signal that meant there was no negotiation. Nothing she said could change his mind. "I must tell him you sided with the stranger against me."

A fire within Sedna ignited, burning with an urgency impossible to understand except that she must not allow death to happen to the Norseman at her people's hands. She didn't know how she knew, but it would change the destiny of all her tribe, of all her descendants, forevermore, if Ogiak kept his promise. It would destroy the Raven Women. They would be no more. Nothing would ever be the same.

Sedna could not permit them to slay Rolv. But she had no idea how she could stop it.

CHAPTER 5

Sedna shed her furs, gingerly rolling the great sword on top, unwilling to touch it, and began dragging the load through the trampled snow of the village. Rolv claimed the weapon was a talisman, and that meant it owned a spirit, just as her Raven Belt did. She dare not take the chance of harming her own powers.

Sensing eyes from each hut watching her progress, Sedna did not pause and no one came out to stop her. She looked back over her shoulder, expecting to see Analusha, Nagatok, and the other hunters swarm over the hill toward the village. She smelled their scent in the frigid air, felt their hot breath on her neck. Aku hugged against her legs, almost tripping her, for she too smelled danger in the wind.

"Raven Mother—Tulunixiraq—Sednah for who I am named—guide me." The sword burdened her greatly, but she hurried down to the shore with all the strength she possessed.

"By Odin's blood, you have brought him back to me!"

She opened her eyes to see Rolv standing at the bow of his ship, shouting down at her. He wore a long, flowing robe with a hood. It made him look as tall as the tallest tree she had ever seen.

"Come! Take your weapon. It is heavy. The shaman is not far behind. You must go. *Now*."

Rolv stood, legs spread, chin in the air, defiant—as if he owned everything including the moon and sun. A slight chill wind blew across the water.

Looking up at him, the truth of how barren, how deprived her life would be without him struck Sedna like a blow.

"I must not bring it aboard myself," he said. "A stranger stole the sword from my possession and a stranger must return it or I will lose its powers in the next battle."

She stopped and let the burden down for a moment to flex her fingers. "It is too heavy to drag it up there."

"You can do it. Call on your Raven powers. For me. Bring your wolf-dog too. She can help you."

Sedna looked back toward the village. Her heart raced when she caught sight of Ogiak going from hut to hut likely telling the people what she had done. Taking a trophy from a stranger, an intruder, was a splendid adventure and worthy of great songs and to be recounted in stories for all time. She had robbed him of this and he would never allow it to go unpunished. She had shamed him. Whatever her fate, she felt certain the people would not deliberately take their ire out on the old ones, but since her mother and father would surely try to help her, that could bring them great danger. These thoughts pummeled through her brain so quickly she didn't have time to sort them all out.

She bent to call the growling wolf. The animal sensed danger, too. The wolf would be of protection, to let her know when they came for her. Sedna would have to be on guard constantly until Nagatok and Analusha returned. Then she would try to persuade them of her loyalty.

Sedna felt Ogiak's outrage along with the vision of an

impending avalanche of hunters pouring over the low hill beyond the village. They would be here before the darkness came.

She squeezed her eyes closed and sensed an ending and a beginning, painful and absolute. There was no going back once she boarded his ship. She felt the one within her urging her forward. '*Go! Go! Do not fear. The Raven is with you.*'

Sedna looked up into Rolv's face, felt those wintry eyes boring into her being, searching for her soul. She touched a hand to Aku's head, a light caress that bade the animal follow. She moved forward, her tread light, the sword no longer heavy with a life of its own. When she stepped from the top of the ramp to the ship's deck, he knelt in front of her and hugged her body to his chest, his lips pressed the top of her head and then moved down to her face.

Sedna pulled back in fright. What was he doing? She had never known the feel of another's lips against her person. It was unseemly.

Still, her heart raced in her breast and she wanted to be close to him.

He held her, preventing her from moving away.

She made a whimpering noise.

Aku had feared the boat and refused to budge from shore. When the wolf heard the sound of her soft moan, the animal snarled and leaped to her side. Rolv let Sedna go, alarmed by the growl and gnashing of teeth so close to his face.

Sedna's feelings warred within her. Never had she felt another's face upon hers in such a shocking manner. Never had anyone touched her without permission. In spite of her distress, she remembered to talk to the wolf, to bid her go sit close by.

Rolv's behavior was upsetting and offensive. She was

sure it should be so. Why would he wish to touch her in such a manner?

"There, do not fret so, love, you are trembling like a captured bird." Rolv drew her close again, gently this time and whispered in her ear. "You will learn what love is. I will teach you."

"No!" She tried to pull away, but not too wildly to stir up the wolf again. "This is not befitting a promised woman. You must not force me to lie with you. It will diminish my powers." She thought of the two times Nagatok had taken her, roughly, hurting her. The last time, she stayed in the shadow of her body for one turning of the moon before her heart had healed and she could accept her fate. Nagatok had been humiliated and threatened never to return to her furs.

Still kneeling, Rolv looked into her eyes. Sedna gasped at the compassion she saw mirrored there, the pity and understanding were more than she was able to accept so abruptly.

He raised from his kneeling position to full height, still holding her arm, and unsheathed his sword to raise upward. "This my solemn vow, my promise as a man. I will never force my way with you. You will be as an honored guest, always protected."

Rolv stood straight and tall. She thought his head might push through the sky.

His voice grew softer. "We share a bond. You know it well. You are in my keep and, thus, will I care for you and protect you until it is time we must go our separate ways."

Tumultuous thoughts and prohibited images rose from the feelings that filled her body, seeping up to deaden her mind. She didn't understand and it confused and frightened her so much, she closed her eyes and let her spirit soar free.

When Sedna opened her eyes, she felt cloth beneath her. Rolv had called it sheepskin. She sat up and fought against closing her eyes again, sensing movement beneath her body.

The ship's tall mast whirled around for a moment while huge square sails billowed and snapped in the morning wind.

Sedna cried out in fear. At once Rolv was at her side. Aku also leaped forward. Rolv spoke to the animal firmly, pointing a large finger at her. Aku flinched and sat close to Sedna. He knelt on the deck and took her hands in his.

She pulled away. "Let me stand. I need to see."

He rose and pulled her up. She stared over the railing of the ship. The sight was so terrifying, it was surely some kind of sign. Her legs barely held her and she leaned into him for support. His strong arm stayed around her, the wolf moved close again, but did not growl.

"Do not be alarmed. They are sails, only pieces of woolen fabric and animal skins," he said to calm her.

They were moving! In a wild panic, she saw the shore line behind her diminish. Not a soul stood on the beach to see them go. She turned to him, her eyes wide with shock and fear. "Is this how you repay me for saving the weapon you hold so dear? Is this treachery the payment for your life which I protected when others wished to slay you?"

His long legs spread against the heave of the deck, the mantle he wore catching the wind. He had tamed his shoulder length hair with a band around his forehead. His face was scraped clean of hair, which he must have done to please her. His hairless face alone made him seem much younger. At the same time, his beard had softened his hard cheekbones, diminished his rigid jawline and now he seemed more of a stranger than ever. His nose like a hawk's, was so different from hers. His eyes, clear like the winter sky, showed open concern.

"I offer no regrets, Sedna. I could not leave you behind. Your betrothed and the shaman will exact a stern punishment from you. They would have to slay you to save face."

She knew the truth of what he spoke; still she did not want to run away from her people, especially with a stranger.

"Your mother and father will be taken care of. Did you not say Nagatok liked and respected them as his own?"

She knew the truth of that, too.

"I cannot go with you." The ever-increasing speed of the vessel frightened her. She warned, "Return me to the beach or I will turn into a raven and fly from you."

His expression was unhappy but resolved as he took her arm gently. "Then I must keep you below until you find it in your heart to trust and forgive me. I am right. You well know it. You must believe in my concern for you. You can stay with me until I find the band of Eskimos who live on the next island. They will take you in among them. I promise I will not keep you a *thrall.* You will be a slave to no man." With a firm grasp he pulled her down a stairway into the bowels of the ship. Aku followed, growling low in her throat.

Sedna could have had the wolf on him by now, but there had to be another way to escape. If she was patient, it would come to her.

"I believe in your powers," he said. "I have witnessed strange practices of the people who look like yours. We, too, have seers who can do magical things. I do not wish to remove your precious belt, so I must keep you safe from yourself."

The area below the ship was dank and dark. She felt the gentle roll of the vessel on the water beneath her feet.

"It is dark here! I do not like it!" In the dim light of the candle he held, she saw a pile of clean bedding against the wall. A chain was fixed to the side of the boat with a wrist cuff on the end.

"No," he said, reading on her face the horror she felt. "I would never chain you. This was a cargo ship, used to tow behind the great vessels since the warriors brought back slaves when they went a-viking to other lands. That was in the time before the king banished Eric from Norway."

She took a deep breath, pulling away from him to stand against the wall with Aku close by her leg. "Leave me alone to ponder this. I will not try to escape. For now."

Rolv hurried up the steps to see to the steering of his vessel.

When he brought her food, Sedna pretended sleep and he left. Later, she fell into an exhausted sleep. She awoke outside on the deck. He must have carried her up the stairs without waking her. The things he had called sails still flapped in the wind as the ship cut through the water like a sharp knife through walrus fat. Sedna sat up and looked around. Night was approaching fast. She could feel the dampness come in through her parka.

"Good. You are awake." He let down the sails until they lay parallel with the ship's bow and threw a heavy object overboard. Immediately, they stopped still. The ship swayed, and turned a little with the sudden change in movement.

He knelt at her side, pulled her close, and kissed her forehead, her cheeks, the tip of her nose, lightly, gently, sending scattered rays of sunlight all through her body.

She sensed his rigid control through his fingers. He was used to taking what he wanted, but he had made a promise to her.

"Little troll, I brought you up here to see the beauty of the sea with me. It is dark for you, and stifling below. Promise not to fly away."

Their gaze held a long time together. "You cannot hold me captive if I do not wish it," she said finally.

He nodded. "I know." He touched his fingers to her chin, in a caressing gesture. "Please wish it," he whispered, his breath sweet and warm against her cheek.

She moved away slightly.

"You do not like to be touched?"

It wasn't so much that she didn't like it. She didn't understand it. Her people weren't touchers. Sometimes a mother touched one round nose to her baby's when she played with the child. There was a feathering of fingers to another person's cheek, lightly, to offer shared sorrow or delight. The problem was, she did like it, very much. She stretched her hand to him, to dispute his claim that she didn't like it.

His stern look softened, his narrow, long lips spread in the expression of pleasure that she had come to recognize. His big hand engulfed hers and brought them to his chest where she could feel his heart beating. Her own was throbbing in her throat, making an odd tightening, hard to swallow.

"My people will find us," she said. "They will come for me. No one dares steal a shaman from a village, especially a shaman who is to be punished."

"Yes. They will come. And if I must, I will fight them. You are my prize. Just as my father brought home my mother, so I bring you back to my dwelling Nordrsetur. I will only release you when it is safe, when you have found people you can live with."

He spoke carefully and she understood his words. Perhaps it was better when she hadn't understood everything he said. Sedna sat up straight, her eyes bright with anger.

"I belong to no one. You cannot own another person. I am a Human Being. I am Raven Woman."

"Someday you can go back to your village. Analusha is old. Even a shaman cannot live forever. Your people will be fortunate to have you back when he is gone."

"Are you so certain, then?" she asked.

Rolv looked unrepentant, but didn't argue.

☙☙☙

In serene grace, the ship slid through the waters, always within sight of a shoreline. Sedna stayed on deck. They slept side by side, but separately, wrapped in blankets, within reach of the moon and stars. Aku slept between them, unafraid of the Viking. She was guardian to them both.

Rolv did not try to touch Sedna again, as if afraid of his hard-gained control.

Sedna liked to watch him navigate, to look for the sun through a strange crystal he called a sunstone. He even showed her how to locate the sun through an overcast day and then made marks on a wooden instrument.

When he steered the ship while looking at the night sky, he noticed her curiosity and beckoned her to come closer. With his arm around her shoulders, he pointed her in the right direction to look. "You see the North Star? The brightest one? Some call it the Guiding Star or Lodestar."

She tilted her head upward and nodded.

"The sun moves up and down across the sky, and for that we need the sunstone. When we are but boys, we are also taught to navigate ships by that star. The others all move with seasons. It stays always in the same place, the one permanence in a moving vastness. It neither rises nor sets, nor circles the sky. The seasons have no claim on it.

Only when a sailor changes latitude, does it appear to move."

That night they lay under the stars. She could tell from his breathing that he was not asleep, but something told her now was not the time to ask his thoughts.

Toward morning, Aku began howling and pacing the deck. Rolv leaped to his feet, chest bare in the wintry morning air, looking toward the shore.

Sedna stood beside him, her breath making poofs of white in front of her face.

She pointed. "There."

"I don't see anything moving," he said.

"Hush, Aku! We must listen for the crunch of snow." Sedna knew the hunters would not make much noise. They probably wore their soft-skinned muukluks that allowed them to sneak up without their prey hearing them.

"There!" She took hold of his arm and turned him in the direction of the slight movement. It was more a slant of moonlight off a weapon than a movement.

"By Thor's mighty breath, I saw it!" He pulled on his fur jacket and grabbed up his sword.

"It would be best to move this ship. They cannot follow."

He shook his head. "It will take too long to pull up anchor and start the sails, there's no wind—it comes at daybreak."

They waited, standing close together, but saw no more movement.

"What do they fight with?" he asked.

She did not want to look at him. The picture of his large body punctured by many lances was too real to her. They would cut off his head and put it elsewhere so he couldn't come back to haunt them. She shivered. "Lances, harpoons, bird bolas, axes, clubs," she finally answered.

"I'm not afraid," he said, scowling into the semi-dark shore.

She knew he wasn't, and that was what frightened her most. She did not think the shaman had returned yet. He had no time to come this far. Without the shaman, the band of men might be merely tracking them, leaving a trail for those behind to catch up.

"I do not think they wish to attack us," she said after they waited a long time in silence.

A pale dawn oozed around the edges of the low clouds. The sun would not venture out for hours and then it would not stay long, but still there was a light of day.

"You think they only follow us?"

"They wait for Analusha and Nagatok to catch up."

"Then we will surprise them. Today I will weigh anchor and leave the shoreline to head for open water." His expression was cold, his voice grim.

Sedna didn't know anything of ships and water, but she knew he did not want to move into the "open water." She thought it better not to know why.

The first wind struck them and Rolv waited until the sails furled so that they swelled outward. He pulled the heavy object out of the water and the ship surged forward at great speed.

Soon the white shore receded and all around her was dark water with chunks of floating ice. He stayed at his wheel, his forehead creased in a frown she took as worry.

"Watch on Aku's side!" she yelled above the whipping sound of the sails. She was learning to help by running back and forth across the vessel to catch sight of large ice formations he might not see. The wolf had given up following her and settled down to nest in a pile of ropes at one side of the ship, well out of the way of her hurried scrambling.

"Ah, lass, you are a fine help," he cried out to her, a grin splitting his face.

He was enjoying this! She wanted to slap him alongside his head until his ears rang.

Sedna stopped in a headlong flight to consider such ill-advised thoughts. No one in her tribe ever laid an angry hand on another person, even a child. That would have been unforgivable. She was terrified by the speed of the ship plummeting across the open water. The ship began to rock more and Sedna's stomach began to roll also. A huge spray of white came over the bow, wetting Rolv to the skin.

"Sedna! Come closer." He had to shout now, with the wind shrieking in the sails and rigging like people from the dead.

She ran to his side. "You are wet! You will freeze."

He shrugged off her concern. "No matter. I want you to take your wolf and go below. It will be safer there for you."

His hands were white on the wheel, holding on with all his strength. His clothes were plastered against his body. He shuddered when a hard blast of cold air struck him.

This was why he hadn't gone away from shore. The weather and water were treacherous for one man to handle. He did it to escape her people, so they wouldn't try to bring her back. She guessed also that he did not wish to slay any of them because of her.

Her hair pulled loose from her customary braid and whirled around her head and shoulders, tangling in her face. Aku stood close by her legs, but leaning against her body to stand upright, not leaving her. The cold arctic rain mixed with soft mushy snow began to pelt their bodies along with the stinging sea spray.

"Did you not hear me, woman? Go below. Now!"

Normally that tone of voice would have sent her scurrying away or made her so angry she would have willingly left him.

She put her small hand on his arm, feeling the hard muscles working beneath her palm, through his clothing. "I must make a seeing. Do not concern yourself with me."

Before he could answer, she sank down behind him on the cold, wet deck, using his body to protect her from most of the spray. She took off her belt and held it to her chest, to let the cold ivory feel her lifeblood surging within her body.

"Sednah of the Sea, you may wish to help
a man who is distressed by your intensity.
Splendid though your creation of violent water and sky,
this Viking has no place in your domain nor do I.
The Raven Mother commanded—he must live.
Why he must live is not a secret
she has shared with me.
It must be so."

Sedna opened her eyes reluctantly. She wanted to stay in her dream world, it was so peaceful.

"Sedna! By Odin's beard, what did you do, girl?" He was shaking her, pulling her to her feet, brushing the hair away from her face with rough, gentle hands.

When she first came out of a seance, she was often empty for an entire sleep. Her mind and body limp and needing to recuperate. She knew she must not give in to it this time. Rolv would be alarmed. He would not understand. She leaned into him, no longer feeling the rocking boat beneath her feet.

"I heard your song, your chant. Are you truly a witch?" His expression was that of respect and distrust.

It was not a sound she wanted to hear in his voice.

The sails flapped above, some were torn. The deck had frozen over lightly with a soft patina of frost. The wind had settled to a mere breeze, but the snow continued to fall.

She faced him, putting her hands on his arms partly to keep from falling. Her legs were still wobbly. "You must hear me with your heart, Norseman. I am shaman and Raven Woman. From that I derive certain powers, but not always what I wish for. I spoke to Sednah. You are not destined for a visit to her deep water, nor am I. I feel that here." She reluctantly released his arm, which emanated heat, and struck her chest with her fist. "If we are to stay together, even for a small passage of time, you must trust me and my powers. You have no reason to fear them."

Rolv cocked his head and looked into her eyes for a long moment before he hugged her close. She felt his heart beat and his wet, cold furs stung her cheek.

"The wind is gone. Now will you go below? I will follow and we will dry ourselves. No one will follow us now."

She nodded and, calling to Aku, hurried to get out of the softly falling snow.

Halfway down the steps she began stripping off her leggings and furs, leaving her clothing lay where she dropped them. Her body was chilled to the bone. Fingers trembling with cold, she lit several lamps and stood naked, rubbing her body down with dry sheepskin Rolv had piled in a corner.

Aku curled up in at the edge of the light, content, licking her fur dry.

Rolv clumped down the steps and stopped. She knew he was there by his sudden intake of breath, but she continued to dry herself off unconcernedly. The people did not flaunt their bodies, neither were they ashamed. They were used to small quarters with little privacy. She ignored his presence as was fitting.

Sedna heard the wet material make a squishing noise on the floor as he threw off his clothes. The air below was chilled, but nothing as cold as above with the snow and wind. Already the lamps had created a golden glow, warming the room just enough to be tolerable.

She heard the sudden silence. Slanting a look in his direction, she sucked in her breath. He stood, legs set apart, arms across his chest. She stared at his body, having a hard time swallowing past the tightness in her throat. He was the largest human being she had ever seen in her life. Golden hair glinted all over him in the lamp glow.

"Woman, does it not distress you to undress in the presence of a stranger?" He appeared confused at her open look of question. In two long strides he was across the room, lifting her off her feet and gathering her to him, holding her close, careful not to crush her.

For a brief moment she pulled back, but her mind and body were confused. One part of her needed to maintain dignity and proper aloofness, but the other part wanted to get even closer to his warmth.

"You are like a flawless little person, perfect in every way." He leaned back and she felt his gaze linger on her body, which suddenly felt warm. Rolv bent and kissed her. She tried to squirm away. This was an unheard of invasion of self.

Her feet barely touched the deck. "I am betrothed," she whispered half-heartedly.

He came up for air. She felt the ice cold chill on her throat where his kisses rained.

"Do you not think that is in the past, Sedna? The next time you see your sweetheart, he may wish to slay you."

His words were true enough, but that was Nagatok's right. She had taken a stranger into her abode and left with him. Willingly or not, it went against all of their laws. He had the right to punish her in a fitting manner. Sedna gathered her strength and pushed Rolv away so there was a cool blast of air between their warmed bodies. "Viking, do you forget so soon? You raised your sword to your god and promised to protect and care for me. I did not ask you to bring me with you. Would you go back on your sacred word to your god—and to me?"

Rolv frowned, clearly unused to not getting his way with the opposite sex. But he reluctantly dropped his hands and a deep sigh came from somewhere inside his chest. He turned away, looking toward the wolf who hadn't stirred.

"Thank you for reminding me. I will not bother you again." His voice was stiff, his back rigid as he walked away with as much dignity as bare buttocks would allow.

She couldn't force herself to turn away. There was that amazing combination of sun-darkened shoulders and chest. Her gaze followed down his narrow waist to the tight bottom and his muscular legs, slightly bowed. That part of him was white, almost as white as snow. But she thought it was not the time to question him about this.

That night, after they and the wolf shared cold, rancid strips of moose he had brought along on his journey, they lay down to sleep.

She thought that not the poorest, most deficient wife in her village would have prepared dried meat in such a terrible manner that it became an embarrassment to eat.

കൂര

The next morning Rolv looked worried. "I found ice clinging to the side of the ship. We must head for open water again, in spite of the storms. If we stay close to shore, we will soon be unable to move."

There were chores she learned to do every day to help Rolv on the ship. Many nights, anchored in still water, they had to take shifts walking around and around the boat with a long oar, churning the water so it wouldn't freeze to the boat, locking them in.

Several nights later, she discovered another reason they should move away from the coast line.

Aku woke her by scratching against her shoulder. She leaped to her feet to look over the railing, out past the water and the quickly forming ice bergs. Aku growled at her side, a low growl, that didn't wake the sleeping Rolv. Off in a distance, on shore, she saw running men. Stealthy, surreptitious, they were stalking the boat. She rubbed her eyes and the men were gone. She'd just had a vision of her people coming after her and they were close!

During the first days, she thought that was what she wanted, but now she knew better. She was not ready to return to her village. Sedna looked at the sleeping man. His head thrown back, eyes closed, Rolv looked so peaceful and different from his waking hours when he had to be ever alert and skillfully maneuver the ship through increasing ice blocks. When they sailed during the day time, the light and the weather could serve as his allies but by night fall the constant battle with the wheel tired him.

She sent her spirit across the blanket to touch his face, caress him as he did her, without his knowing. It felt good. She didn't know why. No use trying to explain some things. They just were.

The Raven Women could accept such uniqueness without challenging the spirit's rights. From the ancient legends passed from mother to daughter down through the generations, she knew this, but without legends, she would have still known in her heart.

Perhaps that was why she went with Rolv. Without recalling Tulunixiraq's words in the glacier, Sedna would never have departed from her parents and her village no matter what lay ahead for her when the hunters returned. Or if she had been alone and the Viking took her away, she could have escaped any time she wished. It wouldn't have been so difficult to step across the great ice to the shoreline while he slept each night under the full moon. Aku could have found the way back to the village.

Sedna knelt and held the she-wolf close to her cheek. With long, sharp teeth, red tongue, and bright yellow eyes, the creature looked anything but lovable. Until it nuzzled its nose into Sedna's neck, snuffling underneath her braid.

"Aku, you are the only thing I bring from home," she whispered.

༄༄

They sat eating a meal, chewing on smoked fish Rolv had stored below. It was a little more palatable than the moose meat. Aku ate the same food in a hollowed out dish Rolv found for her.

Sedna was beginning to feel uneasy about the distance they had traveled. "Where do we go? My clan believes if you go too far in a certain direction, you fall off into blackness."

He smiled.

She had learned the smile was also a way not to hurt her feelings with his opposing words.

"We do not believe that. My people have sailed to the ends of the Earth and beyond and I know there are no such boundaries. The sea never ends—and neither does the sky."

The strange concept made her uneasy. His next words gave her something pleasant and safe to think about, "We are going to Nordrsetur. It is nothing fine, not like Ericks-fjord, but cozy and warm. You will like it."

She looked over the water toward shore.

"Do they follow?" he asked. "I have searched the land, but see nothing."

"My people are not here yet, but they track us. I have seen them in a dream."

"How do they track us? We have not been ashore."

"The shaman can see tracks in the water."

"No one can do that!"

"He taught me some knowledge. The people think he sees tracks, but if he searches the shoreline he can tell from the way the ice lies and the driftwood along shore, that there was movement of the water—that a large object passed through. He knows where we are."

"Your people have the skin boats, why do they not follow in them?"

"The kayaks and *umiaks* are not powerful enough to follow in water filled with ice. That is why they come on land. If it gets cold quickly, if our journey takes too long, they may turn back."

"Turn back?"

"Yes. The seals will be out sunning, the walrus will be playing in the cold water, and the hunters need to hunt."

"They would not harm you now, would they? You could tell them I took you away against your will and I would agree."

She shrugged. "Analusha has listened to Nagatok's father who told them I went willingly. Some will believe him. He has to protect his powers."

"What would they do to you?"

"The shaman might order my leg cut behind the ankle so I cannot run away again. This happens. Or he could order my mouth to be slit thusly," she lifted the ends of her lips, pulling her mouth up to her cheeks in a grimace.

"They sometimes do that with people who lie or with women who go away with another man."

His mouth worked, she watched his throat move as he tried to swallow and, immediately, she knew the depth of his distress. This big, powerful man was afraid for her!

"I will never let them near you," he promised, laying his hand gently against her cheek.

She was not so certain he could keep that bold promise, but it consoled her to know he would try to the death.

"This water is so still, so black, so deep," he said, staring down, caught by its spell.

Sedna shook his shoulder in alarm. "Never stare at the water! Sednah is down there. She can claim your soul." She broke the mesmerizing effect on him. "That is what I saw happening to my father."

Rolv turned from the black, deep water. "Did you cure your father of the kayak sickness?"

She nodded. "I made a journey inside his thoughts. I saw how terrible it was on the black water when he was alone. He thought he must be the only person alive. It is no wonder we lose many hunters because of this."

"Why do they hunt alone? We never do—unless one of us has been cast out." The hurt crept into his voice as it always did when he mentioned his exile.

She shrugged. "It is the people's way. Sometimes they go in groups, sometimes alone. Whatever they chose to do is proper for them. We are guided by inner spirits from ancestors. Are you not?"

He was so quiet, she thought he would not answer.

"I do not know. I never thought of the notion. It may be all of us are." He touched her hand lightly. "You have caused me to think thoughts that never came to me before. I did not like it, at first. Now I find it exciting. I made a poem about you."

"Do you wish me to hear it?"

He looked suddenly shy, his usual strong arrogance gone. "Maybe you will make one for me one day."

As a shaman, she had been allowed to make up stories and songs, normally a man's function. Women who were not shaman were not permitted. From early childhood the course of a person's life was set by what he or she was destined to do or be. Most hunters never composed a song, only when they became old—like her father.

Rolv smiled and looked younger, not so fearsome, without the hair on his chin. She had grown to like what he called a mustache and was glad he left that amount of hair. When he asked if she was ready to listen to his po-em, his voice sounded strong. She could tell he was used to making up songs for his family.

> "A raven came to me, turning into a
> woman-child to haunt my dreams.
> Her hair is shiny black as a raven's wing,
> Her eyes are tilted at the edges,
> to prevent the spilling of the secrets they hold.
> Her body is small and perfect. I imagine
> myself looking upon the soft honey
> of her breasts with wonder,
> touching everywhere, exploring,
> searching out the mysteries...
> Holding her spirit with gentle hands,
> As she holds mine."

The silence closed around them when he finished speaking. His voice, deep and filled with emotion, ca-ressed her senses. She swallowed, uncomfortable but lik-ing the awareness it evoked. "It is beautiful," she said.

"You are the beautiful one." He kept his distance while the words in his poem swept over her again.

"It is but a small tribute after great effort, to say what I feel for you." Rolv held her hands in his and looked into her eyes, questioning her silently.

She had no answer.

He dropped her hands and leaped to his feet. His voice took on a hard edge. "This is wrong. I want to seduce you—make love to you, but we are worlds apart and must separate when I start my journey back to my family and you leave for yours." His voice changed, becoming low and husky with desire. "I thought to take you, to possess your body as my father took my mother captive, but that is not my way."

"Why did you bring me with you?" The words felt torn from her throat.

"I could not let the shaman kill or deform you. I promised not to take your body against your will and I will abide by that."

Startled at his volatile changes, able to follow some of his thoughts, she looked away toward the shore, to keep him from reading her eyes. He was right. This feeling of closeness would evaporate like the morning mist when he left the island to return home, leaving her empty and alone. She felt a close, dark vision of apprehension when she thought of his people and his true home.

He cleared his throat. His manner became more reserved, polite. "It will not be long now. Two more days and nights. We are close. Once we get to my home, your people cannot harm us. A Viking built this house long ago. Perhaps he too was cast aside. I wonder how my father knew about it, but he is a great explorer. The house is strong, if small."

She wondered how he had found their isolated village. All the open water, all the inlets had little fingers reaching out to the ocean, and he went down just that special one to land on their shores. Their meeting was clearly destined to happen and the Raven Mother knew it was so.

Sedna thought seriously on all these matters, as well as the question of whether the ice would claim the ship. Ice could hold them fast in an inexorable grip that would mean slow starvation and death. The ice was treacherous, in that some was thick and impenetrable. And just a little ways ahead, the ice could be thin. If they tried to cross it, they could fall into the darkness forever. He told her the Vikings had been to the ends of the sea and had never fallen off, but still, old beliefs died hard. He had explained to her that on their passageway, the ice was impenetrable in places and if they chose the wrong finger of water to traverse, they could be trapped.

Neither did she know if one night her people might cross an ice channel to leap on board the ship and slay them. Because Aku would tell her of their attack, they could not slip up on her unawares. Also she knew Rolv did not sleep the entire night, but watched over her and his ship in the darkest hours.

She closed her eyes, wishing for her drum so she could make a chant of protection, so she could claim a vision of how her mother and father had fared. She tried to send them mind messages that her leaving them was not from lack of care but was her destiny.

The shaman and the hunters followed, she'd seen their outlines on the shore. But also she needed the vision of how far they would follow.

CHAPTER 6

L and ho!" Rolv's rich baritone awoke her during his watch in the night. They traveled always when the moon was full, hurrying to arrive before the winter closed in.

Sedna rubbed her eyes. The stars looked so close she was tempted to reach up to touch one, but thought better of it. She had heard stories of long ago shaman who had been sucked up into the sky for staring too long at the moon or a particular star. She pushed out of her wrappings and leaped to her feet to hurry forward and stand next to him.

Rolv grabbed her in his arms, dancing around so her feet did not touch the deck, shouting with glee. Sedna laughed, too, enjoying the closeness without worrying any more over the suitability of his actions.

"What makes you so happy?" she asked between laughter and shouts.

He let her down to point. "Look!"

They had left the main body of water and entered a narrow inlet.

First she saw eerie ice shapes, windblown shards all pointing in one direction. They looked like crystal images of magical shapes—creatures, mountains, trees—all bril-

liantly clear with the moonlight slanting through them.
She shivered. "Why does the ice arrange itself so?"

"The wind blows constantly from the southwest here.
If you become lost in the snow, you can usually find your
starting place."

They sailed closer, rounding a bend in the ice.

She saw a strange, tall structure of gray stone piled
upon gray stone and covered with green turf. It was
overwhelmingly ugly, yet strong and arrogant, protruding
like some live entity from the land surrounding it.

They hit shore with a severe bump. Rolv cursed and
leaped out to see if the impact had damaged the ship. He
swung back up on the ship by a series of ropes which she
found amazing. "No harm done." He put down the plank
for her to walk on and led the way proudly while she followed with Aku.

"This is Nordrsetur. At first, I hated being alone. But
after the men helped me settle in before returning to Ericksfjord, I learned to enjoy owning my solitude."

He spoke of how being alone had helped heal his anger and his wild temper. He admitted that his volatile
moods were no longer a matter to brag about, to compare
with his father's notorious ferocity. It had helped, to live
inside his head for days at a stretch without the interfer-
ence of another living human being. If his father had ever
owned the benefit of this time alone, perhaps he wouldn't
have grown so hot-headed, so quarrelsome.

∝∾∝∾

Sedna walked sedately down the embankment and followed Rolv up a rise toward the house. She heard a rushing, roaring river behind the building. In the other direction lay the sea, ringed by tall mountains with snow covering their tops.

"Oh! Never have I seen such trees!" She clapped her hands together in wonder. Only once in her lifetime had she ever traveled away from the land of snow and ice. She was a small child then and barely held the memory of her people's frantic search for food in the woodlands.

"This is different from your land," he said. "You may not be happy here long. People such as you have lived lifetimes beyond the glacier, on an island that holds no green."

People such as you. He did not say it with a critical voice, but Sedna did not like what he said. She tilted her chin with disdain and ignored the hurtful words.

Brilliant green turf had grown up over the stone of the house and outbuildings. The soothing color warmed her eyes, so used to seeing the sharp whites of her own land-scape. "It is…" She held up her palms, with no words to describe the beauty.

"Soon the snow will cover it all." His arms swept over the surrounding turf. "Please enter," he said, pushing aside the heavy layers of animal skins.

"At home, we have entry ways of wood." He looked unable to explain the idea.

She had never seen any opening in a home that was not covered with skins.

"I have no servants," he warned. "When they brought me here I was to fend for myself or die. Harsh, but all must obey the judgment."

Sedna was relieved that they were alone. "What is a servant?" she wanted to know.

"Questions, always questions," Rolv teased. "When Eric went a-viking from the old country, sometimes they captured slaves. He couldn't abide that, so made them into indentured servants who, in time, could pay off their capture and become as neighbors. Many of our neighbors were servants to begin with."

Sedna wasn't certain all that was clear to her, but she filed it away in her head to think about later.

Inside the structure, she panicked at the close, damp walls. Rolv hurried to light lanterns filled with oil, which dispelled the gloom a little but made odd, dancing figures on the low ceiling and walls.

She shivered. It was mystical, like being inside a seance, only her eyes were wide open. The stone walls felt damp and cold, not like her family's warm hut, yet inside it was not as cold as out. The walls were solid, the entryway the only opening. It resembled an extra-large ice hut the hunters built and used on their hunts. She wandered into a little alcove which held a meager supply of furs and other equipment she did not recognize.

Rolv stood in the middle of the room, arms across his chest. She knew he must be waiting for her opinion. She tried the opening of lips, the showing of teeth she learned from him. It seemed to satisfy him. What could she say? That she was frightened? That she'd felt a separation from him—a strange quality of aloneness—since she had arrived.

A foreboding held her in a grip that made it hard to breathe. She would have to make a spell to rid the house of phantoms, of ugly thoughts, of bitterness, or she might damage her powers if she stayed here any length of time.

Rolv knelt in front of the fireplace and began to light the wood piled within.

සාශ

Nordrsetur held a surprising enchantment for Sedna in the days to come. She and Aku wandered around the woods. Rolv invited her to enjoy the solitude. She needed the time to recoup the powers she felt had diminished during the voyage. The trees held a power, a vibrant life that claimed her imagination and soothed her soul. Sedna felt a calm contentment within herself. As if this was supposed to be.

During the day, Rolv fished and set out traps. He didn't catch much, by Inuit standards, but he seemed content with his yields. She privately thought differently. Not the smallest child in her village would have been satisfied with what he harvested. Her fingers itched to grab hold of his lance and show him how hunting was done properly. She didn't think the people's ruling that women could not hunt large animals was reasonable now that she was not with them. But this was his land and he had his own ways, which were hers until she left him. She did not wish to shame him.

"If you had given me time, I might have brought one of my father's harpoons and my bola. I need to make a bola for the birds," she complained one morning as they stood outside the house looking at a sunrise.

"If I had allowed you to think on it, would you have come with me?"

She stretched her lips carefully in what she knew now was a smile.

"What is this thing you call bola?"

She explained that a bola was a line as long as her two arms spread apart, made of twisted sinew from a walrus hide with weights on each end. "The smallest walking child in our village knows how to hunt with the bola. It is a form of hunting women are permitted."

"Can you show me?"

Sedna expected him to be proud and stubborn. But his eager desire to understand, his readiness to learn new ways, proved a constant source of pleasure to her.

She found three stiffened, badly-cured deer hides stacked in the corner of a store room and asked for one.

He watched her carefully cut it into long, narrow

strips. "Walrus hide is better, but this will do. Have you a bone place? I need bones, this big." She took his hand and separated two large fingers.

"Of course." He went behind the house and brought her a bowl full of bones, exactly the sizes she needed. She tied two on each end of the strip of sinew. "Come, I will show you."

She motioned him away from her and swung the bola around over her head with expert grace. When she let fly, it captured an upthrusting pile of stone with ease.

"The bola is for the large sea birds. We also use it on small animals to stop them from fleeing. Soon it will be too late for small animals. Then you must hunt seal and walrus."

"Amazing. I've never seen anything like this. We use lances and knives. Freyda prefers a small ax."

"Freyda?" That name again. Sedna rubbed her arms to get rid of the bumps that arose. "Are your women allowed to hunt?"

"Norse women do as they please. Many go into battle in foreign lands, following their mates. Women can vote in the *Althing*, they can own property, they can leave their mates if they choose. Is it not the same with you?"

She shook her head. *Not since the first Raven Mother relinquished this right.* She wanted to speak the words aloud, but he might not understand and she could never explain.

"So strange, the difference in our customs," he said. "Yet, it does not seem as important as once I thought. We have a legend of a woman named Bibrau who is much like your Sednah. We refer to her as she-who-sits-in-the-blue, meaning at the bottom of the sea."

He leaned forward and bestowed a kiss on her lips. It felt so gentle, the wings of a bird touching her.

He sat back and continued. "This maiden accompanied

warriors into battle and sang them songs to give them courage and support. She vanished one day in the midst of a battle between ships and was never seen again. But we believe her to watch from her vantage point below the water to aid sea-faring men."

She no longer wanted to back away from his touch.

They regarded each other with a long look—sky gray eyes staring into fathomless black.

∽∾∽

The winter storm rushed in, unannounced, while the green grass still covered the Earth. The trees, just changing color, dropped their leaves. Yet, the birds remained abundant. Sedna saw so many birds that she wondered what the warm time would bring if this many stayed when the night temperatures froze shallow lakes. By now, ice would have covered everything in her village, including the shoreline and far out into the water. No birds could remain on the land. The men would ready their weapons to hunt seal.

Before the winter ended, she must make nets of sinew, to catch the small, juicy birds of spring. Once, inside a nearby forest, she looked up toward the sky. Dust motes and sunbeams sifted through the multicolored branches, in a breathtaking array of splendor that brought a tightening in her throat, hard to swallow. Aku ran around, smelling everything, touching her nose to each tree trunk, sniffing in holes in the ground. Everything on this island was different from Sedna's land of ice and snow. Different, but no longer frightening. Was it because she was in the company of Rolv?

Nights were the best to her. Long nights to sit next to the fire inside the house while she and Rolv made up songs and told stories to each other. They slept side by side in front of the fire, wrapped in blankets, close yet separate, with Aku at their feet.

"She would be a fine mate for Legbiter." Rolv touched the wolf's head and his eyes took on that faraway look.

She knew the thoughts of home came to him more and more as time passed. Soon it would be spring and his time of banishment would be over. What would he do then about her?

Sedna brushed the thoughts away. "Legbiter?" The word sounded funny on her tongue.

"He is Eric's dog. I do not know how to explain dogs except to say they are like wolves only tame. And bigger."

It was another one of his stories she thought made up.

"Here, let me show you something from home," Rolv said one night after they had eaten a meal of roasted bird. She did most of the cooking now that he finally understood how terrible he was at the chore.

The main room of the house was long and narrow. Leading off on the sides with open doorways, were small storerooms, icy cold, any time of the day or night.

Rolv had walked to the doorway and returned carrying a large stone.

She could see it was heavy by the way he took pains not to show it.

"I took this from Eric's place—to bring me luck in my banishment. They have more and may not miss this one."

She moved her fingers carefully over markings on the stone. "What is it?"

"It is a rune stone. Our ancestors had them in Norway. Eric brought some of them with us. They bring good luck in our homes."

"Like our door stone." She explained how every Inuit home had a flat stone at the foot of the last step-down inside. When they moved, the family took the stone to the next dwelling. "Do you know what is written on your stone?"

He shook his head. "No one does. It is an ancient language only sorcerers know."

She sat cross-legged near the fire, closed her eyes, and played her fingers lightly over the writings. From deep within, the strange words came. Words she did not understand.

"What has become of the steed?
What has become of the warrior?
What has become of the seats of banquet?
Where are the joys of the hall?
O for the bright cup!
O for the mail-clad warrior!
O for the glory of the prince!
How that time has passed away,
And grown dark under the cover of night,
As if it had never been."

Slowly Sedna opened her eyes and looked across at Rolv. The big Viking had tears in his eyes which he rubbed hastily away.

"That is magic! You could not know these words or know what they mean. Yet I have heard them before, recited from a poem of my father's ancestors. No one knew the words lived on this piece of stone!"

"It is part of the shaman in me," she said

"There are times when I look into your eyes and you seem different. As if you are two people." He touched his fingers to her chin, tilting her face up.

"Is this troublesome? Often that happens with a shaman."

"No. But I want you to stay my little troll, never change," he teased her, pulling gently on her braid.

೧Ꭷ೧

Several days had passed, and she could see he prepared for a hunt by working on his weapons. Sedna sat working on her surprise gift of boots, but she hid them under her furs when he looked at her. "I wish to go hunting with you. I do not want to stay behind alone."

He used what he called a whetstone on his lance tip a moment before answering and turned his head sideways to slant a look at her. "I had not thought of leaving you behind."

She did not understand the material at the tip of the lance, although huge balls of fire had dropped from the sky in the past and left the people hard substances such as this to use in their weapons.

He saw her looking at the lance. "This is forged metal. At Ericksfjord we have metal workers who put pieces of this over fire and hammer it into the shape and size we ask for. The best metal is blue steel from the Arabs. Eric has a sword made of the blue metal. The King of Norway bestowed it upon him in battle."

She wondered if he always told the truth because his story seemed too far from anything in her own experience to be real.

"Is Eric's...is this place where you live the same as here?"

"No." His voice was somber, as it always was when he spoke of his home. "Here we have warm ocean currents and breezes in the summer, spring, and fall. Only a league away, the land resembles your land, white and treeless except for stunted willows and occasional bush. Ericksfjord is much more beautiful than anything I've seen, the land more hospitable."

CHAPTER 7

The next morning they ate a bit of smoked fish, of which she was growing heartily tired, and set off to hunt.

She snared five sea birds with her bola. Aku ran out to touch her nose to them and sank back on her haunches, knowing Sedna would give her one to devour.

Sedna saw that her throwing skills surprised Rolv. It pleased her to show off to this man who seemed impressed with ordinary competence that any woman, young or old and many children easily performed in her village. "It will soon be time for the seals to come out and sun." She pointed toward the ice floes, increasing in size every day in the sea.

He grimaced. "I tried ever since I came here, but only caught a small one who lay on the ice unaware. When I lanced him, he rolled off the ice and disappeared into the water. That is not surprising. My father and the men in our settlement also have a hard time catching any seals."

"The walrus? *Ayvuq*? Do you slay him?"

Surprised, Rolv said, "A man alone cannot hope to kill a walrus. They are like fierce warriors who refuse to be slain. My people have wounded many, killed some, but only a crew of men can bring one down."

She knew him to be brave. He stood up to her clan and faced down certain death. He was always talking about the glory of dying in battle. Yet, she sensed his hesitation to confront those huge beasts. How strange to mistrust animals who were sent to Earth to feed the people and took pleasure in doing so. Did he also fear the white bear, *naanuk?*

When a man feared, his soul was not his own, he belonged to the demons that owned him. She would not let this happen to him.

She needed some of her people's weapons to teach him and to sing shaman songs for him.

"What do you live on then, if you cannot catch seal or *ayvuq?*"

"Winter berries and birds. I set out traps and slay deer and moose. We have cattle. Once I journeyed across the mountains to slay a muskox, but it was too hard to bring the meat home without sleds and dogs."

Sleds and dogs? Cattle? She had much to learn of life outside her village. But so did he have much to learn also. She saw evidence of that in the stiff, hard pelts in the storeroom. He could learn a lot about flensing and curing leather, to begin. A woman would be put out on the ice if she cured a hide in such a slovenly manner.

"Look! Sedna, look, it is one of *them.*"

She turned in the direction he pointed to see a big, fat walrus in the middle of a giant iceberg out in the water. "It is too soon, the ice is not safe. Use a boat." She knew he had a small boat the size of a kayak in back of the house.

"No! It will take too long to go back for it. The ice will hold me."

Sedna believed him to be showing off for her benefit. She closed her eyes, using all her shaman skills to make him stop, but his single-mindedness was too strong for her. His long strides ate up the ground. He advanced across the ice, first quickly, then in stealth, Aku at his side. She tried to move the walrus—capture its interest with a chant.

> "O mighty *ayvuq*, creature supreme in the water,
> Offer your body to this brave man
> who wishes to receive you with gratitude.
> Sednah of the deep, Goddess of the sea,
> mother of all creatures, will bless you as will I,
> O powerful one."

Sedna finished the chant and hit her palms together lightly, a pantomime of using her drum. She did not want to venture nearer, fearful the beast must feel their presence.

Rolv concentrated on his goal so that he no longer spared a glance downward at his footing. Aku skimmed the ground behind him, her belly touching the snow.

The huge animal looked up from his sleep. Rolv hesitated, stepped backward in his same tracks, and twisted his body sharply, as if trying to stave off sinking into the icy water when the ice cracked beneath him. Only the end of his lance showed as he slowly descended into the sea.

Aku snapped and growled at the walrus, lunging toward the large creature until it slipped off the side of the ice and floated away.

Sedna dropped her bola and ran, leaping from ice pack to ice pack, secure in her slight weight and propelled by the heart-smashing fear of his sinking into the cold, black water—to be forever lost in Sednah's grasp.

When she arrived at the edge, his head bobbed to the surface. She grabbed hold of his hair and began pulling him toward the shore, skirting around the ice. Once she had to drag him over a shelf of ice and she made a new grab onto the fur collar of his coat. Aku pranced and howled, circling around her until she had to shout at the wolf to be silent. She did not know if Rolv was dead or alive. All she could think to do was haul him to the house and warmth of the fire. Once she pulled him onto the shore, she knew dragging him was impossible. He was too big, too heavy, weighed down with frozen water. Only her Raven power and her terror had helped her get him this far.

She shook him and pounded on his chest in frustrated anger. "Do not die! You cannot die! I will not permit it!"

"I will surely die, if you keep pummeling me so," he gasped out.

As soon as he had spoken, he began to shake all over in great tremors. His teeth chattered so that he could not speak.

He was alive! She leaned forward and hugged his body to her, barely getting her arms half way around him. "Hurry! Can you stand? We must get you to the fire."

As soon as she spoke, the sky darkened even more, and she felt the prickling of the north wind on the exposed flesh of her hands and face. A winter storm was coming!

"Hurry! We must hurry!" She didn't know if this land was like her land, where the storms brought the deadly white fog that covered everything making it impossible to see your hand in front of your eyes. They could be lost between here and the house!

At the urgency in her voice, he struggled to his feet. He swayed in place, having used all his energy to rise. She knew he wanted more than anything to settle back down on the ground and go to sleep.

"Walk! Damn your eyes, walk!" she screamed at him. Her small fist struck against his back.

This unfamiliar voice with words Sedna did not know

startled them both. They looked at each other, shocked at the strange voice and harsh words from a woman who had never spoken so. Sedna spared a moment to thank the Raven Mother.

It worked. Rolv put one shaky foot in front of the other in an effort to move forward, trying not to lean on her too heavily. The lance was frozen inside his fist and he could not let go, nor could she pry it loose, so he tried to use it on one side for balance.

She looked ahead for the house, so far away. He fell down again, closed his eyes, and refused to move.

His long, thick eyelashes crusted with ice against his pale cheeks. The sun-brown of his skin had vanished leaving a patina of blue under the skin of his face, pulling his lips tight into a grimace of near-death.

She urged Aku. "Come, help me get the *umiak*." They ran all the way back to the house and found the strange-looking thing he called a boat leaning against the wall of an outbuilding. The people's *umiaks* were different, made of animal skin and light weight. This one was heavy and clumsy.

Her half-frozen fingers tried to use the bird bola to make a harness for the wolf. At first the animal looked up at her reproachfully, growling deep in its chest. The instinct against bonds was for the moment stronger than her love for Sedna.

"Please, my friend," Sedna coaxed. "We must save him. I cannot tell you why, perhaps in your wisdom you know, but it is important, so very important. Will you help me?"

Now would be the time to leave him. He could not hold her prisoner. She was free to go, move across the tundra with the wolf leading the way. She had a feeling her people were out hunting on the ice and would find her. By now they would welcome her back.

But no! She could not leave him. Not when he needed her.

With lolling tongue, Aku began to pull the small boat through the snow-crusted grass toward Rolv's prone body. Sedna pushed from behind to speed the progress.

When they reached Rolv, she pondered the problem briefly then rolled the round-bottomed boat over on its side. She twisted and rolled the comatose man inside and struggled with all her might to right the boat. When she achieved her goal, she took her place behind and spoke to the wolf. "Aku! Pull and I will push!"

Together, they pulled and pushed the heavy boat across the tundra toward the house while she muttered a shaman spell for strength. Fear rose in her breast because Rolv looked so still. A thin sheet of ice covered him. Only the thick gold/red hair between his nose and upper lip moved slightly, attesting to his breathing.

He had to live! He had to! It was not only her fervent wish, but the warning the Raven Mother had left with her that willed him to stay alive, that gave her the endurance and strength to continue pushing the heavy boat.

At the door, she overturned the boat again, disconnecting the wolf, stopping briefly to hug Aku in gratitude, and dragging Rolv inside by his collar.

She threw more wood on the fire at the center of the room, leaving the doorway partly open to let out any smoke from damp wood.

By now the storm tore around the corners of the stone house, whistling through the ice outside with eerie noises of anger—as if it had missed its prey. The wind wanted to claim them as its own, to be forever statues in the ice and snow.

Sedna shivered, then knelt and began stripping off Rolv's wet clothes. Layer after layer she pulled away, rolling him back and forth to get the crusted cloth away from his icy body. By the time she got down to the strange material next to his skin, she was exhausted, but did not give up. She sucked in her breath when she saw one of his legs twisted sideways in a strange manner. There was no sign of a bone protruding through the skin, something every Inuit feared. Often it meant they must cut off the offending limb. When they cut, the man usually died anyway.

Taking a deep breath, she began tearing off her seal skin jacket and trousers, then her leather tunic and on down to her bird-skin vest and short trousers. In spite of the heat from the fireplace on her front parts, her backside was assailed by bone-chilling cold in the stone house.

What foolish people these giant strangers were, to build a winter house on top of the ground instead of beneath it!

When they were both disrobed to bare skin, she pushed him onto the bear skin lying in front of the fire. Then she lay down on top of him, and pulled several of the strange materials he called woolen blankets all around them, finishing with another large bear skin lying near the fire place.

Holding him close, she offered the spare comfort of her small, warm body, suffering the spasms with him as he began to moan with the pain of thawing.

Sedna crooned to him in tones everyone in her tribe through the ages used on their children to quiet them, to heal them, to comfort, and also to mourn their passing, although she would not permit him to die.

She whispered the special chant against the soul forfeiting the body. It was so powerful that a shaman seldom invoked it. Far better to allow loved ones to depart in peace and contentment rather than try to hold them through sheer force of power.

The shaman could be drawn into the land of the dead along with the dying person.

Sedna was willing to take that chance. She did not want him to leave her. The wolf lay close, under the covering against her legs, to offer her warmth also.

Exhausted, she fell asleep, waking with the feeling of being watched. She and Rolv lay on their sides, facing each another, wrapped close. She stared straight into his eyes.

"Thank you, my little one. Two times I must thank you for my life," he whispered hoarsely.

"Do you remember what happened to you?" She did not pull away from him, enjoying the feeling of his warming skin against hers.

"Yes. I wanted to show off to you. I should have listened when you said the ice was not ready."

"Men do not listen to women," she said mildly, sensing the sharp pain of awakening feeling returning to his limbs and knowing he talked to keep it at bay.

"We listen. Women are important to us. We do not shame them by making them less important than a man. Our women stand at our side, not behind us." His voice was low, a soft whisper.

As he thawed and his shivering disappeared, a new emotion crept into his eyes. She recognized burgeoning desire. She had seen it in Nagatok's eyes each time, before he laid claim to her body, but she had never felt it herself.

"Do not fear me, Sedna. I will never harm you nor allow anyone to harm you." He murmured into her loosened hair that hung in front of her breasts.

She thought of his promise to his god aboard the ship. Was he forsaking this vow? Something new within her body wanted her to accept his lovemaking this time. But fear of the unknown made her push at his chest.

He was beyond caution, beyond his ability to stop.

The room lost its chill and the layers of covering on them became heavy. He threw them off and using his elbow to hold himself above her, his gaze devoured her from head to toe.

His mouth covered hers in a tender kiss that deepened and grew demanding. She felt his tremor when a sigh escaped her lips. His hands, now warmed, moved over her body and she arched her breasts toward him, unable to stop the heady, heavy feeling that churned in her lower regions. He gently cupped her small breasts, his thumbs playing with her nipples until she wanted to scream out for…for what?

She didn't know, but an unbidden need began to flow through her body, consuming her until she cried out his name, over and over. When she wondered if she could bear another touch, he pushed his leg between her thighs and spread them apart. She felt his hardness against her and gasped. For a moment, reality intruded with the memory of Nagatok's brutal claiming of her, the last time he took her.

"Hush, sweeting, I will be as gentle as I can, you are so small, but I can feel your response and you are ready for me." He had touched her down there with his fingers and while she held her breath, waiting for pain, it didn't come. He manipulated the bud and she felt disgraced by the soft liquid that she felt inside her secret place. The discomfort suddenly exploded with a jagged lights and she arched her hips upward to engage his fingers deeper.

He pressed his erection at the tip of her entrance and slowly pushed it forward. She cried out once, fearful of the pain she knew had to come. When he gently continued to push into her, she relaxed and put her arms up under his to caress his back.

But her need, the unfamiliar craving, overpowered her

and she raised her hips suddenly and encompassed his entire member with a gasp.

He paused a moment and looked down at her in wonder. So fearful he must have been of harming her. After that, he moved inside her with a frenzy of need and when she screamed with the huge tremor arching her body, he spilled his seed inside her with an ecstasy that he'd never felt before with any woman.

When their lovemaking was over, they lay back panting, eyes closed. Rolv continued to hold her close, to keep them as one body. He leaned forward and brushed the hair from around her cheeks, kissing her face and throat in his Viking way.

"You were not my first," she said tentatively, fearful he would be hurt knowing that. "Nagatok took me twice by force. And then he never touched me again, but he was waiting—"

"Hush, my sweet. I knew I was not the first and I am saddened to know you suffered with your first time. But I will never cause you pain."

Moments passed and she heard soft breathing. Knowing he was asleep, Sedna pulled the covers up around his naked body and, only then, the belated thought came that she lay next to a stranger.

She had belonged to Nagatok since she was a baby and had never thought of lying with another man. It was her chosen husband's right to claim her body after the time of her first bleeding. Which he did. But he had never tried to pleasure her nor had she ever felt anything but fear and pain.

What manner of mating was this that wrung out such strong feelings in her?

Rolv felt her slight movement and awoke. He turned slightly and took her chin in his hand, kissing the tears from her cheeks.

"Dear heart. Never has a woman pleasured me as you have."

He caressed her closed eyelids, her mouth and the throbbing place in her throat with his lips, then holding her close, pulled the blankets up around them and fell asleep again.

Sedna lay awake long after. Her body sated, her mind searched for meaning to what had just happened to her. Even as she lay still and happy, a worry nagged at her thoughts. Her people would not give up searching for her so easily. She'd seen that in a vision. They were coming to find her. Would she go back with them? The shaman and Nagatok had time to think on it and realized she did not leave the village of her own free will. If they offered to take her back, would she go?

Her thoughts finally released her to a troubled sleep.

CHAPTER 8

Rolv was downcast and repentant the next morning. He arose from the bed of furs and poked the fire, looking in her direction, waiting and dreading for Sedna to awaken.

He had sworn his allegiance and protection upon his sword in front of his gods. In his blind passion, he could no more have staved off his invasion of her body than he could have stopped the wind from blowing. The craving, the unrelenting desire had been building since the first time he saw her on the beach, bending over him.

It was a terrible dishonor he had committed. How could he offer atonement to her and to his gods?

The only way he could see to atone for what had to be her diminished trust in him was to try not to break that promise again as a reminder he was not to be trusted.

❧❦❧

Sedna awoke slowly, warmed by what had happened the night before. She looked up at Rolv standing by the fireplace. His expression was remote, his mouth a hard line. Did he regret what had passed between them?

She made a small noise to get his attention, slowly

lowering the covers from her naked body to arise.

The look of regret he turned on her made her heart flutter in her chest, her throat tightened and she struggled to swallow past a lump. He quickly pulled on his jacket and went outside.

Sedna surmised he did not like what he saw. She'd displeased him in some manner. Perhaps he remembered lying with his own kind. Did he think longingly of a soft, white body beneath his own? When he touched her black hair, when he buried his face in her neck, did he recall hair the color of sun like his own?

His raw need for her had left her open to his passion, a passion she would have succumbed to even without Nagatok's forceful taking of her. How Rolv touched her last night erased all the sorrow and emptiness she'd felt. Aku nuzzled her nose into Sedna's hand, wanting to be noticed. The wolf sensed her pain and sorrow and offered the solace of her touch.

҂ಬ಼

Winter roared in to claim the land. Sedna watched the trees, bare of leaves, bend into the screaming wind. The stark, bare branches lowered with the weight of snow and broke with loud explosions of noise that shattered the still land. The sea close to the shore turned white with ice.

Sedna sat on the ice, patiently waiting for a fish to snap at the line she made.

"Thank you, my friend for bringing food," she whispered to the wolf who lay nearby. Several times Aku brought back rabbits and ptarmigan, their feathers and fur white with their winter covering. This helped when they were so hungry that even the smoked fish tasted good. The fresh meat nourished their bodies and souls.

While she fished, she thought of Rolv who had hurt

his leg in his fall. When he stood on it, that leg wouldn't take his weight. The big muscle all the way past his ankle to his foot had turned black.

Shaman knowledge advised that he would heal one day, but not if he walked on the leg and foot while it was black. It was hard convincing Rolv to stay off his feet, but she finally succeeded.

He grumbled and groaned like a bear wakened from its hibernation, but he obeyed her, even though their supply of food was low, and fish did not swim to take the lure on her line.

"O Sednah, goddess of the sea, we are hungry. Please spare us one little fish, perhaps two," she murmured.

Aku leaped to her feet growling low in her throat. She looked back at the house, hackles on her back raised. Sedna pulled up her line and stood to look too.

Hunters! Men moved across the frozen tundra, toward the building where Rolv lay inside unaware. Feeling for her fish skinning knife, she slipped it in her pocket and shouted at the men, turning their attention toward her as a mother ptarmigan turns a predator away from her nest.

When they saw her, they switched directions and came out on the ice toward her, bypassing the house. The reprieve was only temporary. They might still enter the house and slay the unsuspecting Rolv, after they killed her. Hunting groups that came so close to a person's abode signified only danger. Otherwise hunters stayed clear of single dwellings because such dwellings could be inhabited by evil spirits.

Closer and closer they came until she recognized Analusha, Nagatok, and others from her clan. Gladness to see them warred with fear. She could not return with them now. If she did, Rolv would die alone and unprotected, a terrible death for a Viking. He would not be allowed in that place he called Valhalla.

She lifted her chin and stretched to her full height. A shaman in her own right, no one could claim dominion over her unless she permitted it by showing weakness.

"Welcome." She was close enough to them to see the expression in their eyes—cautious, curious, not unfriendly. The bright curiosity was a particularly good sign.

"We have come a long way. Does a woman have broth to offer?" Analusha asked, speaking first.

"We have no broth. A man injured himself on the ice, and a woman cannot hunt."

The old shaman and the others sat down on the hard ice pack, as comfortable as if they would have been home in front of a fireplace. She sat across from them.

No one spoke. Sedna recognized the ancient game of intimidation. Since living away from the village, many truths had come to her about her old life and customs.

"The stranger stole my possession, my woman. I will kill him and take her back." Nagatok's strident voice broke the long silence. He leaped to his feet, standing with legs apart, arms folded across his chest in the age-old stance of threatening ferocity. The Inuit imitated the posture of the white bear.

Sedna looked at him with new eyes. She thought of his clumsy mating, his selfishness that left her empty. The future with him no longer was her fate if she dared change it.

As shaman, if she were strong enough, she could return with them as a solitary person, never again to mate. That might satisfy everyone.

She did have feelings for Nagatok—for all of them. The shaman had been a hard, relentless teacher over the years, yet he had recognized the shaman in her and nourished her birthright.

"The Norseman took me away with him, afraid you two would punish me." She looked pointedly at the shaman, who stood trembling, ready to go into one of his dreaded fits.

"You must return with us. I see no sinews on your arms and legs, holding you here." Nagatok spoke in an angry monotone, as if he tried to hold back his humiliation which lay bare for all to see and hear. She knew he took a perverse pride in showing off his disgrace.

She spoke decisively, looking at each man in turn, and ending with the shaman. "I have decided to be no man's possession. I cannot return with you."

"You are shaman. Yet you are also a daughter and your mother and father miss their only daughter," one of the men from the rear said. She recognized Ogiak, Nagatok's father.

She thought of her parents, how she had taken care of them since they had become old, provided for them without their realizing it. With her gone, they must know how much they had grown to depend upon her. Especially her proud father. Being reminded of them made her feel selfish and cruel.

She missed Kuliit and Suutak a great deal, but Rolv had managed to fill every empty space in her when she left others behind. In spite of knowing this, it would be so simple, so easy to return with the hunters. The thought stopped before it had time to mature.

"I know you speak the truth, Ogiak. I regret causing my parents pain. I feel remorse because you saved me for your son and I have disappointed you. You must tell my father and mother I miss them also, and I may return later. My destiny is here for the present. I have had visions."

No one dared argue with visions. The men exchanged looks.

She could see a new expression in their faces, one of respect and more than a little awe.

"I am sorry for the dowry you paid my father for me,"

she said to Nagatok and his father. "I will repay you for that, if you wish, when the Norseman is able to hunt again."

"You said you had no broth. How do you live? Where is the stranger?"

She took a deep breath. Did their new respect for her extend to Rolv? Did she dare tell them his leg was black and swollen and he could not move? If they thought he was unable to fight, it could go badly for him. Yet she might use his present helplessness to make them feel superior and that might go well for them all.

"The stranger comes from people who are not of our land. He does not know how to do the least thing that an Inuit child knows from birth," she told the little group of men.

At first she felt a twinge of disloyalty, talking behind Rolv's back, but she said only the truth and she knew it would appease their wounded pride.

"I may return to our village when he no longer needs my help, but he has a spirit in him that is important. My visions have said I must be patient until the spirit shows why it is of importance. It concerns the Raven Woman line."

Sedna closed her eyes and pulled off the Raven Woman belt always around her, holding it high in her clenched fist. "I am the Raven Woman. As Raven Woman, I have considered hunting. Even though a woman, I am also shaman. I do not think the animals would be angered by a shaman hunting them."

The men whispered among themselves. Only Nagatok and Analusha continued to stare at her.

The old shaman jumped high in the air to make his point. He whirled around and around in place, keening and shouting and gnashing his teeth.

The others moved away from him, for he was in one

of his legendary fits, which increased their fear and respect.

Sedna sat down again, and fastened her belt with
trembling fingers. They all must wait, to see what the
shaman decided.

Time passed, the wind grew chill and many of them
had ice on their eyelashes and parka collars, but no one
dared move. They were all frozen in time, bound together
by watching the ranting, writhing shaman.

Sedna's and Rolv's lives depended upon his decision.

Analusha continued to whirl on the ice. Dancing a
weird dance of death, of abandonment, she recognized, as
did the others, that they were casting her aside. She must
find another village, another people. These would be
strangers to her after this ceremony.

Blood etched the corners of the shaman's mouth and
she wanted to close her eyes against the climax she knew
was coming.

He stopped in mid-whirl, opened his mouth to give a
horrendous shriek and blood spewed out over the ice in
front of them, desecrating the pristine whiteness with the
contrast of stark red.

She forced herself to look. Fear rippled through her
body and she tried to concentrate on how he did it. This
was Analusha's most unusual trick and he saved it for the
special times. She knew he bit the inside of his cheeks
and tongue until the blood ran, mixed it with saliva and
when he was ready, spewed it out on the ground.

As shaman, he'd taught her many things that she was
not prepared to do. This was one. But it was effective and
worked even with another shaman who knew it as a trick.

He collapsed in a heap and lay twitching and jerking.
No one dared touch him. Slowly, with a twitch now and
then, he became normal.

"I have been to the other side," he intoned in the deep

voice of the giant bear, his helper spirit. Everyone waited, barely breathing.

Sedna closed her eyes for a moment, feeling strength emanating from the Raven belt, feeling radiating warmth seep into her mind. She trembled, though she tried not to show her fear. Analusha could command the men to slay her now and her body would be full of lances in a moment, becoming like a woodland porcupine.

Then they would finish off the helpless Rolv. That thought hurt enough to make her open her eyes and stare at the shaman, hiding her fear.

Analusha stared back a long time, studying her, measuring her resolute strength, the calm composure that showed outside. Finally, he uttered a small explosive sound, a grunt. Sedna slowly released the breath she had been holding, for she knew he was satisfied with what he saw.

"It has come to me in a vision as I traveled through the sky on the wings of the Raven," he said. "This woman we call Sedna has surely left us. She has been joined by the *inua*, a soul from another place and time. This new person is the spirit of the ancient Sednah, goddess of the sea. I am forbidden to challenge this new being or I chance losing my own power. Our daughter may return to us when this stranger leaves her—if not in her body as we see it before us, she will return as someone else. She may stay with him until they die. Until then we must leave her in peace."

His prophecy rang out across the ice and encompassed the world of winter and the small group who stood in the middle. He had seen the determination in her eyes. Sedna instinctively knew some part of his words would come true.

She would come back to her people in some form of life, not necessarily her own familiar one. But she didn't think she would stay with the Viking. She stood. Looking into Analusha's black eyes, knowing his skinny, narrow body hid beneath the fur garments, she wondered why she had ever been in awe of him. He was but a man, though with certain powers. She, too, had powers.

"Will you leave weapons to help me?" she asked.

The shaman turned to the men. "You are the hunters. What do you say?"

Nagatok leaped to his feet, his father beside him. "She is no longer a part of our village. Her doings cannot harm our people. What difference if we leave weapons?" The younger man looked very proud, but his expression showed great sorrow and loss.

Her heart squeezed tight in her chest, and she felt his grieving, though her expression did not change. She didn't dare show weakness, or all which had been gained would be lost.

"Nagatok, I have had a vision that you will forgive me one day. You will take another woman and you will have a family."

He grunted and turned away in shame that she had seen the weakness of his pain.

When he turned back, he laid down his favorite harpoon on the ice in front of her. Each man stepped forward unhesitatingly and laid a weapon or an article of hunting equipment on the ground. They were careful to avoid the blood of the shaman that had frozen to the ice and would stay until spring. Not even the heaviest snowfall could cover a shaman's mark.

The shaman also stepped forward and leaned into her face, eye to eye. Sedna smelled the rancid bear grease he rubbed in his hair. She returned the stare while the others stepped back a pace, frightened by the clash of wills. "You left your drum behind. I brought it," he said at last.

She murmured her thanks and closed her eyes to release him from her stare. Minutes later, when she opened them, the ice was swept clean of people.

Sedna and the wolf were alone.

She picked up each weapon and, as she did, she spoke the shaman prayer of thanksgiving to Sednah of the sea and Raven of the air. Each weapon in turn gave her vibrations of acceptance. Her throat tightened with the thought of the sacrifices these people had made for her. After coming all this way to bring her home, perhaps thinking they should have to kill her, they had left without her, and had given up their most cherished weapons, as well. This was a happening that, even with her powers, she could not have envisioned.

She had longed for her special drum. Each shaman had a drum given by the preceding shaman. The drum added strength to shaman powers and meant a great loss without it.

She returned to the stone house, knowing Rolv had no idea of the drama that had transpired outside. She brought in the hoard of weapons, watching his eyes round with disbelief. When his eyes turned away from the weapons back to her, she took them back out into the storage room. They must be presented with some ceremony.

"Where did you get them?"

"My people came for me," she said simply.

He rose from the chair and limped slowly toward her, every step was painful. She could feel his anguish, but he struggled to keep it from showing in his expression.

"You could have been killed! They could have taken you back with them. You might have left, freely of your own will." He hugged her to him and then began to peel off her jacket gently, helping her out of her outer garments.

Halfway through his helping her, he stopped and raised her chin to look down into her eyes. "Why did they not take you away? Why did you stay? I could not have stopped you."

She wanted to feel his desire again, but it was not forthcoming. He did not desire her. He longed to leave her behind, to return to his home and a woman who may have been waiting. "Maybe later, I will go. You need me—you need someone to take care of you."

Pride rose in his eyes and something else she was not so certain of. His expression was stern, but she knew she'd seen a look of regret within his soul. She held herself erect, sorrow warring with pity that he might need her and not want to need her. As a strong man, he must find it hard to depend on someone, a woman, not long ago a stranger, to keep him alive.

☙☙☙

He sighed, released her, and sank heavily into the chair. "If that is what it takes to keep you here, then I am not sorry to be helpless."

What if she had left while he slept? The terrible thought, the desperate sense of loss made him break into a sweat even after days had passed. He did not let her see his weakness. When another human being saw your underbelly, they instinctively slashed out to destroy. The act was animal nature, human nature. He did not judge it, for that was merely the way things were.

Ever since they had made love, he had feared she would slip away some night, no longer trusting him, for he had broken his promise not to force himself on her. She was in his protection. He was supposed to be her sanctuary until she was ready to leave. To cause him even more guilt, he remembered what she'd said about Nagatok using her body with such violence.

Even though he felt her innocent response to his

lovemaking, that again heaped more shame on his head.

"Let me see the weapons again," he asked, getting away from his dour thoughts. His enforced idleness made him restless.

At first, she hesitated. He knew it was because according to her customs, strangers or women were never allowed to touch a hunter's weapon, lest the animals become offended and never give themselves up for food.

Mildly, he reminded her that the weapons belonged to her. She was free to do as she pleased with them. The tribe had offered them freely.

ↄ⳩ↄ⳩

Sedna brought the weapons from the storage room where she had taken them. She stood over them, touching each item in turn and then closed her eyes and let her hands play over her drum. She envisioned the men who had given the valuable weapons and thanked them again for their generosity. She sent a special message for Naga-tok to heal his wounded pride. When she opened her eyes, Rolv had sunk back into his chair, watching her.

"My people gave me fine lances, eye masks carved from ivory to prevent sun blindness, and flint stones for fire. This knife which belonged to Ogiak is made from chipped black stone of the kind of material that falls from the sky."

Rolv reached out, picked up one weapon, and held it out to her. "What is this?"

She took it and carefully unwrapped the thin baleen from the whale's mouth that the hunters had tied around the sticks of whalebone, sharpened on both ends. It sprang apart in her hands.

"This is a special bear weapon. We put a piece of seal meat inside here and wrap the sinew tightly around it, letting it freeze in place. When a bear swallows this, it springs apart inside his body. A hunter then needs but to follow the trail of blood. Some clans use it for wolves, but we do not slay the wolf. He is the helper spirit to our village and brings us good luck in hunting."

She was so proud of her people for giving up this offering to her.

"What is this strange pouch attached to the lance?"

"An animal bladder, blown up so that when a hunter harpoons a seal, it will not sink to the bottom."

"Your people amaze me. We have no knowledge of such things."

"This is our land, after all. We have been here since the beginning of time, while you are strangers."

He took no offense at her speech, knowing it was true.

"I will hunt. Yesterday I saw a seal on the ice," she said.

"Can you slay a seal?"

"How difficult can it be if men can do it?" she teased.

She tried on the sun goggles and danced playfully around the room, holding out her tunic and stumbling because of the thick mukluks she wore. Usually her people removed their outside shoes just inside the doorway and put on fur stockings. She did not do that here because the stone floor was always cold.

He laughed, the first laugh since his injury, and it warmed her from the inside out. After a time of self-consciousness and withdrawal on both their parts, he started holding her in his arms each night again. Many times she had awakened in the morning to be cradled in his lap, her head just under his chin as they slept. Several times she felt his hardness lying against her buttocks and wanted him to make love to her, but if he was awake when she stirred restlessly, he never let on.

His voice broke into her thoughts. "I will crawl outside, if you promise not to watch until I get settled out there. I do not know your weapons, but I can teach you what I know."

She understood a man's pride at not being able to walk upright. She discreetly turned away.

☙❧☙

They spent gray winter days with her throwing the lance and him shouting instructions like a leader of a Viking hoard. He was patient but stern in his criticism.

She knew he was growing hungry, as was she. The poorly dried meat and fish no longer satisfied them. They needed fresh meat.

"You are improving each day," he told her. "The muscles are tightening in your arms and wrists. Soon you will be ready."

His spare praise eased the torment of her bones and back a little, for she was heartily sick of practicing and wanted to get on with hunting.

"We need a sled and proper dogs to pull home our kill," he said. "I had a sled but lost it in the water when I tried to pull a load of fish off the ice."

"My people sometimes make what you call a sled out of driftwood and drag their kill home." She showed him how to tie bits of gnarled driftwood together with strips of sinew as her people had done throughout the ages.

The next morning she brought him a long piece of tree limb which she had been making into a walking stick. While he slept she had carved figures of the Raven and some of Sednah's sea creatures on it for good luck. "Come with me. You can walk if you lean on this stick. I saw a seal last night in a vision. It is time to hunt."

Rolv admired the piece of wood. "What beautiful work you do. Where did you learn to carve?"

"Most of my people know how to do this work. I left behind my carvings on walrus tusks." She struggled to keep the regret from her voice.

"We will get a walrus. You can carve more if you wish," he promised.

They walked out on the ice, pulling the sled they had made together. The black in the fleshy part of his leg had faded until the darkness lay mostly in his ankle and foot. She could tell, from the grimace he tried to hide while he moved along at her side, that his foot still pained him.

Aku stayed close, walking between them, nuzzling her nose into his palm in encouragement.

Out on the ice, Rolv paused, hesitating as if remembering when he had fallen and almost lost his life. Life was glorious to lose in the splendor of battle, but to lie on the floor and perish from frostbite and a blackened leg would have been the most terrible punishment he could have envisioned. His half-sister Freyda would have been ecstatic, had she known that to be his fate.

"You have taught me some of the strengths of your hunting prowess. Let me show you how an Inuit hunter receives a seal," she said.

"There are no seals on the ice," he protested.

"It does not matter. We hunt walrus from on top of the ice, but seals come from Sednah, below."

Some night to come, when they talked and spun their tales and songs, she would instruct him about Sednah, for she was a very important Being and one must not hunt without showing her respect.

Sedna made a place for Rolv by spreading a hide and piling on furs for him to sit on and wait.

He wasn't ready to sit and wait. He wanted to know every step of what she was doing. He followed her, watching her move gracefully across the ice, as she bent often to peer down at the surface.

Finally she stopped and pointed. In a whisper, she indicated, "Here is what you must look for."

"I do not see anything."

"This is ice formed upward from a seal's breathing hole. He will return." She motioned Rolv back and then knelt and began to chip away with a long sliver of flint attached to an antler handle, one of the tools the hunters had left for her.

Sedna scraped away the ice and enlarged the hole until she could see water below. She was ready to lower her net made of sinew and whalebone, also a gift from the men. "This will entrap the animal after it comes up to breathe and dives again," she explained, still whispering.

It was all strange to him. If you couldn't use a knife or a lance on an animal or trap it, he knew of no other way to kill one.

"This way requires much patience. We must be still and not speak. The seal has many holes to return to but he will return to each in time."

Rolv pulled the furs closer, spreading them so they both could sit. She was so serious, so full of pride in her knowledge. He wanted to reach over and touch that sleek dark head, to encompass her slender neck in his hand and hold her close. Hellfire, she was bewitching him!

Unmindful of the seething emotions within her companion, Sedna concentrated on her task. She held the net with a long sinew. When some time had passed, she crept to the edge of the hole and began to scratch the edge with an ivory tool that had four small carved claws.

Without needing her to tell him, he reasoned that was to emulate the sound of another seal.

They waited, both heedless of the fierce cold and the wind, sitting close together, the wolf lying on their feet.

For no reason he could see, she pushed up on her knees and crawled toward the hole, holding the net sinew tightly wrapped around her arm. She knew that was a dangerous move. Hunters had been known to be pulled in by demon seals and disappear forever under the ice, trapped by the tangled line. But she, Aku, and Rolv needed the food. All three of them grew weaker daily on their diet of dried fish, which was almost gone and rationed severely.

The net jerked and the ivory clinkers along the edges knocked together. Her arm wrenched downward. She jumped to her feet and ran toward the hole, fighting to keep her footing.

Acting purely on instinct, Rolv crawled over the ice to her side and held her legs, to keep her from tumbling into the hole while she wrestled with the net. Once she had command of it, she leaned back and motioned for him to pull it up. He dragged a squirming seal up onto the ice with Aku yipping and leaping around. Rolv dispatched it quickly with a lance.

Sedna bent and pushed a carved ivory plug into the dead creature's wound to prevent the loss of precious blood. Then she dipped a wooden cup brought from the house down into the water and poured it gently across the seal's open mouth.

"We offer you a drink of water, oh, brother seal, and our respect for your generous gift of your body for our sustenance. Thank you, Sednah, for allowing us one of your creatures."

Rolv closed his eyes in a mutual thanksgiving to both Odin and Thor. He did not want to leave either god out of the show of gratitude. "Magnificent," he proclaimed.

Sedna smiled with pride at his praise. "We will do this together when you grow steady on your legs," she promised. "I will show you how the people trap. We need wolverine fur for new parka hoods."

"Why wolverine?"

"It is the only fur that does not freeze when our breathing touches it," she explained, watching him load the seal on the makeshift sled. "We have much to do, you and I. The winter will pass quickly."

∽∾∽

Rolv thought of the previous winter, his first spent alone. Each night and day had seemed a lifetime. There were times when he hadn't known if he would survive without going crazy in the stillness indoors, with only the crackling of the fire and the wind outside to let him know he could still hear.

He wanted to hate his father and half-sister for voting against him in the *Althing*, the council. He knew most of the council wanted his banishment to serve as a warning to other hot-headed young men, but his family didn't have to side with the assembly. Eric was chieftain in the new country he had named Greenland and decreed the end of blood feuds. Rolv couldn't blame his father, since feuds and fighting had been his way of life in his native country of Norway. When Eric was banished from his birthplace, he sailed with his family to Iceland and subsequently fought and was banished from there. He sailed on to discover the new country and now he wanted to change his ways. Rolv, younger than his half-brothers, had heard the sagas all his life.

The longing to return to Ericksfjord was deep inside him, an ache that never subsided. His worry was Sedna. What would she do when he told her she could go free? He knew she could return to her village, but the circumstances would be terrible for her. She told him of her talk with the shaman. She would never be allowed to mate again. He thought of her warmth, the passion he had awakened in her small body. The thought of that body being touched by another man was more than he could stand to think about. What he wanted was to take her home with him.

Rolv felt a wave of relief wash over him as he realized the truth he had been hiding behind his worry. He wanted never to part from her, but he couldn't take her. She would not fit in with his family. They would never accept her, nor she them. He closed his eyes, imagining how his noisy, rowdy family would run over her as if she was never there. She would probably refuse to go with him, anyway. She had her own people. With them she was respected and protected as a shaman. Perhaps he could walk over the ice cap to find another village for her.

His heart and mind warred so that he held his head in pain. What was he to do?

CHAPTER 9

Each day, in which the wind did not blow up a storm of ice, Sedna went out with Rolv to hunt or trap. She showed him how to flense out the skins so they remained shiny and supple no matter how long they were kept in the storeroom.

They ranged far from home to bring down the reindeer needed for inner tunics and trousers for the new outfits she planned to make.

Rolv cut and sewed together a proper harness for the wolf out of strips of reindeer hide. Aku learned to pull their sled to bring back the kill and wait for her portion as a reward.

After Sedna showed Rolv the proper way to work, he helped her cut skins with the sharp knife, and even helped sew skins together.

The nights when their work was over, became the best times. He, who had been so lonely in the nighttime, loved the nights now and wanted them to last forever.

When he caught her watching him under the sputtering light of the soapstone and blubber lamps, as he patiently sewed with one of her bone needles, he congratulated himself for bringing her with him. She had asked him slyly once if he didn't think that was woman's work and he, in turn, asked her just as slyly if hunting belonged only to men. She smiled that endearing little crook of a smile which she had learned from him. He knew she would rather hunt than sew.

"I still do not understand why we have to have four sets of clothes plus the outer furs," he asked, breaking one satisfying silence. "It seems a waste of time and material. Do we not remove them every day and air them in the storage room?"

"Yes, and that is good. But we must wear one tunic and trousers with the fur turned in and another set turned out, to keep out the cold. In the warm months we will catch birds and ducks and make underclothing."

"I will never wear a bird next to my bare skin. I don't want you to do that either."

Rolv knew she studied his expression to better understand how serious his words might be. Sometimes he teased and she was trying to learn which was which.

"Every person has a line in the snow another should never cross," she said. "The people recognize this in all creatures. Your eyes are kind but can appear forbiddingly somber when you make up your mind to something. I have tried never to cross over the line. However, in this matter of proper clothing, I cannot be dissuaded."

He knew she already wore underwear of bird skin, no disputing that.

"I do not know how that furless material you call wool can keep you warm on the ice," she said. "Your trousers do not even reach your ankles. You do not have real boots, but skins wrapped around your feet. That cannot be warm enough or keep out moisture."

He listened and agreed. "It is not comfortable out there, but we do not expect it to be. This is the way my people dress. We know no other way."

"You must not fight against the land and the cold. My

people have learned to be one with it. You almost died," she reminded him. "You would have been warm and dry in the water, dressed like a bird close to your skin." She smiled—a bit smugly, he thought—but in truth he did not mind her lessons and welcomed the chance to learn.

"I brought something from home you could use," he said. "Probably it belonged to Freyda. Who can say how it became mixed with my clothing?" He rummaged through a chest in the storeroom and brought the article back. "Try this on."

She undressed in front of him, her actions natural and innocent of coquetry. He couldn't keep his eyes off of her. Her skin glowed with the warm color of summer ale and his own skin remembered hers as soft, smooth, and delicate.

What a puzzle she was. How could one person contain such strength of purpose, such courage to face anything this hostile land threw at her, and yet be so soft and womanly? He cursed himself under his breath. He had made her a solemn promise when he brought her to Nordrsetur that he would not force her sexually. He had a vague, but pleasurable memory of that time they had made love when he was wrought with fever. It tormented him to know he must have forced her then. He had to have even forced her response, which was the most damning of all. What a villainous way to reward someone for saving his life, not once, but twice.

When the tightness in his loins forced him to stop looking at her, he turned away, pretending to ply needle to the fur draped across his legs. Fortunately the heavy material hid any physical sign of his longing. He had a need for her that threatened to tear him asunder at times.

When he turned back, he caught a forlorn look in her eyes before she looked away. He must have imagined that.

Sedna hurriedly slipped the soft wool over her head and let the shirt fall down around her body where it hung on her like a shroud, touching the ground.

Rolv immediately laughed. The sound relieved the tension in the close room.

Before he could take a breath to let out new laughter, she jumped on him, knocking over the chair and falling on top of him, while pummeling his chest in fury.

With ease, he held both her fists in one giant hand and wrapped his other arm around her body to hold her still. "Hush! What ails you? By Odin, you have a temper worse than Freyda."

"You laugh at me. You hate me and you laugh at me! What have I done to earn this disrespect from you?" Tears crowded from under her lashes and she moved to brush them away, but he held her hands tight in his.

"Ah, lovey, I did not mean to laugh, but the shirt is supposed to fit tight to your body and end somewhere around your buttocks. Not wrap around you twice and end at your ankles." Such was the fit of shifts he had removed from women he had previously bedded. "Both you and the great *naanuk* could fit in Freyda's shift together."

She subsided against him, relaxing her arms so he was able to release her hands.

"Do you think we might get up now?" he teased. "This is very uncomfortable, although I enjoy your sitting on top of me."

She rolled off, leaped to her feet, hands on her hips, and began to giggle in the manner of her people, politely behind her open palm. He joined in with his ringing laughter and soon she let loose of the polite giggles and laughter rippled through her body.

She was learning both to smile and to laugh. He felt good about that.

They held each other close for a long time, with the wolf standing by their legs.

∽∾∽

Winter deepened. The furs in the store room piled higher and higher. They trapped the wily wolverine to make the hoods for the jackets and used seal hide to cover the bottoms of their boots.

Often Rolv went inside the storeroom and stood for a long time staring at the stacks of furs and the meat lying frozen next to them.

One day she asked him. "Why do you look in here with such wonder in your eyes? Do you fear our stores will disappear? I am certain the room is safe. The people bury meat in the winter. They dig long holes in the ground during the summer months when the ground thaws on top. You do not have to dig outside. This stone room, without lamps and fireplace is surely cold enough."

"I stand here to marvel at these riches. Sometimes I cannot believe my eyes. I have to look again, and admire. This is a fortune in furs and meat and the winter is not even half over."

"What is this word, 'fortune'? Is fortune of importance to you then? The people treasure a large supply of meat to insure none of the people starve, but they do not save more than for one season. They will take more according to need. It is very disrespectful to an animal when it allows itself to be killed for food and then wasted and not used."

"We measure wealth as the success of a man. How he obtains the wealth is unimportant. Rich men are promised Valhalla when they die, even if they do not die in battle. I will be wealthy when I return. When the *knarr* comes to trade I can barter for salt and wool so my mother, Thornhild, will not have to work so hard spinning and carding. I can barter for iron tools and honey and meat cured in tubs of sour milk."

"What is this word *knarr*?"

"It means trading vessel, ugly ships, not at all like our glorious warships, but they serve a purpose. They are square and deep and hold storerooms of provisions."

She wasn't listening, but only asked the question to make room for her sorrow to pass, thinking of the day when he would leave and she would return to the people. Sedna tried not to think of their parting. Soon enough she would have to think of it.

Would she would return to her village or find a new one? It would be good to see her mother and father once again, but she could never go back to Nagatok. She would have to live alone, as the old shaman did, growing ancient, bent, and wrinkled with no children of her own. The village children would fear her, the adults always respectful but distant. She would die, never knowing what happened to Rolv. Would the Raven Mother abandon her too if she left the Viking?

Sedna turned her face away, so he couldn't read her countenance. He was responsive to her every expression—perhaps because her people were taught not to have many.

☙❦❧

Sedna admired Rolv's quick grasp of everything she taught him about Inuit lore. In turn he told her of the Viking life, including how they plowed the ground to plant food. This plowing she did not understand. She could not see how a person raked aside the ground, put a tiny seed inside and then buried it and expected some kind of food to come up from that. It made no sense and she thought he might be playing an elaborate joke on her. She did not take offense, since jokes were meant to be enjoyed. The people loved jokes.

"Will you make another song for me someday?" she asked him one night.

"I have. I was waiting for you to ask."

Sedna leaned closer to the fire and waited. The people considered it a high honor to have a special song made only for one of them. Ordinary songs could be traded or passed on to others but personal songs belonged between two people forever.

She marveled that over the months she and Rolv had come to understand one another so completely. She had always wanted a companion, but this unity with Rolv was special in many ways. They spoke in her language, Norse, or a curious mixture. Sometimes thoughts were intercepted between them. She had always known how to receive the thoughts of others at times, but it was disconcerting, at first, to have someone do it toward her.

He readied himself to sing, by sitting across from her and closing his eyes. She did the same, waiting for his deep, rumbling voice to caress her ears.

"O for the love of Thor, of Odin,
of Sednah, of all the gods who have
brought us together,
She of eyes like the ocean's depth,
she of hair like a raven's wing,
a woman with the soul of purity
and the body of a courtesan.
A woman-child who has stolen my heart
and given me hope.
I never want to leave her."

His last words were torn from him in a low groan of

old Norse language. Sedna felt elation welling up inside her and yet she did not understand the last line of his song in his strange language. As she continued to sit with her eyes closed, feeling what Rolv felt, the substance of his song made her heart beat rapidly in her chest. She slowly opened her eyes, knowing he watched her.

"A song I will never forget," she said.

Her hand reached toward him. When it touched his cheek, he captured it in his and bent his lips to touch her palm. His mustache felt prickly, his mouth warm and soft. Without explanation, he broke away and stood up, releasing her. Sweat broke out over her face. She bent down and wiped her forehead on the hem of her shift, to delay looking at him. She did not wish to see a lack of desire in his eyes, see clearly, perhaps, that he was only doing what he thought was expected of a man.

And yet he made up the moving, wonderful song for her. Was it a goodbye?

When he fell asleep later, she lay awake, thinking of how empty her life would be when they parted. A knife twisted inside her gut. She wanted to cry and shriek and beg him to let her stay with him. At the same time, she cared too much to shame him—to force him to tell her that he was not able to take her to his home. To tell her in words that he had no desire to take her with him.

She knew this already, without him putting it into hurtful words. His life was separate. Her ways would embarrass him, cause him difficulties. His father was a formidable man who would not countenance a stranger within his camp. This came to her with a certainty—a fatalistic conviction that turned her blood to ice within her body, chilling her to the bone. She must make herself ready when the time came to part.

But often during many nights sleeping so close togeth-er he would pull her even closer to his body, never awakening. She felt jabs of fierce desire inside her, warming her stomach and sliding down to the places he had touched. Did he not feel desire also?

The next morning, he awoke first and pulled her from the snug warmth of her bedding. "It is time we hunted the walrus. You say we need his hide for boot soles. My feet are cold all the time, even by the fire. I wish you to make me a pair of boots such as yours."

She sat up, her hair in disarray around her shoulders, wearing the night shift he had helped her make from Freyda's tunic.

He kissed her nose, then her closed eyes. "I love the way you look in the morning. During the day, with your hair braided properly, you walk with dignity, unless you are giggling at some joke, but in the morning, before you are fully awake, you are like another person and I like both of them."

Nagatok would not have appreciated the thought of her being two different people, but then, he probably wouldn't have noticed in the first place. Because Rolv saw her magic and accepted it, a great warmth of affection swept through her. She gasped in dismay at her revealing her inner self and turned aside to divert his attention with the first thing she could think of. It was unwise to show too much regard for someone. There were always jealous spirits ready to do mischief. Especially now that he spoke of going walrus hunting. That was the most dangerous hunt of all and she didn't think he was ready.

"Your stitches could have been finer and neater," she scolded, holding up the hem of her garment.

She worried he felt he had to prove himself to her. She suspected hunting the walrus was something he had to do and yet he feared it. Perhaps it was a goal he set for himself to conquer before he could go home.

Rolv laughed at her serious demeanor and accepted

her mild scolding. "Soon you will be free to return to your people. I—I do not like to envision you going to Nagatok, but if that is your choice, I know he would succumb to your magic and forget his resentments."

She said nothing, the words pummeling her like stones of ice from the sky.

After a brief breakfast of roasted reindeer, they dressed for the cold, both wrapped in thoughtful silence.

"Since this is the first time we wear the new clothing. We should celebrate," she said.

"They are splendid. You look like a little furry animal, I look like a large furry animal."

"Wait until you see how warm they are. Where it is truly cold, you will not joke about it." Outside, the wind whistled and roared around the corners of the building causing her to shiver. The north wind meant dangerous fog—fog that crept inland from the frozen sea and captured everything in its midst, shutting off the world so one stepped off the end into darkness. In all her world, the white fog was the only thing the hunters truly feared.

"Perhaps it is not a good day for hunting," she suggested, knowing that attempting to change Rolv's mind once he set it on a project was futile.

"It is a good morning. I can feel it." He stretched and blew out a lamp to save oil, leaving one lamp burning, not only to keep away demons, but to guide others to the house who may be lost. She had taught him that also.

He used coals from the fire to start his strange little lights of moss, but they were not as effective as blubber oil lamps and difficult to start from the burning coals. They would never claim a whale so they could have blubber for proper lamps.

They brought their weapons out from the store room. Without light or lamps, the dark room was freezing, a perfect place to keep their winter meat supplies.

As they sorted out their weapons in the main room, under the light of the fire, Sedna spoke. "When the warm season comes, we may have to scratch out shallow holes in the ground near the house to bury this meat," she said, grabbing hold of her favorite harpoon and making a stance to throw it.

"Ah, my heart's breath," he said in his Norse language, "you will be free to leave me by then and not give a damn about my food supplies."

Sedna cocked her head to listen to the strange words, but this time it did not come to her what he was saying. He looked so sad, she wanted to comfort him. While he slept peacefully at night, sometimes Sedna leaned her body against his to gather strength from him.

"Taking you home to my boisterous, troublesome family is one thing, but facing Freyda with a stranger from another culture is quite another. I can only imagine the consequences of exposing you to that."

So she could understand, he continued in their mutual language. "By far the best solution is to help you find your village, or next best, find a village like your own, where you can blend in and begin your life."

That said, she nodded and turned away to busy herself with cleaning the weapons. Yet the winter was passing and still he'd made no move to go out on the ice and look for her people.

If she had wondered about his moody silences occurring more and more often as the winter progressed, she didn't speak of it. In her people's passive way, she waited for him to act.

Her dour thoughts were halted by the wolf running to greet them when they stepped outside the house. The full force of the wind struck and Sedna backed up into Rolv. He held on, steadying her until she could gain her footing.

"It is grateful I am that I took your advice and stayed off my leg, giving it time to heal. I can walk as good now as I did before the injury."

"I too am grateful that your leg healed. Sometimes the bones do not go back the way they started." She listened to the whistle and whine of the buffeting wind. "The north wind may be trying to warn us not to go out today," she shouted.

Rolv braced, tall and fierce, into the gale as if forcing his strength against the elements. His thick golden brows were laced with ice, his long eyelashes coated with white. His mustache was already hidden by little flakes of ice from his breath. The golden red disappeared under a patina of white. His wide shoulders and magnificent height seemed to disappear into the clouds above her.

Once he had told her he was the runt of his family. She knew he was joking. No man could be taller, more magnificent.

He grabbed her mittened hand and danced around her, the wolf barking and dancing too. "My leg is healed. I love this weather. I am part of the wind and sky. I have stayed inside too long, sewing and preparing skins like a woman. I need fresh air."

She laughed at Aku and Rolv, her misgivings buried beneath her pleasure at their antics.

The fog lifted with the shifting wind, moving it away from them in their advance toward the shoreline. It was hard to know where the water and the land left off now; the ice was covered with a crust of snow and only a thin line of near-light entered the horizon, reflecting off the endless white.

The wind roared and shrieked through the *sastrugi*, the natural ice carvings appearing around them. The shapes were so distinctive they used them for landmarks to know the way home.

"These furs are amazing," he enthused. "I don't feel this wind or cold, only in my feet."

She smiled, smug in the knowledge that her ways, though crude by his standards, had much to recommend them. The work on his boots had already begun.

They walked straight out onto the frozen sea. Away from the land and trees, the wind calmed, the temperature dropped even lower. The world surrounding them was immersed in white silence. They waited, side by side, to spy a huge dark shape on the ice.

"Look! Over there!"

Fear mixed in his voice with excitement and gave her a brief flash of a troubled vision. She saw her father lying on the ice, his leg pierced by the sharp tusks of the giant beast. She saw the blood splayed across the ice, the blood mixed with the slushy mire beneath the hunters' boots as they waded in to dispatch the roaring creature.

Her nostrils flared with the smell of blood and excrement. She sensed the force within her body stir as she, too, felt and heard the death bellow of the dying walrus, mixed with the shouts and screams of the attacking men. Sedna brought herself back to the present, staring out toward the dark object

She moved between Rolv and the frozen sea, arms outstretched to stop him. "Wait! Leave it. We cannot do this, not alone. He is a bull, in the prime of his life."

Rolv pushed back her parka hood, kissing the ice from her eyebrows and eyelashes. "Do not fear, sweetling. I have worked it out. The wolf will attack first, get the beast off balance. Our dogs are used for this. Aku can do it too. Then you come from behind and sink your lance in his back to let blood and weaken him. I'll get him from the front."

"But it is not the time, I feel—"

"We *need* this kill, Sedna. We need his fur and hide

for strong sinew and boots. You told me yourself how valuable this animal is. When my father and his men managed to slay one, we only used the meat for the dogs and threw the rest back into the water. I see now that your way is better."

Beneath the strength of his voice she again heard the tremor of doubt. He was not as sure of their prowess as he pretended. Why was he taking this foolish risk?

In that moment, when she was about to argue more strongly, she felt something coming from behind, stalking them. The hairs on her arms stood up, beneath her jacket sleeves. She truly sensed a presence—an evil, dangerous entity behind them that soon would block their retreat. "We must leave this place. Now!"

She began to chant the song of protection, hoping to shield them within the perimeters of an invisible boundary line. The wolf also sensed danger and stayed close to her legs, growling low in her throat.

"You will frighten our quarry," Rolv protested. "Even now the walrus looks around, but cannot see us yet." Rolv's hand on her shoulder, pressed through the thick fur as if nothing lay between his strong fingers and her skin. She flinched at the steady pressure but did not cease chanting.

Without warning, the walrus gave a mighty roar and slid off into the water with a huge splash. The wolf began snarling and barking, facing back in the direction they came from. Both Rolv and Sedna turned in unison.

Not six feet away, a monstrous polar bear towered over them, standing on hind legs, his black eyes and black snout were visible against the snow and ice. His mouth gaped open showing yellowish-white teeth and a blood-red tongue with spittle forming at the edge of its mouth.

In a split second, before the terrible roar hit them, reverberating off the ice, all these colors and impressions collided in Sedna's brain, mixing with sheer terror.

"By the blood of Odin!" Rolv blurted and stepped back, pushing her behind him, shielding her with his body.

Sedna's breath came in painful little bursts of fog in front of her eyes. She expected the crazed animal to kill them both if she did not break her paralysis. She ducked forward under Rolv's protective arm to stand in front of him and reached beneath her jacket to pull off the Raven belt. She held it high, brandishing it in front of the bear. Struggling

Careful not to lose her concentration, she spared a hand to touch to the wolf's head to quiet her.

Knowing the movement at the corner of her eye to be the Norseman's fist tightening on his lance and his body tensing to spring forward, she began a chant.

> "Aya, aya, great white creature, brave *naanuk*,
> Does a long-ago ancestor possess your body—
> inherit your spirit—or did you arise
> fully grown from the snow and ice?
> You do not need to slay us to prove your prowess,
> nor do you need our bodies to nurture yours.
> You are strong and powerful.
> A mighty hunter are you who seeks
> not the company of human beings.
> Leave us now to live in peace,
> and we promise to do the same for you."

The creature shook its head and gave a mighty roar, making the ice tremble beneath their feet. The roar echoed across the frozen wasteland, creating a series of echoes that came from ever widening circles.

The bear lowered his forefeet to the ice and stood for a

moment, deciding whether to charge. If it did, life would end painfully for the three of them. Sedna felt, smelled, and tasted the beast's hot foul breath in her face. Already she felt his sharp teeth ripping into her skin, his long claws tearing at the furs protecting her body.

"Ayee! Ayee!" she shrieked in outraged frenzy.

She was not ready to die. Her life was important to many people besides herself. She had others to think of.

She was Raven Woman.

At her explosive movement and shout, the monster bear reared again on his hind legs. His mighty roar shook the snow off barren rocks nearby. She saw Rolv's fist tighten again on his lance. At this distance, it would be a sure hit. He could put it through the beast's throat, killing him instantly. She willed his hand to stay.

A decision had been made.

When no one moved, the bear spun, agilely for a beast of its size, and loped away, blending into the oncoming white fog.

Rolv and Sedna released their breaths in great gulps of mist in front of them. He reached to pull her close, hugging her tightly.

"You could have slain him, I felt it. Thank you for honoring my promise to him," she said.

"A promise must always be kept." Regret tinged his voice. "The bear would have provided much meat and invaluable fur and you spoke true, I could not have missed the vital place with my lance. What a pity to have had to send him away."

"Come, we must go before the mist grows thicker and we cannot see," she urged.

"By what magic did you know the bear stalked us and how did you turn him away? Was it your song or your dreadful screaming? Did you cast a spell on him?"

Rolv took her shoulders and bending his head, looked

at her searchingly. She read the emotions crowding through him. Relief and frustration, respect and fear, teasing, and seriousness—it all showed in his eyes while he stared into hers.

Sedna wanted to tell him she did not turn the bear away by herself. "The Raven's power is with me as a shaman," she answered. "I knew we could not slay the beast. Even Inuit hunters do not attempt to kill the white bear face to face. *Naanuk* is the only creature, except for the killer whale, that the hunters fear. He has been known to hunt man. Later, I will show you how to use the special weapon for the bear."

She recognized that although Rolv had been nearly turned to stone because of fear, he had pushed her behind him and stepped forward, ready to do battle to save her. A tightness filled her throat. She knew he cared for her. She knew he took pleasure in her body. Why then, did he wish to cast her away? Oh. The answer struck her with the force of a blow. She was not a proper wife for him when he returned to his home. She was not good enough to be a life companion to him.

He moved forward, pulling her along behind him, unmindful of her distress. The wolf bounded ahead, happy to go home.

"We will slay a white bear," she said when her voice came back to her. "Soon we will also slay a walrus. When it is time. You are right. We need what they can provide."

They began striding with long steps toward home.

CHAPTER 10

The furs and meat in the storeroom piled higher and higher. Sedna and Rolv ranged far from the house, hunting the huge, tame musk-oxen and black bear in hibernation. Although Sedna didn't understand why Rolv needed so many furs and so much meat, it was such a pleasure hunting side by side with him that she didn't question it.

The wolf gladly pulled the sled, and if the burden was heavy, Rolv helped pull it and Sedna pushed from behind.

Often packs of wolves followed, sneaking along the perimeters of the scrub willow trees, weaving in and out of the snow-covered brush. Aku stopped occasionally to hear their cries, but she seemed content only to listen.

"When Eric's men brought me here I saw a glacier on the way. Will you explore it with me?" he asked one day.

"Glacier?" A chilled premonition sped through her body.

"You call it *sermisiraq*. I have heard you speak of it in your stories."

"Yes. But none of the people would willingly go near one," she assured him. "It is a place of enchantment, where both good and evil spirits dwell."

"Did you not say a glacier was the home of the Raven Mother? How then can you fear a glacier?"

His words made sense, in the way that a man's sometimes did. Still something warned her to stay away. This glacier was not the home of Tulunixiraq, Raven Mother. When he would not be dissuaded, Sedna promised to go with him to a certain point but no farther.

"I only want glacier ice to bring home and keep in the storeroom," he explained. They trotted beside Aku pulling the empty sled. "When spring comes to the land, the meat will thaw on my journey back to Ericksfjord if I do not have ice."

Ericksfjord—that ugly name again. She hated the sound, signifying the finish of his exile and the end to her contentment with this life, with this home. With him.

The light of the winter day was murky, because the sun would not return for a long time and then only a short while every day, each day staying longer. Her happiness in anticipation of the sun's return to the land was spoiled because it meant he must leave and return home. She pushed the thought away.

Sedna heard the glacier before she saw it. Its low, humming noise from afar, and closer the groaning, crunching sounds, convinced the people that spirits lived inside.

She stopped in her tracks, arms across her chest.

"This is what I wanted you to see." He pointed straight ahead to land beyond the glacier.

"I see only ice."

"Yes! I could walk to Ericksfjord in the winter from this island. Of course it is too far, with deep land ridges and bottomless chasms. Yet the thought of the ice-filled channel making it so close has comforted me these two years of exile."

"The people know of a body of water in the direction

you pointed. It has wind and water currents that move in a circle day and night, never freezing. The Inuits save it for special times, when they are in need—when starvation faces them—and have named it *nunavit,* water of plenty. Animals are always there to welcome us. Game is plentiful, no matter how scarce elsewhere."

"I have never heard of any place such as that," Rolv said. "Surely, if it was there, we would have found it. Eric and his sons go sailing every spring to explore new land."

"His sons? Does that mean you do not also go?" She didn't miss the tone of bitterness in his voice.

"Eric expects me to stay home. He claims he needs one son to watch over the place in his absence. I think it is just that I am his bastard. My difference irritates him."

"What makes you different?"

"My eyes are not blue or green, but the color of smoke. I have my mother's eyes and I am smaller than Eric or his sons. I told you I was the runt. He commands me to sing and compose songs while the others joust and maim each other in rough play. Even Freyda goes with him on some journeys, although she hates the water. Water is the only thing she fears. It is unnatural in a Viking to fear water, but perhaps Thornhild tried to drown her as a baby. That would have been wise of her to do."

Sedna peered into Rolv's face to see if he was joking. His expression was hard and grim. Someday, he might tell her why he hated his half-sister so. "But are not what you call sagas of value to your people? We respect and admire those few of our village, who can compose a good story or song, more than we value a hunter. There are as many hunters as there are men, but only a chosen few can make up stories and songs."

"I never thought of it that way. They do enjoy my sagas. Your stories and songs cheer me when I am in one of my black moods. Is it for certain you will not come to the glacier with me? It is very beautiful."

She folded her arms across her chest, raised her chin in a stubborn tilt, signifying the end to their conversation.

"Wait here, then, Lady Stubborn. I will return when I have loaded ice on the sled. Aku, stay with your mistress."

Sedna hid her smile politely behind her mitten. It pleased him to think her wolf obeyed his commands.

He strode toward the towering mountain of ice. Sedna trusted that the spirits would not harm Rolv, since he was not of this land or one of the people. Perhaps outsiders were invisible to the dead souls of clans who lived in the glacier. Turning away, she began scraping snow off fallen branches. The dried wood would be good for the fireplace. Once, while she worked she thought she heard her name called.

"Sedna...Raven Woman..."

It was the sound of the wind slicing through the ice formations on the beach. The second time she thought she heard the name of the sea goddess called out softly, hauntingly.

"Sednah...Sednah..."

The sound came from the direction of the glacier.

Sedna pulled her hood closer around her face and scraped the knife against the crusted snow on the wood, louder to drown out the seductive sound that she knew emanated from the glacier. She began a song, a low whisper of a chant to overcome the temptation to follow that voice.

'*Do not listen. Close your hearing to this siren voice.*'

It was the first time Tulunixiraq had spoken to her since their meeting in the glacier.

'*The voice can draw you inside, but I have an undertaking you must do within your lifespan. You must give birth to a daughter so the future Raven Woman will survive.'*

Hypnotized by the groaning of the glacier and the sound of the wind, Sedna waited for the voice of the Raven Mother again. Something grabbed her shoulder, her knees melted like ice on a summer day, and she fell in a daze. When she opened her eyes, Rolv was holding her head on his lap, kissing her face.

"By Thor's sweet breath, I thought your soul had departed. What happened to you?"

She struggled to sit up. They faced each other, sitting in the snow. It was so cold and so dry that the ice beneath their bodies did not melt.

"It is the glacier. The spirits inside the glacier coax me to come to them. But the Raven Mother cautions against it."

"But no one can go inside a glacier and live," he exclaimed. "It constantly changes, moves. It would grind you to bits." He held her tight. "We will not come here again," he promised, helping her to her feet.

She said nothing, but knew someday she must face the glacier and its mysteries. On that day, perhaps the spirit within her that was the Raven Woman would leave, never to return. Perhaps that would be the time of her own death. Since being with Rolv, her sense of prophecy, her ability to look into the future had diminished. Perhaps she had too much happiness and not enough meditation time alone. She wanted to be near Rolv every moment. To store their time up for the future that would be empty without him.

Slowly they made their way back to the house. She felt weak. Something had sucked out her insides, as a child might suck out the marrow from the bone of a caribou. Even so, she had won the battle and stayed away from the glacier.

ભ૭ભ૭

Days and nights gradually turned warmer. The wind sweeping across the ice brought a different feeling with it, a feeling of renewal.

"Back in our village, the warm does not happen quick or strong," she commented one morning as they sat outside the house, watching the sea.

Icebergs had begun to shift and crunch; every day fading away a bit, growing smaller and smaller. Sedna wondered what happened to the parts that disappeared. They could come back in the next time of the cold, but when there was no ice to be seen, they must exist somewhere, waiting to return. Did they sink to the bottom of the sea? She did not wish to appear ignorant and ask Rolv.

"Your land is different," he agreed. "I do not see how anyone survives there. Even this is more formidable than Ericksfjord. I expect when the council chose this place, they thought I would either return with my tail between my legs like a whipped dog, or disappear into an ice storm."

"Who could wish that of a kinsman?" she asked. He had taught her the word, which was the same as clan. She liked the sound of kinsman on her tongue.

"A Viking can. To a Viking, the law is all-important. We must abide by it and the rulings of the assembly, for the good of all the people."

"And does everyone obey?"

"This is something my father has a hard time learning, yet he believes in it. He has been banished from Norway and also Iceland for fighting. Even so, if he is challenged, he must fight to keep his honor undefiled. It is a curious business, not to kill and yet to keep one's reputation for courage, which is the most important matter to any Viking."

Sedna understood his words but fog surrounded his meaning. Bravery did not concern her people as much as working together to achieve a rewarding outcome of a hunt. Everyone shared in the kill. To prevent hunger was the importance of hunting. "We have a saying," she said. "Those who hold their heads above others are singled out for misfortune."

"That is a wise saying," Rolv commented.

"Tell me more about your family," she continued, enjoying that pensive, thoughtful quality in his voice.

"I told you about my two half-brothers, Torvald and Torstein. They are cheerful, overgrown children. Always playing tricks and joking. Leiv, the oldest, is smarter than all of us, and generous too. He helped me while I was growing up, when I could not go to Eric for one reason or another."

"And your mother?"

"Thornhild, Eric's wife is not my birth mother. She is a strong woman. She has to be to mother the lot of us, but she is also kind in a distant way. Eric, he is a man, a leader."

Was he also a good father and husband? Sedna didn't ask, but waited for Rolv's words to catch up to his thoughts.

"He gets something in his head and it is impossible to remove. Like when he killed his best friend in Iceland. We were happy there, but his banishment turned out well and we are happier in the land he named Greenland. In this part of the world, he makes the laws. He is the most powerful man there, since he found Greenland."

Sedna hadn't realized the land had been lost, but didn't question him, primarily because she never knew how to begin such a discussion. "Does your father hunt or move from one land to another in one of your great boats or lie about in the village, eating and sleeping?"

Rolv laughed. "He does not go in the ships much anymore and he never eats or sleeps to excess. In Norway and Iceland, the stories say, he did drink to excess, but we do not allow it on Greenland. Thornhild said drinking was the cause of his banishments."

"He hunts?"

"Oh yes, he hunts. He is obsessed with capturing a great white falcon. Ever since we arrived in Greenland he's been trying to snare one of those birds. He thinks, since the nobility use them for hunting, especially the King of Norway, he should be able to own one. We've managed to shoot several down by winging them, but they never lived long."

"I know their nesting places. In the beginning of warm weather, I will catch one for you."

He kissed the tip of her nose as one would do to a child. "That is a good idea, Sedna."

She knew he thought she had made an empty promise. Sedna could picture his whole family, to a point. "Freyda?" she asked, not wishing to say the name yet not being able to avoid it.

"Freyda—I do not wish to speak of her."

Sedna pulled on his sleeve. "Please. I need to know of your half-sister. I want to know why there is so much hatred within you toward this person."

Rolv took a deep breath and put his hand over hers on his sleeve. "Very well then. It started when we were children. She tormented me because I am a bastard, even though she is one also. Eric has spoiled her since she was born. She is the only daughter and, admittedly, a beauty. She looks just like him. Even acts like him.

"She—she came to my bed one night, when we were young. It turned my stomach. We were kin after all, even if our mothers were not the same. She never forgave me for rejecting her. When I and my friends sneaked alcohol and, in a drunken brawl, I hit Olaf too hard and killed him, Freyda testified in the *Althing* that I did it purposely, that I hated him."

Sedna could not look in Rolv's direction. By his voice, she knew he had never shared these terrible remembrances with another person. His hands clenched and she felt anger and bitterness surround him. She knelt in front of him, taking his hands in hers, moving her lips softly across his callused palms. "You harm yourself by holding such thoughts, by treasuring each wrong and hurtful deed this woman does. She cannot hurt you if you do not permit it. She triumphs when you waste your strength beating against the destructive nature, which is hers. She cannot be otherwise. She bests you each time you permit her to drive you to anger."

He bent his head downward for a moment and then tilted his chin up to look at her. She never tired of those smoke-gray eyes, rimmed in the golden outline of his lashes. She had to turn away, to pat the wolf, to take a breath.

"What you say is true. I never thought of it before, but you are wise. Your counsel is well beyond your years." He held her hands to his flushed face, kissing each palm as she had done to him.

"When you return, try to remember my words. You are a Viking and let no man best you. Why then do you permit a mere woman to do so?"

He kissed her on the mouth and drew her to nestle on his lap.

She pressed into him, but before he could deepen the kiss, he pulled away. They sat and watched the sea birds fly overhead. The birds were gradually returning to land. A good sign.

꧁꧂

Rolv began hauling some of his belongings up the plank onto his boat every day. He had brought the vessel up a little finger of an inlet near the house, which offered some protection from the elements. On very cold days, they had to go out and stir the water around the boat to keep the ice from forming and crushing in the sides. Neither of them spoke of what he was doing until he stopped and looked at her. "Before I leave, I will accompany you and your wolf to a place two day's journey from here where there is an Inuit village. From there you can decide if you wish to go home or stay with the new people. I know you miss your mother and father, even though I believe you take mind-journeys to visit them at times."

How perceptive of him to think that and yet leave her alone in her shaman doings. There were times when she did take a journey through the star-filled sky at night and although she could not speak to her parents, she saw them and knew they felt her spirit surround them and were comforted. The clan took care of them, making sure they had meat and her father joined the hunt at times.

Was Rolv in such haste to rid himself of her? To return to his home without her?

When Sedna helped him ready some of the frozen meat, he said to her, "Do you wish to take half the hides? Perhaps the meat? You can have the sled and the harness. Aku can haul it for you."

That was very generous of him, since he had so admired the contents of the storeroom and wanted to take the furs home to show his father. But he was in such a hurry to leave her, he needed to make an apology offering. "No, they are yours. I would shame my village if I went home with furs and meat from you—an outsider. If they knew I killed some of the beasts, it would be even worse for me."

"I do not understand this. My family would be surprised and pleased to learn of a woman's hunting prowess. Not many of them care to try hunting, although they are not forbidden."

"Amongst my people, no one would approve of changing a custom. They hate change of any kind and think the people's way is the only way."

He smiled and touched her cheek. "I know. My family is the same in other matters. They do not accept change well, either."

One morning, the three of them went out onto the ice. There in his majesty, afraid of only the white bear, sprawled a large male walrus. Like Sedna had taught him, Rolv pulled the animal skin over his head and body and crept toward the beast, stopping whenever the walrus raised his head.

The eyesight of a walrus was poor, but he had a keen sense of smell, so the animal skins helped hide the encroaching hunter.

Aku slunk around behind the sleeping animal to cut off his escape to the water. When Rolv dispatched the creature with his lance without a fight, Sedna gave thanksgiving, and they knelt and poured the melted snow water she'd brought with them gently into its mouth to show that they had treated him with respect.

After they had harvested the walrus, Rolv seemed to gather more confidence and Sedna hoped he would not become too sure of himself, or it could prove dangerous. They used the bear weapon to slay *naanuk*, a much smaller polar bear than the one that she'd made the promise to.

At first Rolv thought it strange to offer a sea creature more water when they killed it.

"The people know all animals are put on the land to serve as food for humans, and for this reason the animals take pride in giving of themselves. But if they are not accorded proper respect, they will abandon humans, and the people will starve."

"Has this ever happened?" he asked. "We have plenty of food in Greenland. No one will ever be hungry there."

Alarmed at his boast, she said hastily, "Do not tempt the listening spirits with your bragging. Starvation is ugly and can happen to all people. In the span of only my life, starvation came upon us two times. We ate the harnesses of our sleds and our boot soles. Anything in the village made with hide, we devoured. It was said a husband had looked upon his wife at her birthing time and for this reason the animals were offended and refused to give their bodies for food."

"What do you mean?"

When Sedna realized he did not understand the taboo, she explained. "We have a separate room for birthing. Away from the village. The woman goes there alone or with another woman. If any man looks upon the woman at that time, it is sure to harm a hunter's prowess, sometimes for a season, maybe forever."

"We do not regard a child's birth as shameful," Rolv said. "We have great celebrations and sometimes the whole family is present at a birthing. Yet your tribe is so clever, so intelligent in so many ways with your spirit at one with your conditions, perhaps there is a reason your people think thusly. The Vikings fight the land, fight the weather, fight one another."

He sighed as if these new thoughts hurt his head. "We live what I had never questioned to be a full, rich life of excitement and danger. And yet, sweetling, you have taught me control and to embrace a time of quiet." They sat on the ship, looking out over the water. "I should have thanked you for teaching me new ways of looking at things."

Sedna could hear the gratitude in his voice mixed with

sorrow. "There is no need to thank me. You have taught me much also." She wanted to tell him she longed to explore that new word he spoke of as love. Was it the same as what she felt for her parents? She thought so. A warm affection that lingered and gave happiness.

"I fear I have taught you what you have no need to know back in your village. I have taught you to smile and to kiss me back.' He laughed at her nose wrinkling.

"It is true." As if he'd read her thoughts. "We have no words for goodbye or what you call love. We have what we say is *kunik*, a rubbing of noses on a cheek. To us that is sufficient to express our feelings, whether it be a mother toward her child or a husband to his wife."

"Sometimes words just confuse," he admitted. "Still, I do thank you for the great riches you have helped me win. When I return home a wealthy man, I can hold my head high, instead of sneaking in at dark so as not to be noticed as everyone expects." He picked up her hands that lay in her lap and rubbed the palms gently against his cheeks and lips. "By the blood of Thor, how I will miss you!"

She longed to speak, to beg him not to leave her behind, but her heart was too heavy already, weighed down with grief, and she couldn't find the words.

c/ɔc/ɔ

The sun came up earlier every day and stayed longer. They worked together, side by side until he had everything loaded, except for the few furs she was taking with her and the weapons of the people she thought her duty to return to the hunters. Many objects he had copied, although perhaps not made as well or as strong as those she made for him.

On the eve of his departure, he pulled her down on the

fur beside him in front of the fire. "I wish I dared tell you how much I love you, little troll. I've never said this to another woman, but I truly love you," he said in his Norse language.

By the deep sorrow in his voice, more than the words he uttered, she knew he was bidding her goodbye. The tears pushed behind her eyes and she willed them away. The people never cried over what they could not change.

"Dear one, I made you a gift. For all you have given me, taught me, it is poor thanks."

She accepted the wood from his hand. He had taken a gracefully gnarled piece of driftwood, rubbed it with oil until it shone up and down the length of it, and fashioned a staff. He had carved the top into the head of a raven, smooth and shiny and stained black, and removed the two largest jewels from the breast buckle that held his tunic together to use for eyes.

"Oh! This is very beautiful! As fine a carving as I have ever seen. But these stones came from your buckle. Your favorite buckle."

He shrugged. "I want you to have something of me with you. Something that matters to me."

She reached down into the furs she had packed for her journey. "I had these hidden away. I was going to leave them behind for you, but now you must have my special gift, also." She handed him gigantic boots that would have served three men of her clan if they could have worn them at the same time. The thought made a giggle well up to war with her pressing tears.

She had made them from sealskin, lined them with soft moss, and fashioned the soles from tough walrus hide.

"I thought you had forgotten my boots!" He ripped off the leather thongs holding the wrapping around his feet and pulled on the boots. "Perfect! I will be the envy of everyone in Ericksfjord with my new furs and now my boots." He leaped to his feet and did a crazy jig all around the room, kicking up his heels. Amazing agility in such a large man, she thought.

He reached for her, pulling her to her feet. Around and around he swung her, lifting her in the air, holding her close, kissing her neck and her cheeks and the tip of her nose.

She laughed and pushed futilely at him. If he continued in this manner, she wouldn't be able to keep away the tears. She had held out this long. She didn't want to give in now and show her silly womanly weakness. They were saying goodbye, each to return to a different life.

CHAPTER 11

That night, Sedna pulled quietly away from Rolv's sleeping embrace and closed the door behind her. She walked toward the boat. The air was cold on her bare skin, covered as she was with only the woolen shift she wore at night. Barely acknowledging the discomfort, Sedna moved numbly, in a trance from which she wished never to awaken.

She walked up the plank and stood for a long while gazing off toward the sea at the full moon rising in the distance. Only the continual whisper of the wind through the tall ice formations made a sound. Beyond the light of the moon, the land lay shrouded in darkness. The *sastrugi* had melted, the weird shapes of ice pooling back into the land or the water, whichever they rested upon, for the wind was much warmer than it had been. Yesterday they discovered the ice had melted from the opening in the water between the two lands. They both had seen it, but neither spoke of it.

Her Viking was ready to sail down that water, past the glacier, and the length of this island, until he reached Ericksfjord at the tip of the big land that lay parallel. Leaving her forever alone.

She needed to leave with him part of her essence, a

piece of her soul to keep him safe forever. She separated a large fur from the pack on board and stretched out on top of it, hoping to fall asleep again. Brother moon looked down at her without pity. She should not have given her heart to someone who refused to accept it.

This might have been how Nagatok felt when she deserted him. This might be the same ache her mother and father felt at losing her. How cruel she had been, for it was as if someone had yanked her insides from her body. She looked down at the deck, expecting to see her entrails there before her, bloody and pulsing like those of a fresh killed animal.

The pain within her middle—the hollow emptiness—threatened to burst her asunder and she clenched her fist against her mouth to keep from crying out loud. Sedna allowed the tears to run freely down her cheeks for the first time—experiencing their cleansing relief.

Rolv had told her in the beginning he would teach her what love meant. He had succeeded and she never wanted to feel it again because of the pain of parting. What value did living have without him? How could she return to her village and take up her life as before? Everything had changed. *She* had changed.

She tried to commune with the Raven Mother, but did not feel her presence. Had Raven Mother abandoned her, too? Loving Rolv with all her heart, she didn't see how it would be possible to continue living without him, without his fierce protectiveness, his readiness to do battle for her, in spite of the fears she knew he hid away. He gathered courage from protecting her. He faced down the towering bear, shoving her behind him. He would never again suffer a fear of an animal, no matter how huge and destructive. She loved his eagerness to learn from her about living with the elements.

He had taught her mating wasn't just a taking of a

body, but a sharing of a spirit, of two bodies sharing one soul. She leaned against the wolf and poured her heart out in great wrenching sobs.

"My love, what are you doing out here? Are you harmed? Why do you cry?"

Rolv had come up behind her and , immersed in her sorrows, she hadn't heard his footsteps or sensed his presence.

Under the full moonlight she saw the open look of alarm in his expression, his eyes filled with concern. She was the shaman, with the power and spirit it took to keep them both alive this long winter, but to him she was a woman and he feared for her. She turned away, ashamed of the tears, but he knelt in front and, lifting her up, raised her chin to look into her face.

"Why are you crying, my sweetling? You are free at last to return to your life. I stole you away against your will and now I release you. I love you too much to keep you any longer, to take you away from your people. You are like a bird that must be uncaged. Like your wolf, you must be free."

She wrenched away from his big, warm hand and shivered with distress.

He immediately took off his woolen cloak and wrapped it around her. He wore nothing underneath but the flimsy woolen trousers he called underwear.

"I am not cold," she cried out and leaped to her feet, angered at her inability to speak the words she needed to, angered that he had not guessed what had troubled her for so long. Everything boiled to the surface and she paced the ship's deck, hair flying about her shoulders. "I am filled with sorrow. I do not wish to be free, nor to leave you. Not ever. This love you speak of—I feel it in here." She pounded her fist against her chest. At last, the truth was out. She could pretend no longer.

Sedna stopped pacing and reached up to take his head between her hands to look into his eyes. "I was never captive, except in here," she said, touching his chest with her fingers.

Rolv lifted her and sank back on the furs with her in his lap. He looked down at her for a time that seemed to last forever, gray eyes gazing into black. Then he rubbed his thumbs across her cheeks to brush away the tears, following up with warm, tender kisses.

"Am I hearing you true, or is it something that I have longed to hear for so long that it is coming to me in a dream? Sedna, I need you more than the Earth needs the sun," he whispered hoarsely. "I never wanted you to leave. I thought that was what you desired above all. I thought it best for you."

She pulled his head back gently by thrusting her hands into his hair, entwining her fingers, her eyes filled with such love he could not mistake it. "I did not wish to leave. As a shaman, my spirit has always been free. I could have left anytime. That should have been clear to you. Do you forget I sent my people away when they came for me?"

"I gave my solemn promise never to force my way with you. While in my fever, I must have taken you against your will. Do you forgive such a broken promise so easily?" His voice was harsh with emotion.

Sedna owned no words to tell Rolv of her feelings. She was unaware of his promise being broken when she had wanted—no begged—him to love her. She didn't know what to do next, only that she needed him so badly and now she knew he needed and wanted her, too. If she let him leave her behind, he would be lost to her forever.

The people were not known for lengthy speech. Somewhere from inside her blossomed a new feeling of space, of freedom of expression, and she did not question from where it came so effortlessly. With a burst of energy welling up within her, a strong force threatening to rip her apart, Sedna felt the power to speak. Her love warmed her insides, pulled her back together in one piece again, whole and new. "You never took me against my will. I gave myself to you. You have taught me your love. I wish to show you mine." For a brief second she hesitated, not knowing where the shameless speech came from or what to do next.

He pushed aside her flimsy covering and ran his hand down her back, encircling her small waist with his hands splayed around it, then he moved to rub her breasts teasing the nipples and moving downward until she thrust her hips up to meet his seeking fingers. The touch of his hands flooded her with heat. She gasped as he lowered his head to kiss her belly. He put his hands under her buttocks and lifted her slight frame to meet his seeking lips. She twined her fingers in his hair and pulled him up her body to claim his mouth in a long, shuddering kiss. When he entered her, she felt her hot, moistness close around him. They moved together as one and once, when she opened her eyes, she saw the stars above her and the pale, golden moon to witness the rapture.

He brought her close to the edge of a precipice, then backed off and rubbed his fingers over her nipples again until she moaned his name, wanting more. She bent her head down and licked and nipped at the little hard buds of his nipples. He groaned, an almost anguished sound that startled her, yet brought a heady surge of gladness that she could please him so easily. When he must have known she was almost beyond ready, he thrust hard inside her, holding her small buttocks close to his body. She felt his rapture as much as her own in one blinding moment of bliss.

Finally exhausted, they lay back, letting the frigid air

condense the sweat, adding a delicious chill to the throbbing nerve ends covering their bodies. When he caught his breath, he turned to her, bringing her within the circle of his arms.

"That was as close to Valhalla as I may ever get." He pushed her hair back from the side of her face so that his tongue could tease her ear. His hands roamed over her gently, as if to make certain she was still there for him.

Sedna couldn't have spoken if she'd wanted to. What had just happened?

"A Norseman could not sail without the North Star. You are my North Star. You will be my permanence in this life. I knew that from the first time we looked into each other's eyes."

Sedna knew it, also.

"Will you come with me?" he asked her. "I want to be with you always, to protect you. I promise I will serve you as a faithful husband. I will care for you and shelter you and never will I treat you as my father treats a woman."

She twisted her hair around his neck and held him to her. "I never want to be away from you. It has been my desire since we met."

He groaned and held her closer. "To think I nearly left without you."

The Raven Mother had warned that the Viking would be important in Sedna's life and for future generations of Raven Women, and yet Sedna had to be the one to keep him with her.

The Raven Mother could not interfere. Sedna understood that now.

They lay on the deck, watching the moon sink into the horizon. "Brother Moon has finished his work on Earth for this night and is satisfied," Sedna proclaimed. *And so am I.*

They left at dawn. He showed her what to do. Each of them stood on a side of the boat and poled through the narrow channel, making the turn and heading directly south toward the mainland.

"When my father named this Greenland, he did it perhaps with his fine sense of mockery," Rolv said with a laugh.

"Can you never return to that place you called Iceland?"

"Maybe we can, but not my father. He is permanently banished for killing. I hardly remember why he fought now. Over some livestock, I think. He was always hot headed."

She laughed at the description, as if he might be different.

"He is also a leader among men, but with that temper—out of control. That is why I try so hard to contain mine. All of us do, except Freyda. She takes pride in being wild like Eric."

"And you are honored because you tell stories and recite songs. Among my people, we are only what our ancestors want us to be."

He stopped pushing and stared at her. "By Odin's blood, that is the same way we think! We are not so different then."

She had never thought they were, but said nothing, only admired his beauty and power. She still could not quite believe there were others in his world not just the same as he, but larger.

The journey was one of languid enjoyment for both of them. After two years of dreaming of little else, he was in no hurry to return.

They made love often, anchoring in mid-channel when

they felt the urge come over them. Each time was exquisitely new and satisfying.

One morning when he began to pull up anchor, she
stopped him and pointed. "Look over there. In that cliff
edge is a nest. It is large enough to belong to a white falcon."

Rolv looked in the direction she pointed—off shore
not far away from a tall escarpment abruptly poking out
of the ground. The stone mountain had begun to be covered in green but the tip was still wrapped in snow. He
shaded his eyes. "I do not see a nest."

"Come with me and I will show you."

They beached the boat, descended the ramp, and made
their way toward the mountain with the wolf between
them. Their destination was farther than it appeared from
the ship bow. A half day passed before they reached the
foot. He looked up. "I do not see anything yet."

"I see a very big nest. You are too heavy to climb.
Wait here for me." She shucked off her light outer furs
until she was down to the thin woolen tunic. She had
worn the tunic under everything else ever since he had
given it to her and begged her to discard her precious bird
skins. "I can climb easier without these," she explained,
laughing at his devouring eyes. "Stop that, or we will
never get to your home."

He laughed ruefully and kissed the top of her head.
"This is dangerous. I can help you."

"No. It is not dangerous. Often in the warm months, I
have climbed crevasses to get bird's eggs. The children of
my people learn how to do it early in life to help feed
their families." She began to find toe-holds in the mountain and gracefully moved upward so fast he could hardly
believe his eyes.

When she was alarmingly high, hanging onto tiny pro-
trusions of rock, she moved the upper part of her body

into a fissure and disappeared for an instant while he held his breath. She came out with something clutched in two hands and, teetering on her meager support, put her booty in the sealskin pouch hanging on her shoulder.

"Sedna! Look to your back!"

Rolv's strong voice, filled with panic, made her swivel around, swaying dangerously, her feet still toed into the slight outcrop of stone beneath her. She saw the shadow of the great wings first, before she smelled the strong fish odor and felt the brush against her head. The female falcon had returned!

Sedna crouched as small as she could make herself and began to climb back down slowly. The bird soared over her nest and instinctively knew one of her fledglings was missing. The others in the nest made loud sounds of hunger when they saw the wings above them.

The falcon gave the screeching, angry cry that Sedna as a child had heard many times when she'd robbed bird's nests. She calmly continued descending, her feet searching for the holds she passed on the way up, trusting not to miss one.

The giant bird struck at her, tipping her sideways. Sedna stopped moving to cling and chanced a look toward Rolv, who was unslinging his bow ready to loose an arrow at the bird.

"No!" she shouted at him. "Do not harm her! She is fighting for her young. They will die without her. It is a bad omen to slay her."

Rolv released the slack on the bow, but kept the arrow ready. No matter what Sedna commanded, he did not intend to see her torn apart by the falcon.

Aku had raced forward and, snarling and howling, tried to climb the mountain, her long nails scratching toe holds in the slippery rock. She slid back, tearing her pads on the sharp shale.

The bird continued to pummel Sedna, who moved slowly downward. The baby bird in her sack answered its mother plaintively, which stirred the female to greater fury. Once her great talons nearly grasped Sedna's arm. She jerked back just in time. Warm blood spurted from the long wound, but Sedna dared not lose her concentration.

"Do not hit her. I am nearly down," she cried out to Rolv below. She looked down at his concern while he stared up, his bow readied. "Find a rock. Throw it upward toward her nest."

For a long moment he searched the ground for a loose stone. Most everything was already covered with lichen and a tight green web of moss. Finally he straightened and aimed high over the flapping bird's body toward the crevice.

Hearing the smack of rock against rock, the great bird abandoned her fight and flew upward to protect her nest.

Hurriedly, Sedna continued downward until Rolv reached out to grab her. The wolf, bloodied and panting, tangled between her legs.

She knelt and hugged the animal close. "You're bleeding. Good Aku! Thank you for trying to help me, too."

Rolv pulled her to her feet, holding her tight against his chest.

"Oh, my love, never do that again. How could I live without you, now that we are together?" He rained kisses on her face and then, aware of her bleeding arm, he stopped. "Come, let us return to the ship. I will take care of that."

He emptied one of his leather pouches and wrapped the soft material around her arm to stop the bleeding, then helped her into her furs. They hurried toward the ship, carrying the little bird wrapped loosely in a sack so it would not cry out for his mother.

After a time, weakened from the loss of blood and weary from her ordeal, Sedna walked slower and slower. Rolv picked her up and carried her in his arms the rest of the way to the ship.

ഗ്രൈ

Days later, sitting on the deck, they watched the young bird eat fish. Already it ate out of her hand, while she talked to it in funny little noises made between her teeth.

"This falcon is for your father. I hope he will like it."

"My love, for the white falcon, he will welcome you with open arms."

They continued to talk of light matters, as if he knew she needed to take her mind off the throbbing in her arm. No doubt the wound would leave a long scar, but it was worth it if Eric, the bear of a man who terrified her sight unseen, accepted her as Rolv's wife.

Many questions, Rolv tried to answer truthfully, without embellishment. "One thing, my love, be ever watchful of Freyda. She is treacherous. She has formed a perverse infatuation toward Eric. I fear I am the only one who sees it unless others know and refuse to speak of it."

"She sounds like a terrible creature we would put out on the ice. The people have little patience with destructive persons. It only takes one to destroy a clan's unity, and everyone suffers. My father tells stories of this happening in the old days with entire villages split and blood feuds lasting for generations."

"Does it work when you put a trouble maker out on the ice?"

"Oh, yes. It is better for a man to perish than to be cast away. Other villages will not accept him, and he is invisible until he dies. You were only sent away for a time. That was lucky for you."

"Olaf was not worth my banishment. He was but a pawn of Freyda's, groveling at her feet like all her playthings. She torments and teases men until they will do anything for her. I have often thought she put him up to the fight."

"There was also a woman in our village who was said to cause trouble with gossip, even though her husband warned her to stop. He split her tongue like a crow's. I have seen this myself. That sometimes solves a problem."

Rolv held her close and kissed her. "I well know you mourn the loss of your people, especially your mother and father. I pray to Odin I can make it up to you over the years to come."

಄ಌ಄

In the passing days, Sedna patiently worked with the baby bird, which grew more feathers every day. Now the bird would perch on her wrist with no thought of flying away. It took longer to get it to settle on Rolv's arm, but it had to learn not to fear a man if she wanted to give it to Eric.

With mixed feelings of apprehension and enthusiasm, Sedna thought of Ericksfjord. Alone, staring out over the night while Rolv slept, she mouthed the strange syllables of the different names of his family. Would she ever learn to pronounce them or remember who owned each name?

She leaned on her elbow to look at Rolv next to her on the fur mat. Their time together during the long winter, their explorations of each other's mind and thoughts, were almost as delightful to remember as the explorations of bodies that had come later. They truly belonged together. With all her being, she wanted to be his North Star. She *was* his North Star.

Sedna knew her destiny and that of future generations

of Raven Women was tied to this one man and him to her. She also felt a warning that a danger worse than any she had faced loomed nearer as they approached Ericksfjord.

CHAPTER 12

The overcast sky threatened a wind and rainstorm the afternoon they arrived at Ericksfjord.

"There it is! There is Brattalid!" Rolv shouted to her as he sailed closer to shore, avoiding the many sharp rocks with the skill of a born sailor.

When they fully rounded the tip of the island, Sedna's eyes widened. Her breath escaped with a gasp of astonishment. Many people busied themselves at work in nearby fields while children played on the upward slope in front of the water. Strange animals grazed, animals Rolv had named—horses and cows and sheep. She remembered the names well, but thought he had made them up to amuse her on the dark nights.

Eric's home, Brattalid, lay sprawled across the slope leading up from the water. Behind it, a rich setting in the distance, stood mountains tipped in snow, holding off the gathering storm by impaling dark clouds on their tips.

"Will you permit me to show the falcon when I choose?" she asked him.

"Of course, my love. You have earned that right." He touched the long narrow mark on her arm that was gradually healing. There would be a thin white scar.

"My eyes are unaccustomed to the colors of your

home." She knew he was concerned for her safety among his people, but they were only human, weren't they?

As if in answer to her unspoken question, he turned her to face him, his expression somber. "Do not lose heart if my family refuses to accept you at first. They are generous and good in their own way. I cannot yet believe my good fortune that you have come with me. We must base our trust in each other, no matter what transpires. If they fail to support you, in time, we will return to Nordrsetur."

Sedna reached up to touch his cheek. "Do not fret so. I have fine thoughts about your home. We will be accepted."

"Did your Raven Mother tell you this?" Rolv asked, half serious now, half joking.

That he had not only believed in the spirit that made her a shaman, but welcomed it, never ceased to amaze Sedna. "It will be well with us, my love. I will make them like me. Am I not a shaman woman?"

They hugged each other before Rolv blew an eerie blast from a horn made of a giant sea shell. She spared but one glance at the running people, so awestruck was she at the splendor spread before her eyes.

The sunlight shining down on the meadows exposed bright wild flowers in more colors than she ever imagined existed. Nearby green fields flourished. Green caressed her eyes everywhere she looked. The thick stone house of Brattalid was covered with rich green turf of grass, moss, and heather, the whole of it blending into the surrounding green as if it sprang up on its own, out of the ground.

The cry of sea gulls overhead broke her from her state of trance-like wonder. She heard Rolv talking to her and felt his strong arm around her shoulder as the people crowded around the ship. Men threw up a landing plank against the vessel.

Her first thought was that he hadn't lied to her—about

anything. Everyone was a giant—women and children, too. Many of the loud and laughing children were taller than she. And their hair! She had to be having a vision. The rays of sun struck against brilliant red, gold, and white heads and men's beards. She tucked herself closer into Rolv's side. He bent down and bestowed a kiss on top of her head, a habit that she loved. It appeased some of the tumult he must know she was undergoing.

Two young men, taller than Rolv by a head, crowded in closer, pushing aside the hesitant crowd to run up the plank. She saw everyone else had hung back, waiting for this signal that Rolv was welcome.

Sedna recognized Torstein and Torvald, Eric's other sons and Rolv's half-brothers. They slapped Rolv's back, lifted him up as if he was weightless, and laughed with the crowd. The sun-crested man who stood with serene dignity next to Eric must be Leiv, Eric's favorite son. He smiled at Sedna, and she liked him at once. She could tell by the way the people appeared so overjoyed and excited that they loved Rolv and had missed him.

"We had no one to recite the *skaldes* while you were gone," someone in the crowd complained.

"I have returned, bringing you many songs to relate on long winter nights," Rolv promised, still holding Sedna tight to his side.

She stared at the way his people dressed, much the same as Rolv had when they first met. The men wore leather jackets and woolen leggings below their knees. Their lower legs were wrapped with the cloth he called "wool." Leather hides covered their feet, wrapped with leather thongs to hold the skins in place.

Women wore long, flowing gowns and capes with hoods. Each gown had a white apron attached, that extended almost to the bottom of their hems, with decorations of colorful flowers. The heads of several older women were covered with a piece of bright material wrapped around their hair. Children were miniatures of their parents.

Eventually Rolv and Sedna stepped off the boat. The crowd parted and they stood before four people slightly separate.

Sedna's heart cringed at the sight of the massive man with a countenance like Rolv's, yet not like. The older man's eyes were fierce blue with thick brows above. His beard and mustache almost completely covered his face. Everything about him bespoke an amazing vitality, an intensity of spirit that she knew she would have to fight against every day of her life to keep her own self whole.

"So. My youngest son has returned."

"Yes, Father." Rolv went forward and knelt in front of his father, waiting for the hand on his shoulder that was as much of a caress as Eric ever bestowed on one of his sons.

After his father touched him, Rolv stood, and they spoke quietly, earnestly. Sedna looked toward the two women.

One she knew was Eric's wife, Thornhild. Tall and stately, she appeared full-figured with delicate age lines just beginning to show on her translucent skin. She wore a cape and hood, but Sedna was certain her hair, too, was golden.

Sedna felt the stare of the one she knew as Freyda. The woman's bold eyes were like shards of the hard stones from Rolv's buckle, the stones he called jade. Freyda stared long and hard, as if trying to find a weakness in Sedna to pierce through. Sedna was thankful for lifelong training in not showing her feelings. She could not afford to have anyone know of her numbing terror at that moment. Freyda's piercing stare attempted to invade Sedna's spirit. The force within Rolv's sister was ma-

levolent and threatening. Sedna turned away, breaking
the hold between them.

So much energy to be loosed at one time, so much
emotion—so much confusion and turmoil, so much
laughter and shouting—all of it mixed together in this
crowd of noisy, boisterous people. Sedna never imagined
anything like it. Her people would have been horrified at
such disorder and tumult.

Rolv stepped back and pulled her closer to his side.
The other two sons arranged themselves on either side of
Leiv.

"My, are you not dressed in fine furs?" Thornhild exclaimed, touching her fingers to Rolv's jacket in her first
gesture of greeting. Her fingers trailed lightly across his
cheek and chin. Sedna felt warmed by her welcome as
did Rolv.

He bowed his head and, lifting Thornhild's hands,
kissed them both.

She touched his head briefly, as if giving him her
blessing.

Even though it was warm, barely weather to freeze
water, Rolv had insisted they wear their finest winter furs
on arrival. Sedna was thankful for the protection they af-
forded, the confidence with which the furs wrapped them
both.

The crowd separated as a small group of men and
women stepped forward to touch and feel the furs, to admire their boots. Freyda stood back, apart, watching. She
seemed to devour Rolv with her scowling gaze, which
made Sedna uncomfortable.

Freyda did not have the look of a sister to a brother.
Sedna would have known this without the words from
Rolv.

"Is this your *thrall*? She looks too dainty to do much
hard work." One of the brothers flipped Sedna's jacket

away in front, exposing the thin tunic she wore underneath for the journey.

Rolv knocked the hand away and stepped protectively
in front of her. "She is not my slave. She is my woman.
We are mates." He turned to his father. "If this in unac-
ceptable, we will return to Nordrsetur. Now."

Eric's brow wrinkled for a moment. The boisterous
crowd near the family fell into a hushed silence. Not
many spoke to Eric so boldly and lived to tell stories
about it later.

Sedna held her breath, waiting for Eric's reply, knowing Rolv would soon grow bitter and old with another
banishment.

"Can she speak?" Thornhild asked mildly, her calm
voice interceding between father and son.

"I speak her language. She understands mine." Rolv
put his hand on Sedna's shoulder proudly. "She is a
shaman of her people—like a *skalde* is with ours. She has
brought me much good luck in hunting. She made this
fine attire for us and…" He trailed off, to let his next
words fall on the hush surrounding them. "…she can read
a rune stone."

The crowd, who had stilled to listen to the family
drama spread before their eager eyes and ears, surged
backward. Even the family moved away slightly, putting
a little more space between themselves and the stranger
Rolv had brought with him.

He had told her in one of the long nights of storytell-
ing that a *skalde* was a high priestess who accompanied
the warriors into battle, reciting poetry to bolster their
spirits. It was as close to her word shaman as he could
come. She also knew that reading the stone was as magical to them, as it was to her, for she had no idea of how it
came to her.

"Torstein, Torvald," Rolv spoke to his brothers. "Go

to the ship and bring back some of what you see there."

Only moments passed before the two brothers shouted from on board the vessel. "It is a treasure! There are more furs here than we have seen in the market back in Iceland! Meat enough to last everyone here until the next cold season!"

The brothers shouted and laughed as they brought out the bounty.

Eric and Thornhild watched as men helped to pile the furs at their feet. They bent and felt them between their fingers.

"You could not accumulate all this on your own. Did she do it with her magic?" Eric spoke at last, after nearly everyone touched the furs to see for themselves.

Rolv shook his head. "It is not magic. She is a bold, fearless hunter. Her people are wise in the lore of this land of ice. I have learned much from her."

Eric turned to Sedna, his fierce eyes calmed now to a mild probing. "You know how to hunt all of these creatures?"

She nodded.

"You cured these hides so they are flexible and not hard."

It wasn't a question and she continued to meet his stare without flinching, with her chin high.

"We thought our brother might die, banished alone in the wilderness. You return him to us a wealthy man," Freyda said into the silence, her voice a rich contralto, at odds with the harsh lines of her mouth and her eyes so hard with cunning. "We are forever in your debt."

In spite of Rolv's warning not to trust his half-sister, and in spite of her involuntary tremors each time Freyda spoke, Sedna felt warmed by her praise, the first she had heard from any of them. There was a warm, golden aura surrounding everyone but this woman. Sedna saw a blood-bright mist when she looked at her. She could not be sure if it was a warning, but it was a sign.

Eric turned to his sons. "Bring the furs and meat, store them in the cold house. No one is to touch them again. They belong to Rolv and his woman. The *knarr* is due in from Norway before the summer is over. After the trading ship comes in, he will be able to have his own land and house. Come, son, we will dine and you shall stay with us until then. We wish to hear about your adventures. On the morrow we will begin looking over the land for a site for your home."

Sedna was puzzled at the significance placed on the stacks of pelts and meat and walrus tusks. Belatedly, she remembered Aku. "Wait." Sedna tugged on Rolv's arm and whispered to him.

"Did you see an animal aboard ship? A live animal?" he asked the brothers.

"Oh, yes! A wolf has stowed itself aboard. We let it be, thinking what a superb joke if someone tried to come on your ship without permission." The two men laughed like overgrown children.

Sedna walked toward the ship and the people in front of her parted into a pathway. She made a low growling noise deep in her throat. At the sound of her voice, Aku leaped off the side of the boat and, in a furry blur, ran to stand at her side, red tongue lolling, yellow eyes unafraid of the crowd. Sedna knew Aku was used to her clan crowding about, even if the people were not noisy like these people.

"A wolf!" The cry went from person to person. The family looked at her and at the animal, and stepped back even farther.

With no warning, a tremendous roar came from behind the crowd. A huge animal ran forward, snarling and snapping in fierce disregard for anyone nearby.

"Legbiter!" Rolv knelt and the dog, still snarling and watching Aku, allowed his head to be caressed. "Behave yourself. Aku belongs here now."

The animal with short bristly hair, not long and silky haired like the wolf, stood stiff legged, challenging Aku, ignoring the crowd.

Someone yelled "Dogfight!" and the voices soared in-to the sky with shouts of approval.

"No!" Rolv shouted to be heard above the crowd. "Legbiter is three times her size and trained as a fighter. Aku will not be made to fight him. Sedna has had this wolf since it was a pup. She prizes her above all else."

Eric held up his hand for silence. He stared into Sedna's black eyes with frosty blue ones. The expression on his face held none of Rolv's gentleness. "What say you, little troll? Is your wolf a coward?" Are you a cow-ard, also, he was asking her.

Sedna stood straight and returned his stare. "She need not prove herself for me. It is her decision if she chooses to fight." She knelt on the sandy beach and pulled the wolf close, whispering in her ear.

"You don't have to do this!" Rolv protested. "She is all you have from your home. I know you love her."

That strange word again. Love. Sedna knew what it meant now and agreed that she did love Aku but, since she had met the Norseman, she had also learned that love included freedom of choice.

The crowd surged away, forming a large open ring. Legbiter ran into the center, knowing his place. He was champion of Ericksfjord and all the beasts challenging him died or made their peace with him at the price of their pride. He made a lunge toward Aku, his large teeth snapping. A violent gnashing sound and low growls is-sued from him.

The wolf looked tiny. Her winter coat was still full but

her legs were fragile and thin compared to the big dog.

Rolv held Sedna in front of him, encircled by his arms. She leaned against his body, never taking her eyes from Aku, concentrating and speaking to her through her thoughts. *Our spirits are entwined, my friend. Be strong, for together we must prove ourselves here in this strange land.*

Before the dog made contact, Aku dashed forward, her small body a blur as she slashed and dashed, slashed and dashed.

The white and brown dog soon had blood seeping from shallow cuts on his legs, lower thighs, and ribs. The crowd went wild.

The fight seemed to go on and on, although Sedna knew it only lasted moments. Aku rushed in once more, leaped, and struck against the big dog's shoulder, knocking him off balance and onto his side. Stunned and winded, Legbiter lay on his back, exposed his throat, and gave up.

Aku stood over him for a second, growling low in her throat. Then she turned and stared directly at Eric, as if she knew he was the one to satisfy.

No one spoke for a long moment, even the rowdy children were awed.

"What did you whisper to your wolf before the fight?" Freyda's voice intruded in the silence.

"I asked her not to harm the dog," Sedna said with a smile.

Everyone broke into laughter and excited shouts.

"Get an ax, someone. Kill Legbiter. We will tolerate no cowards here," Eric ordered, not breaking the gaze between him and the wolf.

"No!" Sedna moved from the circle of Rolv's protecting arms, hoping she could command enough of the language to make him understand. "Do no harm to the dog.

It was not his fault. Aku is my *tunaraq,* my helping spirit. No mere animal could win against her."

"Let this be a lesson, a lesson I have already learned well. Do not be quick to judge the worth of anyone by her size," Rolv said, his voice strong and filed with pride, carrying over the heads of the crowd.

ℰℐℰℐ

Sedna sat in front of the fireplace beside Rolv, who had been given the place of honor next to Eric.

The main hall of Brattalid was longer than it was wide. Two fires blazed in the center at each end of the room. The group of invited people surged inside to be near the fires and warmth. Firelight threw itself against the thick stone walls and smoke rose in ethereal wisps upward through a hole in the roof.

The family and close friends sat around the room on rough benches made from driftwood or lolled on reindeer pelts spread over the sand and earthen floor. Children crawled on the floor and played with carved toys, laughing and teasing one another, not subdued like children of her tribe.

It was said that evil beings were drawn to laughter, especially children's laughter. The evil spirits might conceive mischief if they heard too much. Therefore children in her village played quietly, and apart, enjoying their play just the same.

Lamps hung along the edges of the wall, flickering with the soft glow of burning moss. Later, when Rolv's people accepted her, she could teach these people to use melted blubber from seals and whales. It put out a much better, more constant light and did not smoke.

Up on the wall, near Eric's huge chair, a long metal bar with rings attached hung in a prominent place. She noticed that upon entering, the first person shook the bar, creating a clanging as the metal rings struck against each other. After that it was shaken every once in a while by someone passing by.

"What is that?" Sedna pointed.

Rolv's smile vanished; he answered seriously. "That is the Magic Holder some call the Ringing Bar. The first person entering the room is obliged to ring it, to frighten away evil spirits and magic potions that might be used against us. The last person to leave also does it. It has protected this family ever since I can remember."

The Ringing Bar made perfect sense to her. She began to like these new people, losing some of her fear. She smiled up at him and he looked as if he wanted to kiss her. Gazing into his eyes, she understood his thoughts and felt the same. He wanted to hold her, to lay her down on the rug and make fierce, mad love to her in front of his gods and his family, to let them know the depth of his feeling for her. He was proud of the way she handled herself. He knew she was frightened of the enormous differences between their worlds. She sensed these thoughts as if he'd spoken out loud.

He was pleased that she had not shown fear of his father. That would have had dire consequences, for Eric demanded fealty and obedience from all he met, but hated above all fawning and fear in others.

Someone called out to Rolv and he tore his thoughts away, separating himself from the images Sedna visualized coming from him.

Sedna smelled the pungency of the damp wood burning, warm animal hides, and human bodies, the same rich smells as in her old village, in her home, which brought bittersweet remembrances of her mother and father.

"Why is there water inside instead of out?" she whispered to Rolv, who never strayed far from her side. A narrow channel carved in the ground and lined with rocks came from outside beneath one wall and traversed the room, bypassing the fireplace and ended under a huge dining table.

"It is a cistern," he explained. "We have a trough from the river that flows in here so that it does not freeze in winter. We cover it to keep it clean and have water for cooking and drinking."

These people could have shown her people new ideas also.

Rolv might have explained more to her, but everyone claimed his attention while he wove tales of their adventures on the ice during the past season of the cold. She listened with half awareness, admiring the rich baritone of her man's voice, but watching others and noting details.

Freyda sat close to her father, on the other side of Rolv, where Thornhild might have sat. Freyda ignored the younger, unmarried women her own age who clustered together around the edges on benches, giggling.

Thornhild sat apart on a little stool, listening, but busy working with wool, which she turned on a wheel to string out in long sinew-like pieces. This she wrapped on a wide piece of stick held by a child.

Sedna felt comfortable with Eric's wife. Thornhild had a stern demeanor, showing she was strong-willed. She would have to be to keep a man like Eric at her side all the years they had been together. Rolv said his father had a roving eye for the women when he used to go a-viking.

Sedna's head nodded but she painfully struggled to stay awake. Among her people it would not have been impolite to doze, but would have shown that a guest had been made comfortable enough to allow himself to appear defenseless in front of his host. She did not want to be exposed, in spite of Rolv's nearness. When one was

close to sleep, creatures both good or evil might choose
to enter one's body, invade a spirit. That was a shaman's
greatest ability, to put people into a trance so that he
could do as he willed.

She awoke sometime in the night. Rolv must have carried her into a room and removed her clothing, for she lay
bare but for her thin tunic, cuddled close in his arms, his
big, warm hands cupping her breasts. She sighed and
wearily dropped off to sleep again.

೧⬝೧⬝೧

The next days were filled with a bewildering barrage
of surprises. Thornhild saw to it that Sedna received a
dress from one of the taller children, which fit her.

Sedna liked it. It was long, touching the ground, but
still permitted more freedom of movement than the fur
tunic and trousers she usually wore. The garment was a
deep yellow in color with a white apron attached in front
and trimmed in colorful flowers, which had become a
part of the material, all around the edges. Thornhild
called it embroidery but that word was hard for Sedna to
even think, much less say out loud.

By the smoldering look in Rolv's eyes, she knew he
approved of her new apparel.

"My father has called for a banquet to be held in our
honor," Rolv told her. "There will be much celebration.
Does that frighten you, little one?" He kissed her mouth
lightly, not caring if anyone watched.

They had made love many times since they arrived.
She was thankful—for, in spite of her exhaustion, her
senses bombarded continually by new and unusual people
and sights, she needed Rolv more now than ever. His
need for her was unmistakable, and he never tried to hide
his feelings from his family.

"First there is something I must say to you," Sedna said. "I walked behind the house this morning, before you awoke. I thought to see the place where Aku slept. What is the reason for keeping live animals in cages? I saw three fox and a wolf, and even a young *naanuk*, the white bear. They cried out to me to be released."

"No! Eric would be furious! Do not even think such a thing. The men have worked long and hard to trap these animals unharmed. The King of Norway wishes to keep them in his court for the entertainment and education of his people."

"But no living being should be owned by another," she protested. "The other animals will witness this and grow angry from the lack of respect shown them. They will tell one another and soon your hunters will find no food."

"Sedna, you do not understand. These animals are treated with respect. They are fed and cared for better than if they had to forage for themselves on the ice. If they survive the ocean journey, many people will look upon them with admiration. They may live out their lives in comfort with all they desire to eat. Did you not capture the white falcon for my father?"

He was right. She had done that. But the falcon would not be caged once it was trained, nor would it be sent away from its homeland like these sad creatures. Her chest weighed heavy, sharing as she did the fear and distress of the creatures in the pens. Some cages had not been cleaned and the animals lay in their own excrement. It was tragically improper behavior for the Norsemen to treat animals in such a manner. One day, the humans would have to answer for this offense.

"Why do you need the ships from other lands to come here?"

"We cannot exist on this island without the ships returning each spring and fall. Sometimes they skip a year and we are fearful for our lives, although we can sail to Iceland during the summer to trade, I suppose."

"We live without any outsiders and we have survived longer than your people here on this land," Sedna reminded him gently.

"You have spoken of this before. We are strangers to this land while you belong here. We cannot live off the land as you do. Perhaps in future generations, after you teach us how…"

He pulled her close, kissed the top of her head, and then tilted her chin to kiss her eyelids, her cheeks, the tip of her short nose, and finally settled on her lips.

When they broke away, breathless, he said, "I do not wish us to quarrel, sweetling. I promise you, I will never capture a live creature to put in a cage, but I can do nothing about the actions of the others. It is their right."

She never again ventured out behind the barns to look at the caged animals, but in her mind's eye, she saw them often in their suffering and knew someone would have to answer for treating the animals with such disrespect.

❧❦❧

"I wish to talk to you, my husband."

The word felt strange on her tongue, but sounded good to her ears. He had taught her the words husband and wife and, though there were no counterparts in her Inuit language, she understood the meaning quite clear. They were a family of two, the same as when a man and woman came together in her clan, but still it was different. Her people would never have permitted such open affection such as his constant touching and kissing her. It would surely call in vindictive, jealous spirits. Yet Rolv and his people, though understanding the *other world* and with many beliefs and superstitions, did not believe such. She

would have to change her views if she wanted to be satisfied here and to make Rolv happy.

They had climbed to a promontory above and at the
side of the main house. Below them the panorama of the
fjord with white water in the middle swept in front of
their eyes, moving up past the beach to green pastures
and wild flowers on both sides, separated by the turf and
sod covered house.

Men and women worked in the fields. Horses pulled a
large object through the rich soil, which turned the
ground over while children followed, putting something
inside the turned soil.

"They are planting seed," Rolv explained.

"Yes. I know someone else who has done the same."
She had wanted to tell him, did not know how. Sedna
moved closer under the protection of his arm, touching
her lips to his big hand as she held it between hers

She was not certain what the words meant that came
from her mouth, but Rolv knew. He held her away, to
stare into her face, then began kissing her. He pulled the
string away from the top of her garment, bent his head to
the throbbing place in her throat he liked to caress, and
then knelt before her, holding her hips. He put his cheek
against her belly, as if already he felt life.

"You are carrying a babe! I had not dared hope our
mating would produce a child. A son, I pray to Odin for a
son," he enthused.

Rolv leaped to his feet and pulled her up, holding her
close and dancing his little jig around and around as he
had done once before. "We must make the announcement
at the feast. Eric has long wanted a grandson, this will be
as exciting to him as it is to us."

This time she couldn't laugh. Her excitement in his
joy evaporated upon hearing his words. She knew she had
told Rolv that Raven Women were not allowed to keep

male children when she first told him about the Raven
Woman legend. Surely, he would not pretend to forget.
She knew him better. His nature was open, containing no
trace of subterfuge or deception. The idea had never
come up in their many nights of conversation and love
making. He must have forgotten or had not taken her seriously.

She put her hand to her stomach, wondering if she
could feel what sex the child might be, imagining the
babe making its first movement inside her. She put
Rolv's hand to her stomach and held it there for him to
feel too. The look of stunned gratitude on his face moved
her to tears and she turned away, frightened.

If it was a boy child, Eric and Rolv would never permit her to give it away even though she would lose her
Raven heritage and jeopardize all the Raven Women to
come, if she tried to keep it. Until this moment, she had
been content, unworried about the future as long as she
had Rolv at her side. Now that contentment might be her
undoing. She put a trembling hand on her belt, and closed
her eyes, concentrating on the power within her.

Was her power enough to contend with Freyda, the
caged animals, the overstocked storeroom? Sedna sensed
harmful forces building around her as if she were the center of a winter storm. She strove for a glimpse of the future but her intuition was empty of pictures. She could
see nothing.

She asked herself if it was a warning of adversities to
come.

CHAPTER 13

Neighbors from nearby farms cheerfully helped to work on the feast, which would take days to prepare. Freyda held back, lofty and judgmental, a princess in her own eyes. Thornhild threw angry looks her way, the brothers teased her good naturedly, but no one else attempted to encourage the haughty young woman to join them.

Before they arrived at Ericksfjord, Rolv had explained the inner workings of the small clan of mixed Norwegians and Icelanders. While everyone tolerated Eric's legendary fits of temper as a chieftain's right, Freyda's mirrored outbursts were uneasily overlooked through fear of reprisal. Once Freyda had thrust a servant's hand in the fire and held it because the young girl had spilt hot soup on her arm.

She had demanded the slaughter of her favorite horse because he dared rear back and throw her to the ground. For this, Torvald and Torstein should have taken the blame, having put cockleburrs under her blanket before she got on the horse, but they only confided the truth to Rolv later, afraid of their father's and Freyda's wrath.

These incidents that Rolv had confided to Sedna had happened many years in the past, when they all were young. Sedna privately thought Freyda fascinating. She felt certain Rolv's dire warnings of his half-sister's treachery were greatly exaggerated. He was overly protective, especially since the baby was coming. So far Freyda had been attentive and complimentary, gracious to a stranger. As a shaman, Sedna felt she could take care of herself. Yet a thread of uneasiness attended every look Freyda turned her way.

Aku had hated Rolv's half-sister from the first. The wolf's hackles rose and she growled low in her throat whenever Freyda came near.

Servants, family, and neighbors brought in garlands of flowers and lay fresh green straw on the floors. They buried great chunks of reindeer, bear, and other wild game in pits and roasted on hot coals. Rolv explained that they never ate their milk cows, as long as they had plenty of other meat and fodder for them in the winter. Only young male cattle were enjoyed as veal. He took her out in the fields early in the mornings and, while they walked, he explained what each animal was called and what they took from the animal. Some, like the ones he named sheep, mostly gave up their coverings of white to be used to make what Thornhild wove into cloth. Sedna would have thought the animal would be ashamed to be treated thusly and not grow another coat but he said no, that didn't happen.

Clouds descended, rain pelted the buildings. A soft thudding on the ground outside was all Sedna could hear. The roof was so thick no sound penetrated from above. Sedna loved the rain in summer. She and her parents had often stayed indoors and talked, or sang, or her father recited old stories during bad weather. Here it was magical. When she looked outside, her eyes could not fill with enough of the sight. Green hills blended with a soft transparent fog after the rain, while flowers of many colors seemed as though they ran in streams down the hillsides and onto the valley floor.

She went inside to await Rolv who was in the barn with the men.

"Come here, child. Let me look at you," Thornhild commanded Sedna who sat across the narrow room, watching Eric's wife work on the loom.

Sedna obediently walked forward and stood in front of the giantess, looking up at the thick golden braids and the stern blue eyes, betrayed by a gentle smiling mouth.

The older woman reached out to lay her hand on Sedna's belly. "You are with child."

Sedna was not surprised, because this woman's eyes reflected much wisdom. Wisdom and pain.

Thornhild laughed, but the sound was harsh, and had no humor in it.

"Why do you laugh?" Sedna asked.

"Ah, little one, it is because I enjoy a huge joke on Freyda, who will not be amused. She has forbidden her brothers to marry or have children until *she* decides to. She wants the honor of bearing Eric's first grandchild. She will not be pleased that his bastard son has out-done her."

"Oh. That is unfortunate. Does she have a man, then?"

"No! Many men have wanted to court her, many have bedded her. She is beautiful in a wild, animal way, I suppose. But what mortal man can stand up to her? She is her father's daughter, and thankful I am that she is not mine too."

"Neither Rolv nor Freyda belong to you. Does this not shame you?"

Thornhild motioned for Sedna to sit near her. They were alone in the large room, for once. The others had stopped making ready for the festivities to gather the harvest before the rain came down in earnest.

"In the beginning, I felt dishonored by my husband's conquests. The first time he brought home a slave from the Westmen, the Irishers, I hated her. But then it came to me that it was not of her choosing and she could no more help her condition than I could mine. Eric cares much for me in his way. Since he has grown older, his eyes wander less and less. I am content."

"What was Rolv's mother like?" Sedna was elated to realize she could understand most of the older woman's speech. She had grown used to Rolv's slow, deliberate talk. He wanted to make sure she understood each word. These people shouted and laughed and argued, all at the top of their voices, their words flying faster than a hare in front of a fox. Being shaman could help her understand Thornhild.

"Rolv's mother was so beautiful, so gentle, no one could ever have hated her. Black hair and small boned, delicate, she was something like you, except her eyes were gray and round, like ours. She was the only one of all Eric's conquests who truly threatened my status as a wife, although she wouldn't have meant to harm anyone. Eric doted on her, much to Freyda's exasperation. Even as a child, Freyda always was jealous of her father's attention to anyone but herself."

"And Freyda's mother?"

Thornhild shivered, her mouth turned into a straight line of disapproval. "Sigrid was a whore. A conniving, mean-spirited slut. Some of us thought her a witch. Eric told his daughter a lie, that her mother died of fever, but that is untrue. None of my sons were told the truth. I can trust you, I see it in your eyes." She hesitated and looked around, as if Freyda might have been listening somewhere in a corner of the room. "Eric captured her mother on a raid to Britain. She was wild and willful from the start. When we were banished from Norway for Eric's temper, we went to Iceland and he brought her with us as a house slave, even though I begged him to leave her behind.

"In Iceland, she ran away with Eric's friend, Gunnar. Eric found them coupled together and split Gunnar's head from top to shoulder. That was what caused us to be banished from Iceland. She was not worth the death of his friend or the banishment."

"Did Eric also kill Freyda's mother?" Sedna had to ask, since Thornhild, lost in thought, seemed to forget the conversation.

Thornhild sighed. "No. But Sigrid became hysterical and never regained her senses. One winter night she disappeared into the darkness and we never saw her again. I hope she fell into a crevasse. Maybe the night demons took her away."

Sedna considered the woman's fate. It did not seem harsh justice for someone who spoiled the lives of many people. At the same time, pity tugged at her heart for the poor, lonely child that Freyda must have been.

"Does Rolv know about his child?" Thornhild asked.

"I told him. He wants to make an announcement at the feast."

Thornhild leaned down to Sedna. "You and I must speak with Rolv, warn him not to tell Freyda. The longer we can postpone it, the better for all of us, the safer for you."

Discouraged, Sedna doubted anyone could stop her man from telling his family and friends at the celebration. Why did even Thornhild fear and despise Freyda? The few times the woman had come close, she only had good words to say to a stranger. Sedna believed none of them took the time to try to understand Freyda.

"Ah, I am an old woman carrying on, depressing you with my gossip. Forgive me."

"I am grateful you told me about the family. I am both saddened and glad to bear Rolv's child."

"Saddened? I do not understand. Are you fearful because you are so small compared to us? You seem very sturdy, in spite of your size."

Sedna put out a tentative hand to touch Thornhild's arm. "Oh, no. We are hardy mothers. I have never known any woman to die while giving birth." She had to confide in someone. "I want to share a secret with you, but you must tell no one. I am a Raven Woman. We are not permitted to keep a male child. Rolv wants this to be a son, and I fear it is so."

Thornhild looked stunned. "All men wish for a son first!" She knelt and touched Sedna's slightly, slightly rounding belly. She closed her eyes, her palms flat, her fingers spread to lightly encircle her stomach. Their eyes were on a level as she stared into Sedna's face. "It is a male child. I can tell by the way you carry it, so high. Why are you so certain you cannot keep him? I cannot conceive of either Rolv or Eric giving the child away. Nor you, if you are a true mother."

Sedna gazed into the fire, watching the glow, thinking how at night a servant scraped up each coal and placed it in a container to keep for the morrow's fire. In her village, that had been her mother's sacred duty, to keep the lamp trimmed so that they did not have to light it anew at the beginning of the day. It was a bad omen if it went out. Thinking these cozy thoughts made Sedna remember her heritage. Something she had tucked out of her thoughts since their journey to Ericksfjord.

"My mother explained to me just as her mother explained it to her. The people believe the Raven created the Earth, the sky, the sea—and the people. We are called Inuit, which means 'the people.' In the beginning women were the powerful ones, the men submissive, dependent on our hunting skills to survive. Our superiority and our downfall came with the ability to bear children. Our task was to bear women descendants—Raven Women. By doing this, our clan was not diluted. The girl children were strong with everything we had poured into them—"

"How did you plentify without males?" Thornhild asked, reluctantly interrupting.

"Only a few of the women were selected to be Raven Women. All others were permitted male children. One of the first Raven Women disobeyed, bore a male child, hid him away until he was near grown and then kept him at her side, angering the Raven Mother. From that day on woman became subservient to man and only one Raven Woman was permitted at a time, and not from each generation. One line of Raven Women came down through the ancestors."

Thornhild breathed a huge sigh. Rolv had told Sedna how much the Norse loved stories. This was evident from his mother's strong interest and sad smile.

"Does Rolv know?"

Sedna lifted her palms in a gesture of perplexity. "I told him when we first talked, but he has misplaced my words."

"He has chosen to forget them. You need not remind him. I lost three children before I bore the first. Then I was blessed with four sons, but always longed for a daughter. It may be the opposite for you. I do not wish ill for you, but you may bring only a daughter into this world."

"It would be terrible to lose a child at birth, but it does happen. Your words are honest and sensible. No, I will not tell him that a son must be given away," Sedna promised.

This was the second request for promise of silence. Was she becoming false to her Raven blood or was a

voice within speaking for the Raven Mother, urging caution? In times past, before Rolv came into her life, the
Raven Mother spoke to her, but it had been a different
kind of exchange. But why had the Raven Mother said
the Viking was important to the Raven line if she must
not bear his child?

❧❧❧

Sedna awoke the morning of the feast day and looked
out the narrow window of their room to see sunlight.
Turning to shake Rolv, she paused a moment to watch
him sleep. He often came to bed in the morning hours, for
he sat and talked late with his brothers. She could hear
their laughter from out in the great hall. He was so happy
here, so content. She thought everything in her new home
extravagantly unusual, but longings stirred within her for
their quiet, contained life at Nordrsetur. It would never be
that way again. She would have to learn to appreciate this
if she wanted to share in his life.

His golden eyelashes, darker tipped at the ends, reminded her of a grizzly pelt. Long and thick, they lay
against the tan of his cheeks. His jawline, square and taut
during the day, relaxed in sleep, as did his long, well-
shaped mouth. She leaned closer. She loved him so much
it frightened her with the exquisite pain of it. She reached
down below the covers to caress his manhood, which was
already beginning to swell. While she watched, his lashes
moved and she stared into his opened eyes, the color of a
storm at sea—smoke in a campfire. How she loved to
look into those eyes.

"What are you doing, wife? Staring at a man whilst he
sleeps? Not fair, not fair! And what did you do to my
staff? I have taught you too well, wench." He laughed
and pulled her close. She struggled to disentangle herself

from the covers, embarrassed to be caught fondling him and staring so at his beauty.

They made love then, wild and intense in the beginning, then, a second time, slow and gentle. Finished, they clung together while he whispered soft love words and she basked in the warmth of their essence.

They heard the family stirring from beyond their door. Rolv released her and leaned away, looking at her for a long moment, while she accepted the caress of his eyes.

"Ah, you are unique. Have you any idea how beautiful you are? My life is content as never before because of you." He gently touched her face, holding her chin so he could look at her. "By Odin's breath, I do not know which moves me most when I look at you, your tilted black eyes or your small, trim mouth." He reached to brush away the hair from the side of her face. "You know, your hair black as a crow's wing is the envy of the blonde women living at Ericksfjord. Thornhild told me."

"Shame for your stories. How could those with hair the color of the sun envy mine?" Sedna did not believe him but it sounded good to have him say that because she often compared her darkness, her slender body to the splendid women of Brattalid and doubted that Rolv could love her best.

He lifted her tunic and rubbed his hand slowly over her rounding belly, letting his fingers reach upward to her softly filling breasts and then he bent over and lay his head on her, to feel the body within her.

"You smile, my husband." She entwined her fingers in his thick hair and pulled his head up to look into his eyes.

"I smile because you have managed to wrap my entire family around your fingers. To think I feared they would devour you."

"Wake up, you lay-abouts!" Torvald rushed unannounced into the room with Torstein not far behind.

Rolv pulled the covers back over Sedna and sat up on the edge of the bed. "What are you boys up to so early in the morning?"

"Early? We have been working since the sun came over the mountain and here you are still a-bed. Mother decided to start the banquet outdoors. The day is so bright, it hurts your eyes. It will be much better out there."

Excitable Torvald always spoke in short bursts of speech. Torstein was a little more sedate, but not by much. They were two huge, overgrown children. In spite of their clumsy behavior, they treated Sedna like she was made of fine porcelain. Respect and admiration shone in their bright blue eyes each time she caught them looking at her.

Sedna smiled at them and nodded solemnly at Leiv who pushed by them and entered the room. Leiv, the handsome, she called him privately. His beauty seemed not of this world. He was as good as he was pleasing to look at. He would be a better leader one day than his father. Others often teased him because he was as serious in demeanor as someone twice his age, especially in comparison with his two unruly brothers.

She looked at Rolv's wide shoulders, his bare, tanned back. He was a mixture of them all. Serious at times, he could be rowdy. He had moods she was just beginning to notice and they could be dark moods into which she did not intrude. She worried about telling him of the baby boy.

∽∾∽

Outdoors, when they saw the laden tables, Rolv looked around and the words exploded from his mouth. "It is so good to be home. I missed this with the sparse, austere life at Nordesetur. It contained good things about it, especially when Sedna came to join me," he told the family who had gathered around them to listen. "But I wanted more. I wanted to be a special person like my father. Since I would never be so physically powerful, great riches would help me fulfill my dream." He encircled Sedna with his arm. "She helped me achieve this end."

Sedna did not understand all he spoke of about riches and dreams, but if it made Rolv content, she was happy with it. Everyone clapped at his speech and disbursed to help or hinder the progress of the meal.

The table was nearly as long as the room. Women sat at one end, men at the other, and children with a table of their own, a little ways off so their raucous laughter did not disturb the adults. Servants ran back and forth with platters of food—meat as well as cooked and raw greens gathered from the nearby hills by the young people.

Sedna's eyes were wide as she beheld all the abundance. Rolv must know she did not approve of such displays of food at one time, but he eventually rescued her from her dark thoughts by assuring her there was plenty of game and had been since they arrived in this land. Eric named Greenland, land of plenty. Why should it change? It was indeed a cause for celebration.

Sedna's thoughts wandered to the young people she had watched yesterday as they went to gather the last greens of the season to grace the table. Most of them of the same age, they roamed with their baskets, excused for a day from their chores. It was a time for them to practice being adults, to explore each other, to a point, but they all knew not to overstep. Thornhild had told her about the practice of giving them time alone. She said there were very few children born to unmated women. They knew how far they could go with their loving.

Gracing the table were piles of flatbread, something

Sedna had never seen before, and racks of lamb ribs and roasted fowl, along with the wild game that had roasted in the ground for days.

"We celebrate many things today." Eric stood to make a toast. "Leiv, my beloved eldest son, has decided to leave before the ice comes. He makes a journey to our old home in Iceland, but he also has an idea to find the land we passed on our way there from Norway." He clapped Leiv on the shoulders with a bear hug that must have shaken the younger man to the soles of his feet.

Leiv's handsome face split with a wide smile of satisfaction. "All of you who will may come, with my father's permission. It may be a long journey, but we will find new land, new exciting country."

The people around the table buzzed with the news. Leiv was always going off somewhere to seek new lands, but this was the farthest he had ever proposed to journey without Eric the Red accompanying him.

Sedna glanced at Thornhild. The mother's expression crossed between anxiety and pride at the news of her favorite son's departure.

Each person owned a brass spoon or carved wooden spoon and a knife to eat with. Sedna remembered the first time she watched Rolv eat with them instead of using his fingers. He had taught her, and she was glad he had, for she would not want to embarrass him. Still, she saw no benefit to eating this way. Her people would have laughed at the sight of such awkwardness.

As the meal wore on, Sedna tried to hide her dismay at the wasteful bounty. Much meat went on the ground to dogs who lay underfoot.

"You look shocked," Freyda commented from the seat next to her. It always seemed to happen that Sedna found herself close to Freyda when Rolv was otherwise occupied. Sedna had begun to question if it was accidental.

Since none of the others were cordial to Freyda, perhaps she was looking for a friend.

"I am amazed," Sedna admitted.

"Why? Do your people not make feasts?"

Sedna spread her hands, wondering how to explain. "Yes, we do make feasts. But we fear bad fortune more than we dare to celebrate good fortune. If you use all of your food at one time, what if starvation follows? We believe in saving for the dark season, the time of cold."

Freyda stood and clanged her metal spoon against her plate. "Listen, everyone. The wife—" Her voice rose slightly in mocking condescension. "—the wife of my dear brother wishes to express her fear for tomorrow."

The table of laughing people quieted. Freyda patted Sedna's shoulder reassuringly as if she had just done her a tremendous favor, while everyone waited for Sedna to speak.

The stillness was interrupted by the ominous ringing of the blessing bar someone had brought out from the hall and hung in a nearby scrubby tree. They were afraid of her! She swallowed past a dry spot in her throat. The eyes suddenly focused upon her caused a nervous feeling in the pit of her stomach, somewhere behind the baby. She had a hard time looking in Rolv's direction, but when she did, a frown of concern had appeared between his eyes, which looked troubled.

"What are you up to, Freyda?" Thornhild spoke into the silence. "Leave the girl alone."

"Oh, be still, Thornhild. I am just trying to make her feel at home. No one is paying any attention to her. Do you not agree, Eric?" Freyda never called her father anything but Eric, even though his sons would not have dared say his name so familiarly.

At the kind words, Sedna forgave Freyda for drawing her into the center of unwanted notice.

"What does our sister mean about a fear of tomorrow?" Leiv wanted to know.

Sedna took a sip of water while the group around the table regarded her with serious eyes. She knew from her talks with Rolv that they believed in magic and accepted the idea of powers beyond their understanding. When she knew they were not going to return to their former joviality without her saying something, she cleared her throat, hoping for the right words to put them at ease.

"It is a matter of different customs," she began, searching for what she needed to say. "We have had seasons of the cold when seals abandoned our shores, when the fish that live beneath the ice vanished, when the hunters searched almost to the end of the land so that some never returned, and yet no one found food. We left our babies and old ones out on the ice because we had nothing to still their cries of hunger." She paused and, looking in the direction of the children's table, saw that even they listened raptly without a sound.

Eric stood, his eyes bright with anger. "And why did this happen to you? My son said you were expert hunters, even better than us."

"The reason, I believe, that we had good hunting was our prowess, but also we did not anger the creatures who gave themselves to us for food. You keep cages with pitiful animals who will die before they reach their journey's end. Their souls will also forever remain captive because this is how they died. That is wrong. You live on top of the land, cutting long strips out of it to change it, to work your own way with it. You cut down the trees which to me are magical, and I see pieces of them lying around rotting and falling apart that you have discarded. Everything has life. We must value and protect this life and learn to live with it, not against it." Her voice rose and swelled as she grew more passionate about what she was saying. She wanted to explain *inua*, the soul of every living creature and some not living, like stones and rocks, all had a place and a being, but that was too hard for her to put into mere words that they could understand.

Eric pounded the table, his eyebrows jutting downward in fury. "This is foolishness. Your hunters are clearly not as able as ours. If they are no larger than you, it is understandable."

Rolv watched the proceedings, torn between embarrassment and distress for Sedna. Like a chessman on the board knocking into its mate and then another and then another, he saw the gathering break into relieved snickers and then loud laughter ripple down from his father's head of the table all the way around and back again.

He wanted to push back his chair and rush to stand by his beloved's side, she looked so serious, so forlorn, so alone.

Of course, it was nonsense, what she said. Game was plentiful both winter and summer, they would never be without food. Perhaps she had heard such stories over and over in her childhood so that she believed it. Her father was known by her clan to be a great storyteller, surely that was the source of her fright.

"Enough!" Eric proclaimed, his voice gentler. "She is a guest in this house, and she will be honored as such."

"But she is not a guest, Father," Rolv protested. "She is with me. Whatever I am to this family, so then is she. Soon we will be one more."

Eric's mouth opened in a wide O and the group was stunned into silence for a long moment. Rolv heard Thornhild's indrawn hiss of breath and he felt Freyda's eyes boring into the side of his neck, as if she held a heated knife there and pressed it into his flesh.

Damn Freyda. He knew of her desire to have Eric's first grandchild but that was ignorance on her part to think all of his sons would wait until she decided to marry.

Rolv pushed back his chair and moved to stand behind Sedna. He put his hands on her shoulders, his fingers pressing into her to offer his strength. He knew she accepted what he offered, but also knew that she would need her own courage, more than she ever had, in the coming months.

CHAPTER 14

As the afternoon wore on, the festivities continued. Eric ordered horse fights and dog fights to entertain the men, along with wrestling and games to show off their skills as hunters and warriors.

The women, tired of the raucous sound of men's voices, settled on a grassy knoll below the house, overlooking the bay. They talked quietly. Thornhild and some of the older ones continued to work at carding or winding wool, their hands never idle.

The young girls, soon bored with the sedate, placid women, went back to watch the men, or found interests of their own.

Below the women, children laughed and tumbled on the gentle green slope leading down to the beach.

"This is a beautiful place, your home," Sedna said. She held a long walrus tusk in her hand and had been showing the older girls how to carve on it. She would show the boys, in time, but on this day they would not suffer the company of females.

Thornhild nodded. Pushing back the cowl covering her head to receive the sunlight, she spoke into the waiting silence. "When we first came here, I was sad and hated it. I was forced to leave my family in Norway after Eric took us to Iceland. Then he brought us to this place, which seemed the end of the Earth."

"I know what that is," Sedna said. "We call such a place *tununirn*, the place beyond the back of nowhere. We think it is where the *wiivaksaat* live."

"*Wiivaksaat?* What a strange word," one of the women from another farm said.

"It means those who come around again or, some say, spirits of the dead."

"What a beautiful way to express the dead," Freyda said, edging closer to Sedna. "Did you tell these words to my brother? Rolv is so good at composing sagas and reciting them, he should include those words."

Sedna shook her head. "No, it never came up. He has learned much of my language. It seems easy for him."

"Easy for you to learn ours too," Thornhild commented. "It is difficult to believe you only started learning this past winter while you stayed at Nordrsetur. Rolv's mother never did learn to speak Norse beyond a few words, nor did Freyda's mother."

Sedna didn't answer, perplexed at how to explain that the Raven Mother, Tulunixiraq, bestowed certain powers to help a Raven Woman preserve the line, but not enough to make it too easy. That was why only few women through the ages were chosen.

"Is that a magical belt you always wear?" Freyda asked.

"Perhaps it is magic, perhaps not," Sedna hedged. No one in her clan would ever have asked such a question. "The belt was given to me by my mother and she inherited it from her mother, passed down to us from the beginning of our time. The first Raven Mother gave it to our line."

"Let me look at it," Freyda commanded, reaching out her hand.

Sedna shook her head. "Nay. I am the only one permitted to touch it." How could this woman be pleasant one time and offensive the next? This puzzling aspect to Freyda's personality had a way of drawing Sedna closer, as though to figure her out. Part of her remained terrified of Rolv's half-sister, the other part intrigued. There were times Sedna sat alone, with her thoughts, trying to discover what the Raven Mother was trying to tell her, but it didn't always come through so that she could understand. Perhaps the sweetness of holding a child inside made it more difficult to allow shaman thoughts to come to her. It could be now she was more woman than shaman.

"Will you tell the others as you've told to me of your Raven heritage?" Thornhild asked. "Rolv mentioned it, but said it was a matter for you to speak of. They would like to hear of your family too and where you lived."

Sedna told about the beginning of the Raven Mother in the glacier and everything that had been passed down through time to her. She left out the part about not accepting a male heir.

It was not the time to go into that, and she hadn't missed Thornhild's frantic looks, warning her away from that subject.

Do not worry, I will not tell them, she wanted to assure the older woman. "My mother and father were old when I was born. I miss them and I know they miss me, but the people's way sometimes is to go afar for a new family."

"Does she not have beautiful glossy hair, Thornhild? It is like the tail of Eric's favorite stallion." Freyda reached out to touch the tip of hair behind Sedna's ear.

Freyda had offered Sedna many compliments today. Perhaps she felt badly about causing her embarrassment at the feast. Sedna looked into Freyda's eyes but could read nothing in the deep green.

"Her hair *is* beautiful," Thornhild agreed. "You are the

envy of all these yellow-haired women. They claim you make them seem pale, like a well-washed gown."

The women smiled and laughed, good naturedly agreeing.

"Now I know you are teasing," Sedna scolded, joining in with the game she had learned to play with Rolv during the winter months of inactivity. It came easy because her people teased much also.

Freyda reached out to take Sedna's hand in hers. "Rolv is comfortable with you as a seeress, a shaman. You have spoken out at the dinner table. When it gets dark, we all go inside and then it is just boring chess and checker games between the men, unless Rolv or someone tells a saga. Can you show us something that a shaman does?"

They both looked down at the contrast between the shapely large white hand with rings on almost every finger, holding the small, compact dark one.

"Perhaps, if it is expected of me," Sedna answered after hesitating. The hand imprisoning hers felt cold as a smooth, wet stone from a river, and Sedna wanted to shake it away, like some vile limpet from the water that attached itself to a leg.

Thornhild rebuked Freyda. "Nonsense, child. You do not have to earn your supper. Freyda, where do you get these ideas?"

"It's not that she must earn her supper! It would be entertaining, is all. What is wrong with that?"

"I do not mind, if everyone is receptive. I would not wish to frighten anyone with a shaman's magic." Sedna was not sure Rolv would approve. She had gone her own way all her life, and now it seemed strange to worry about someone's approval. She had been taught since childhood that she was special and could do as she pleased. That was not without problems, since freedom held a certain responsibility that robbed her of any care-free childish whims. She liked the new idea of holding another person's feelings in such regard and did not feel it harmed her freedom.

"Freyda, stop such nonsense!" Thornhild ordered. "It would go ill with her if our family and neighbors fear her powers. In Norway, she could be deemed a witch."

"You are a selfish old woman, Thornhild," Freyda challenged. "You know our people value witches. We do not destroy them as Eric has said other foreign places do."

Sedna watched Thornhild's lips tighten against the brazen disrespect Freyda displayed in front of the family and neighbors. Aside from an occasional disapproving sound made with their tongue against teeth by a few older women, the others politely pretended not to notice Freyda's insults.

Sedna wondered, if it came to it, which woman Eric would side with?

"I will hold a magic spell so that I may talk to brother moon, if you wish it," Sedna said into the heavy silence, not wanting to see another argument erupt between the two women.

"What of the *Althing?*" Thornhild's voice, carrying an edge of fear, rose above the tittering of the excited women.

Rolv had told Sedna of the assembly gathered to dispense justice. They were the ones who banished his father from Norway and then Iceland and cast Rolv from here for the turning of two seasons. She had thought it a fearful name, on hearing it the first time.

"Why should they assemble to judge her? She is but a guest at our home," Freyda jeered.

"Why indeed?" Thornhild countered. "Because it is their right to do so if they decide someone may be a threat to our settlement. And since she is wife to our son and carries his child, she is not merely a guest."

"Does the *Althing* always make a good decision? Are they always right? We have no need of a gathering of men to make decisions for us," Sedna said, as politely as she could.

Thornhild shrugged. "What matters? They are the law. What they decree we must obey or there is chaos and disorder among us. We must live by certain rules or we are barbarians. It is admirable that your people can control their actions without help. I doubt we could do that."

"Forget it then," Freyda pouted. "I only wanted entertainment for us all. It is so boring with the men playing their silly games and you women sitting about like sheep in a pasture. I don't fit in anywhere."

"You never did, Freyda, you never did." Thornhild's calm voice broke into the vortex of Freyda's anger, dispersing it into the air above them.

"It is growing dark," one of the women said.

"Yes, I feel a dampness settling into the grass. We should go inside," someone suggested.

One by one, the women departed, until only Sedna and Freyda were left. Thornhild appeared reluctant to leave them.

"Go inside and sit in that moldy old hall. We will be in directly," Freyda said.

When the women had gone, Sedna turned to Freyda. "Why are you so disrespectful to your mother?"

"She is not my mother!" Freyda' green eyes lit from within with a ferocity that stunned Sedna. "Never say that if you wish to be my friend. She is not my mother! I hate her! She sleeps with my father, she bears his children, but he does not love her. He loved *my* mother, and he loves me. I know she had my mother killed. She called a secret meeting of the *Althing*. They drove my mother out into the ice fields alone to die."

"You do not know that," Sedna protested because that wasn't the way Rolv and Thornhild had told the story and, according to them, Freyda, then a child, had not even been with her mother.

As quick as the sun setting behind a tall mountain peak, the paroxysm of rage Freyda had displayed disappeared. Her voice turned soft and cajoling as she patted Sedna's arm.

"Please, I need a friend. From the moment I saw you on the beach, I knew you were the friend I waited for all my life. You are not like these cows who fear me. You make your own decisions. In the future, I promise not to say things that bother you, even if they are the truth."

Sedna drew away, trembling from Freyda's touch. A part of her felt sorry for the lonely woman, but a warning crept over her, challenging Sedna's own desire for friendship. Part of her insisted on keeping a distance between them and she couldn't help by be troubled by Freyda's closeness.

Sedna rubbed her arms, suddenly cold. "Thank you for your offer of friendship. Now we had better go inside. Listen to the wolves in the distance."

"Are you afraid of wolves? Yours never leaves your side, except at night when you go into the house." Freyda glanced toward Aku, lying curled next to Sedna seemingly asleep, but the creature's yellow eyes were opened to slits, watching Freyda intently.

"Anyone fears pack wolves," Sedna replied.

"Our hunters do not. They wade into them with spears and knives and slay them. The fur is splendid for trim on clothing. We feed the meat to the dogs."

Sedna was troubled at words spoken so carelessly. How could she make them understand that when animals were not treated with respect, they did not return. She kept quiet about her fears, not wanting Freyda to laugh at her and tell the others again. "We slay wolves if we need their pelt, but we never use the meat. We bury the carcass in the snow out of respect."

"How curious you are, little troll. You rail at us against waste but do you not think that is wasteful?" Freyda brushed back the thick short hair across Sedna's forehead. Her second touch made the skin on the back of Sedna's arms crawl, but she held herself tight, not to show it. Rolv had begun calling her little troll from the first and Sedna loved to hear it coming from his lips. It did not sound endearing when Freyda said it. Yet Sedna longed for a woman friend. She'd never had one before.

She wanted Freyda as a friend, in spite of the growing inner alarm warning her to stay away from Rolv's sister. Perhaps the baby inside her body blocked some of the rapport she'd had with Tulunixiraq. Sedna sensed the foreboding swell within her sometimes, as if someone was desperately trying to get through to her.

She wanted to enjoy her new life, her new family, her beloved husband, and soon her baby. She decided to ignore the foreboding.

CHAPTER 15

The family and guests had come inside by the time Freyda and Sedna entered the great hall. Sedna walked toward Rolv who looked at her searchingly when she sat next to him on the bench.

"I asked you to stay away from her," he whispered, his voice containing subdued exasperation.

It was the first time he had ever spoken even a little harshly and Sedna felt a cross between hurt and anger well up inside her. Why should she not like anyone she pleased? She was a person in her own right and not to be controlled.

Even her own father never tried to control her. He had too much respect.

"We want to hear sagas tonight, but not from you this time, Rolv, my son." Eric stood up to address the assemblage. "If your woman does not object, we wish to hear from her."

Freyda had been whispering in her father's ear, in spite of Thornhild's objections, or perhaps because of them.

Sedna thought Rolv was aware of her resentment for what she perceived to be his arrogance in warning her away from his half-sister. She tilted her chin, in the stubborn gesture that must have become familiar to her husband.

To pacify her, Rolv spoke. "Ask my wife to read the rune stone at the hearth."

Sedna's expression softened at his obvious attempt to regain her good graces. Reading the scratched straight marks on the stone came easy. It was hard to understand why these people did not understand their own words.

Two stout men carried in the rune stone and set it before her on the floor. The crowded room grew hushed. The snapping of the two fires and the cracking of embers floating into the air were the only sounds to be heard.

She left the bench and knelt in front of the stone, rubbing her fingers lightly over the markings. Her speech took on a lower timbre—a shaman's voice.

> "Beasts die,
> Kinsmen die,
> Thou diest likewise.
> One thing I know
> That never dies
> Is judgment on a man who is dead."

"Ohhh!" The hushed sound radiated from the mouths of the listeners.

Eric wiped his massive hand across his eyes and, to clear the air, thumped the table with his fist. "By the blood of Thor, that is said exactly as it was written. Everyone knows it comes from the words of a *kvad,* a great saga written for the king of Norway."

Rolv and Sedna smiled at each other, their quarrel dismissed.

"Do you wish to hear of Sednah, goddess of the sea? We call her *she down there*," Sedna asked Eric, who sat across the fire from her in his giant chieftain's chair.

"Is she like our own 'Bibrau, the maiden who sits in the blue'?"

"Does this Bibrau have magical qualities?" Sedna wanted to know.

"I suppose so." He turned to the others around the fire. "What is your judgment?"

"The inscription about her was found on an ancient rune stone. No one knows what it meant but many songs and sagas have been fashioned about her," Leiv answered.

Rolv moved restlessly and Sedna felt a surge of satisfaction at his discomfort. She had promised to tell him the story of Sednah but he had forgotten. "Husband, will you bring my drum to me?" she asked, enjoying saying the word husband out loud for the first time so everyone heard her. They waited for Rolv to go into the room and return with her drum.

"Tell me about your Sednah," Eric commanded.

Sedna leaned back to stare up at the smoke hole in the roof. As she expected, everyone leaned back and did the same. All eyes watched the smoke slowly curl upward through the roof.

"A long time ago, before anyone's beginning, there was a beautiful maiden who lived on an island as a captive of her father who had a secret, unnatural love for his daughter."

She waited a moment while everyone settled down to listen. The children lay on furs around the fire, for even in the summer, the evenings were cool.

"One day a handsome hunter lost his way and passed by. Since Sednah was very lonely for someone of her age to talk to, they became first friends and then lovers."

Sedna's voice rose in a sing song cadence, soothing and forceful at the same time. The silence made her turn her gaze from the ceiling to the listeners. Heads nodded, the children already lay asleep, scattered on the floor like pieces of shells on the beach.

"The lovers conspired to run away, to leave the old man, but he discovered them one day when he crept upon their hiding place. As he watched them mating so tenderly, jealousy consumed him. He wanted to slay them both where they lay, but this would cause them but a moment's pain. They must suffer, as had he.

"He waited patiently, until he caught the handsome hunter alone. He shot him with a harpoon and buried him beneath heavy stones so that wild animals would not disturb his body.

"First one full moon, then another passed, and poor Sednah felt certain the hunter had abandoned her. Her heart was torn to pieces and she could neither eat nor sleep. Seeing her so sad and lonely, so tormented without her lover, the father, instead of feeling sorry for her, became even more enraged at her betrayal. Coaxing her into his kayak, pretending to show her something special, perhaps a white falcon's nest high on a cliff, he poled far out into the sea.

"There he pushed his daughter overboard. She clung to the edge of the kayak, crying pitifully for mercy, until one by one he cut off her fingers and she sank to the bottom. In the dark waters at the bottom of the sea, she found where she belonged. She became goddess of the sea, her fingers are the animals, the seals, the cod, the whale—the sea creatures all created by her and under her dominion forever."

When Sedna had finished the story, everyone's head was tilted back, or their chins resting on their chests with eyes closed. Snores resounded from the front to the back of the crowd.

Next to her, Rolv slept as did the others, even Eric, his fierce eyes closed, nodded his chin against his chest.

Sedna looked toward Freyda and felt the first tremor of real fear travel up her backbone. The woman's eyes were closed to slits, but Sedna felt her looking out, as if she hadn't been touched by the shaman power. Only another shaman or someone with very strong powers could have resisted.

Sedna's soft voice entered the room from behind Eric's chair as she had been taught.

"We are lying scattered on a soft green field like the flowers beneath us. The earth and grass is soft and giving, the pale sun caresses our closed eyes as we dream on and on."

Her voice grew slower and lower as she gently thrummed on the drum with her fingers. She dared a glance toward Freyda and was rewarded by the sight of her slack jaw and closed eyes. She, too had finally surrendered to the spell of the shaman.

Sedna continued to drum softly and, as she did, frightening scenes sped before her closed eyelids, so quickly that she might have been inside a dream. First, she saw the pitiful caged animals, their eye sockets empty, unable to see, their tongues missing so they could not cry out. She saw wolves, running about skinned and bloody, their pelts taking on another form of life and dashing up to hurl themselves against the naked wolf bodies as if trying to mate. She saw the piles of discarded meat on the floor at the banquet. They took forms of strange animal creatures and rose up to cry out their pain and humiliation.

Scenes of disaster rushed before her. Children crying in hunger, women boiling grass, men hunting far from Brattalid and finding nothing.

It was so terrible, she didn't want to see any more. She arose and slipped outside, leaving the door open so her spirit would stay in the hall.

She hurried down to the ship and brought back the

cage with the bird. If she pleased Eric, perhaps he would listen to her warnings.

By now the falcon had turned into a beauty, growing full feathers, and was tame enough to eat a piece of fish from Sedna's hand.

Rolv had showed her how to tie a leather strip on his leg to bind him, allowing him a certain amount of freedom.

"I regret your bondage," she whispered to him. "I am remorseful at being the cause of it, even though we all are bound in our own way. They will show you much respect. You will be honored here and free to fly above seeking prey. I promise I will not permit them to cage you except at night, for your own protection, since you have grown so tame."

When she re-entered the great hall, she noticed the children tossing restlessly on their furs. She hurried to Eric's side.

Standing there a long moment, she could hardly bring herself to touch the giant as he sat, fast asleep. Even with his eyes closed and a low snore emanating from his lips, he was impressive—a superior human being who would have been equal to Sednah or any of the people's symbols of power.

Quickly, before she quailed at the task, she tied the sinew loosely on his wrist and bent down to instruct the bird. It sat in quiet dignity, at the edge of the table in front of the Viking.

Sedna returned to her place and began to speak, a little louder as she went on. "You have heard me on the roof. I have visited Brother Moon and he imparted vital wisdom. It is time you listened to what he has related to me." Abruptly she stopped the drum beats.

The children first and then the adults slowly woke up and stretched, yawning.

It seemed to Sedna that everyone at the same time saw the falcon.

"What manner of magic is this?" Eric knew immediately not to frighten the bird, but spoke softly, reaching out his hand to stroke it.

The bird arched its neck, ready to strike with its sharp beak. Sedna made a noise with her tongue against her teeth and the bird stopped its attack and began to preen its feathers.

Everyone turned to stare at Sedna, expressions showing respect and wonder. She looked at Rolv, but he shrugged. "It is your moment, do as you will," he whispered.

Sedna stood and regarded them, one at a time, ending with Eric. "You have heard me on the roof, have you not?" One by one up and down the table they nodded, their expressions awed.

"Do not be afraid. My magic is never harmful. I have been to the moon and brought back a gift for your chieftain." She gestured toward the falcon.

Eric cleared his throat to speak, but for once had no ready words.

Should she warn them of the coming starvation? What if it never came to pass, would they mistrust her then? Rolv would surely be angry. She took a deep breath. It was a shaman's right and duty to tell.

"I also bring back a sorrowful message. The coming cold time will be very harsh with the ice thicker than you have ever seen it, covering everything. Even the seals who love cold will go to another place because their food, the fish will not be here. The animals will disappear from this land as if they never had been. Brother Moon did not tell me why this is. He does not have to explain his message as mortals must." She wanted to tell them of her dream about their wasteful ways and the capture of animals to keep in cages, but she thought it might be a good thing to get past one idea at a time.

"Will this starvation time last long?" Leiv asked, his expression solemn, believing.

"Only until the ice melts in the time of the sun," she said. "Then it may never happen again in our lifetime."

Freyda stood up. "Why should we believe you? Are you still vexed by my father sending live animals to Norway? If your soothsaying is true, perhaps you will cause it to happen."

Sedna felt Rolv stiffen next to her, and start up to answer. Around the table, guests and family sucked in their breaths at the insult. Without knowing, Freyda had come very close to the source of the problem. The creatures were outraged and angry at the wasteful squander of the gift of their body and fur, they were angry at the disrespect shown them.

Before anyone could speak, Eric stood and faced his beloved daughter. "What nonsense you prattle, Freyda. Sit down and let adults talk if you have nothing better to say. This person my son treasures has come into our midst offering friendship—even to you—I notice."

"But—"

"She has brought a gift of this amazing creature—all of you know how long have I lusted for a falcon, but never thought to own a white one. She is giving your brother a son and me a grandchild. How can you hint of evil?" He pointed a giant hand with finger extended. "If you ever speak up against her again, you will answer to me!"

He sat down amidst a room filled with stunned people.

Rolv, along with the others, held their breaths. Freyda was spoiled and willful because of her father lavishing affection upon her since birth—sometimes to the exclusion of all else, including Thornhild. Never had he spoken so to her, especially in public.

Freyda visibly swallowed her fury and turned away to speak to Torstein. But not before she shot a look of pure malice at Sedna, who felt a spasm of shock as if the woman had stabbed her in the chest with a lance.

❧❧❧

On the day the *knarr* slipped into the harbor, Rolv and Sedna were the first to spot the huge trading vessel. They had been standing on the edge of the swell of land that led down to the water, looking out toward Nordrsetur, remembering their time alone on the island.

"Look at the strange boat!" Sedna pointed at the larger ship berthed next to Rolv's small boat and Leiv's large sailing ship.

"The *knarr* comes!" Rolv shouted back toward the house and the fields where people worked. He grabbed Sedna's hand and they ran, laughing, down the slope toward the harbor.

Soon everyone on the farm joined them, except Eric, who waited with heavy dignity at the top of the hill. With much backslapping and good natured taunts and banter, the captain and crew made their way up toward him.

"Send word to the neighbors," Thornhild commanded her two younger sons.

Sedna watched as they ran beyond the house, the barns, and the fields to climb the promontory behind and both blasted away on their horns so that even such a long way, the people on the beach heard them. It was a signal for all on the neighboring farms to come to Brattalid.

After the crew and captain ate and drank their fill, Eric and Rolv, along with everyone who had something to trade, brought their goods out into the meadow, close to the outbuildings.

At first, Sedna was charmed by the sight of the people

gathered together, laughing and sharing the excitement. She watched Eric, standing a head taller than anyone, the white falcon from which he was hardly ever separated, on his arm.

"You must give him to me," she heard the captain say, pointing to the bird with a light in his eyes. "The king is waiting for one such as him. He will pay you handsomely."

Sedna felt relieved when Eric shook his head emphatically. "Never! The wife of my son gave him to me as a gift. Perhaps she will show us how to trap others and next time you come we will have some for you."

"Never, never, never," Sedna echoed with a whisper that not even Rolv heard.

Sedna was deeply disturbed by the sight of all the winter meat she and Rolv had brought from Nordrsetur spread out along with the furs.

"Husband, I wish to speak with you."

"Later, sweeting. This is important. I must have first pick after Eric of the treasures the ship brought in for us if you want us to have a place of our own."

"But that is why I wish you to hear my words. We must not trade away the meat. We will have need of it in the cold time. We do not need a place of our own. To cut more trees to make room for another stone house is wasteful."

He rose from his kneeling position of spreading of wares and turned to take her shoulders in his big hands. His fingers pressed gently, but firmly into her flesh. "Lovey, your prophecies are of importance to you. You are important to me. Therefore, your visions carry weight, to be sure. Yet, as much as we believe in magic and visions, we must survive in this harsh land as best we can. If we do not have trade goods to offer the captain and live animals to please the Hakon, the King of Norway, he will not permit ships to return to this island. That would be a grave tragedy. We would perish without the ship. Do you not wish me to provide well for my family?" He looked pointedly at her stomach.

"My beloved, it is not important, this wealth you covet. What is important is that we obey the spirits who give us food. The spirits tell me that we have injured them grievously."

The words came from a source within her, a desperate need to make him understand. Otherwise, they could all be destroyed.

Eric moved forward to stand before Rolv and Sedna.

"What is the difficulty? Now is not the time for a lover's quarrel."

"It is no lover's quarrel, Father. Sedna wants us to keep the meat, trade the furs only."

Eric looked back at the frozen meat, stacked like wood on the grass, then glared from under his bushy red brows at her. "The people of Norway love to eat game. They pay well for it. We cannot use all of this bounty. What is the matter with you, woman?"

Any other time Sedna would have trembled and slid back behind Rolv, but too much was at stake now. She stood to her full height and raised her chin, her eyes staring into Eric's, never flinching.

He seemed almost ready to listen to more of her arguments when Freyda walked forward, the handsome captain on her arm.

"My word, Captain. Can you imagine Eric the Red letting this slip of a girl push him around?" she taunted. "And you, my brother Rolv, what say you to being led about by your nose like a bull to slaughter? You who were untamable and would suffer no permanent woman to your bed before her."

The people close by sensed the strife in their midst and

the jovial laughter and banter stopped as everyone turned to watch and listen.

"Enough!" Eric bellowed, he turned toward the captain. "I say trade—that is what we are here for. My son has his own goods. He may do as he pleases with them."

Sedna knew Rolv had been trying not to turn his anger toward her, though because of speaking out about the hardships to come she was at the center of the conflict.

"She helped me slay the animals. I will not trade without her approval. As for you, Freyda, mind your tongue. You may talk to our father as you please, but not to me with such lack of respect, nor to my wife."

Freyda glared at him, expecting Eric to champion her, but he had moved away, bored with a dispute he obviously felt was beneath his dignity.

Outraged anger twisted Freyda's face, making an ugly mask that people turned hastily away from. She glared at Rolv and Sedna before smoothing out her expression to a insincere smile and dragging her enraptured captain along, back to the trading ground.

Sedna touched Rolv's arm, hating the dissension that had sprung up between them, wedging them apart. "My love, trade if that is your desire. I, too, wish our own place, to be alone." Her premonition could be wrong. It was the first time she had known a shaman to disregard a message, but this life was so different and confusing.

It was possible that she'd read some of the signs wrong and that no harm would come from Rolv being given land from his father. Even if the idea of owning the land was foreign to the Inuit, did that make it wrong? Thornhild had promised to teach her to weave and card wool. They could have their own sheep. Eric promised to help build them a house when they found the land they wanted. How strange it was to own the right to live on land that she and her people had always thought belonged to everyone and to no one. She knew in her heart this went against her beliefs, but she had to make compromises to live here in peace.

Rolv bent his head and kissed her soundly, before trotting forward, like a young boy, eager to join the noisy group of people crowding around the captain and crew.

She watched long enough to see the brothers slap Rolv on the back in good humor, and Freyda look over her shoulder with a spiteful smile of satisfaction.

Then Sedna, with Aku beside her, walked away.

ಲ⁊ಲ⁊

After the ship left to return to Norway, Sedna, with Rolv's help, showed the Norsemen how to fashion weapons for bears and how to carve ivory swivels for the ends of their harpoons to enable surer kills. She showed them how to make sinew nets for snaring birds and small animals.

Nothing more was said about the altercation during the trading day. Rolv showed Sedna their pile of treasures in the storeroom, which he said would help them begin their own household. Iron, timber, barrel staves, pots and pans, cloth in piles along with tools, acorn flour and honey, He pointed everything out to her, more excited than she had ever seen him.

How strange were these people to make such importance out of possessions. The collection seemed a clutter of no significance that she couldn't make any sense of. But if he was so happy about it, she would quell her uneasiness, attributing her feelings to carrying the child.

Later, when Sedna told Rolv that Aku would have puppies, the whole family became enthused about the event.

"It's that wily old Legbiter," Eric laughed. "He gets them all, sooner or later."

Sedna thought he sounded a little envious.

The night the pups were born, Sedna woke up in a sweat, her hands clammy, something calling her. She knew as soon as she cleared the sleep away that the wolf needed her.

She crept out of bed, flung on furs over her sleeping tunic, and moved quietly outside. An early frost chilled the night, leaving a soft white patina on the outbuildings and fences. The moon hung suspended in the sky, just over the tree tops. Inuit legend said reindeer poured out of the half moon and descended to Earth to feed the people. Sedna hoped so, for they could have need of reindeer soon.

When Sedna neared the barn, she heard the wolf panting and her low whine. Most of the dogs slept out on the meadows, but some preferred to stay close to the house. Aku always slept just outside Sedna and Rolv's window where one of the boys had built her a shelter.

"Aku. Are you hurting?" She knelt at the wolf's side and drew her head onto her lap. The pups were huge, Sedna felt their outline in Aku's belly. For a long time Sedna crouched, wanting to help and not knowing how. She removed her Raven Woman belt and laid it across Aku's belly as tears streamed down her cheeks. Her loyal friend was dying, that was plain to see.

Aku's eyes followed Sedna's every movement, their expression pleading for help.

She had no idea of what to do for her beloved wolf. She'd never been around an animal birthing before.

"My love, Torvald said you were here." Rolv lifted her up and held her close, soothing her, whispering in her hair, wrapping her in an extra garment he had brought. "Come, step away, and let me see to it. I've helped birth many a colt and lamb." He motioned for his brothers to move Sedna away.

Rolv knelt and stroked the animal. If he was worried, he tried to hide it, but Sedna saw the frown lines between his eyes. He had to know how much the Aku meant to her, and he had always valued how the wolf watched over her so fiercely. "Bring me some sheep's oil," he commanded.

After rubbing his hands well, he slipped his fingers carefully into the birth passage of the struggling wolf. She was so worn out by the this time, she didn't notice, but lay still, her great yellow eyes focused on her mistress.

The Raven Mother seemed to whisper frantically to Sedna, for the first time. The hairs on the back of Sedna's neck turned cold and damp with the ethereal sound. Sedna's legs trembled, almost causing her to fall. '*The wolf must live!*'

Sedna sensed that desperate need coming from inside her body and mind. "My drum, I need my drum," she murmured.

Someone went for it.

The sound of Rolv swallowing through a dry throat came loud in the stillness of the barn. Only animals at the other end made any noise, stamping and munching hay. She accepted her drum from an out-of-breath child and closed her eyes to drum.

Able to see what Rolv had to do to help Aku, Sedna merged with his thoughts.

His fingers touched the legs of the first pup ready to be born. She felt his concern. It should have been the pup's head in place. Rolv's strong fingers began the arduous task of turning the creature within Aku's body and doing the least damage to her. Blood seeped out over his hands as he worked. Even though the barn was chilled, sweat poured off his forehead, and Sedna bent to wipe it away with her skirt.

What if this kind of birth happened to Sedna? His thoughts burned in her head and she closed her eyes again to receive them. *I wouldn't exchange my precious woman for all the babes in Norway. We don't have to have children. What if my mating with this woman-child caused her to suffer as does Aku? We never should have let Legbiter near the wolf.*

Sedna set down her drum and opened her eyes

He gestured toward the sheep oil and, when she had rubbed it over her hands, he pulled his fingers away from the wolf. "I'm no good here, it is not the same with her as it is with a sheep or a horse, my hands are too big, my fingers clumsy. You do it. Try to reach as high in as you can, careful so you won't damage her, and turn the pup around so that the head is in the opening."

Sedna felt Rolv's closeness and drew from the strength of her Raven ancestors. Aku had to live. Something, some force deep inside told her that Aku's dying carried consequences going far beyond the death of a dear companion. It could signify the life and death of the Raven Woman line.

Time passed slowly in the barn. A crowd of neighbors and family had gathered. Thornhild ordered a warm brew to pass around while everyone waited. Their frosty breaths looked ghostly in the light of the lamps scattered here and there.

"It is no use, my love," Rolv said, his quiet voice loud in the hush of the large open room. "She is too weak to birth them now."

"No! She can do it!" Desperately, Sedna reached in higher with her small hand and, as Aku gave a pitiful keening cry, Sedna pulled the first bloody pup from her body. After that, the others followed. While Sedna saw to the wolf, Rolv worked the mucous away from the pups' muzzles and pushed them toward the source of milk.

When it was all over, Thornhild brought water and towels so that Rolv and Sedna could wash.

"Thank you for sharing your strength with us," Sedna said to the gathered people. "It would be best now if you went back to bed. I will sit awhile here and wait."

Thornhild motioned to the crowd who seemed reluctant to leave the drama, as if fearful it would be played out in the end without them. When everyone left except Rolv and Sedna, he sat down on the straw, leaning against a bale of hay and gently pulled her into his arms so that she rested between his legs, her head against his chest, her hand touching Aku.

Sedna gratefully closed her eyes to communicate with the Raven and Sednah. It was not finished yet. The wolf had lost much blood and was very weak.

The last thing she remembered was the sound of busy mouths suckling milk from the panting mother. When she awoke, Aku had crawled closer to the sleeping Rolv and Sedna. It was those yellow eyes that burned into Sedna's soul and wakened her.

Sedna sat up and shook Rolv gently awake. She hugged the wolf. "Look, my husband. She will live."

The big pups lay satiated with milk, sprawled on the straw. Rolv reached to examine one. Aku snarled deep in her throat, her mouth opened to show her teeth.

"Aku! Shame! He saved your life," Sedna scolded.

As if she understood, the wolf looked away, offering the pup for inspection. Rolv held it up and looked at it in the light of the dawn that had spread over the courtyard.

"Is he not beautiful?" Sedna said, touching her hand to the pup's head. She thought the pups very large, but there were only three. She thanked the Raven for that— otherwise the wolf would never have survived the births.

The pup had thick gray fur like a ruff around its neck. The eyes looked back at her, black instead of yellow, but tilted up at the outside corners like Aku's. The ears were small and pointed, but the legs strong looking, not fragile and delicate like the mother's.

"We all did well tonight," Rolv said, holding Sedna close, the pup in her lap.

Sedna rubbed the wolf between her eyes, something Aku loved. She strongly sensed the Raven Mother was satisfied and had left for now. Putting her Raven belt back on, Sedna rubbed it in gratitude. A combination of many things had helped tonight and she was grateful for them all. She tucked her hand in Rolv's and, together, they started to leave the barn. Abruptly Sedna groaned and dropped Rolv's hand to hold her neck with both hands. The pain was excruciating. She couldn't see and felt suffocating, as if a blanket had fallen over her head. Out of the corner of her eye she caught a glimpse of a long dress, as if someone rushed away. What could it mean?

Rolv stopped in his tracks and peered into Sedna's face. "What is it?"

She drew her hands away from her neck but it still hurt all the way down her shoulders. "We must hurry! Something has taken place in the great hall that will have terrible consequences." She led the way, her worry about Aku put aside for the moment with the violence of her shaman vision.

In the great hall, Eric sat in his chair at the head of the table, his big head bowed, resting on his crossed arms on the table. At his feet lay the bird cage with the white falcon on its side, its head curved back at an unnatural angle. A black cloth lay nearby. Thornhild sat close as did Torvald and Torstein. Only Leiv and Freyda were missing.

Eric heard them enter and acknowledged them with a grunt when he raised his head. "The wolf will live?"

"Yes. And three pups. The image of Legbiter, except for the long wolf fur." Rolv answered.

Sedna ran to the bird cage and knelt in front of Eric. She stared at the lifeless body. "What happened to your falcon?"

The big man sighed, a deep sound that welled up from his boots. Everyone knew how much he admired and enjoyed the bird. He had just taught it to return to his arm without the tether. He had been so excited showing everyone several days ago.

"I slept through all the excitement with your wolf, though Thornhild told me when I awoke at daybreak. I came in here, this is what I found."

Sedna reached in and brought out the bird, touching her hand to the beautiful white plumage. She looked up at Rolv.

"By the blood of Odin, this was no accident," Rolv thundered.

"No." Eric agreed. "But who? I have enemies, true, but no one I know would dare enter my house as I slept."

No one but Freyda, Sedna's thoughts came unbidden, but she could not have stopped them. Why would the girl kill her father's most precious belonging? Jealousy. Freyda was jealous of the bird and jealous of Sedna's influence over Eric for giving it to him.

Rolv's eyes mirrored her thoughts and he opened his mouth to speak. Sedna stood and put her fingers up to his lips, shaking her head.

"We will dispose of it," Torstein offered.

Eric motioned them away impatiently. Sedna put the bird back in the cage and handed it to the two young men.

"I will catch another after the season of the cold," Sedna promised.

Eric shook his head. "No. It will be for naught. I want no other."

He knew. At that moment, Sedna felt certain Eric suspected who had done the deed, but he would rather cut out his heart than accuse his daughter of such a terrible crime against him. He had to deny it to others, just as he tried to force himself to deny the truth.

When Rolv and Sedna went to the privacy of their own room, they sat on the bed.

"You had a vision, didn't you? Just before we came inside?" He asked.

She couldn't look at him. "Husband, my coming here has caused consequences that I do not know how to prevent. You should have left me behind."

Rolv held her to him and rubbed his chin on her head gently. "No, love. I could not exist without you by my side. It is not you who made trouble. We know who the guilty one is. Why did you not let me tell him?"

"In his heart, he knows. Now is not the time to add to his pain. She cannot escape the harvest of her deed. It will come back to her. But we should not be a part of it."

"You are wise, my love. I will abide by your resolve."

Sedna hoped she was right and that Freyda would pay for what she had done, but nothing was certain.

CHAPTER 16

Shortly after Aku's ordeal, and the death of the falcon, Sedna offered to take the women and older children out to the cliffs to show them how to catch special birds. They had little time before all the birds took flight. The birds would soon migrate to the lands of the tall, evergreen trees.

"Freyda never comes with us when we look for berries," Thornhild grumbled just out of range of Freyda's hearing. The mother turned to look back at the sullen girl, walking alone as usual.

"I noticed she hardly goes near her father since the death of the falcon," Sedna answered. "Is she still fearful?"

Thornhild made a face. "She fears nothing! She knows her father suspects her of destroying the bird and waits until his suspicions wear away with time."

They walked across meadows and up and down hillocks covered with wild flowers and grasses, until they came to the dark cliffs looming against the bright blue sky.

When Sedna and the group arrived, the air above and surrounding them turned black as thousands of birds blocked out the sun with their flight. The women and children stopped in awe, no one speaking or moving until the birds began to settle back restlessly in place on the sides of the mountains.

Sedna climbed up the closest crevasse, moving with clumsy slowness because of her rounded body and the burden she carried. She motioned the other women to stay back until she showed them. When she grabbed her first bird and stuck it down in the bag she carried tied to her waist, the others followed.

The more agile women and children climbed quietly, steadily, and then swooped and caught nets full. They dropped them in pouches and continued.

When they had captured all they could carry, they crawled back down and sprawled, panting on the grass.

"Now we must wring their necks?" a boy asked.

The birds had quieted down in the bags.

Sedna shook her head. "No. There is no need to cause the birds greater distress. They gave themselves freely to us for food. We must respect that. Gently reach down into the pouch and bring one out like this." She held a bird in her hand and pressed her fingers lightly into its breast. The bird died in an instant, its head flopping over lifelessly.

"What magic did you do?" Thornhild asked.

Sedna felt gratitude for the older woman's accompaniment. Usually Thornhild stayed home, working on her eternal loom. Sedna assumed Rolv had asked Thornhild to stay close. Freyda had been polite and friendly since the seance and subdued since the death of her father's falcon.

She fooled no one into thinking she was over her jealous destructiveness.

Sedna's powers of insight and foretelling had waned since the time of the banquet when the family and visitors had fallen asleep and under her control.

It was always thus, after a shaman's visit to Brother Moon. Sedna had used up her powers and they needed to be renewed by the passage of time.

She looked at the boy, his blue eyes wide in awe at what he perceived as her magic power. Touching his head lightly, she expected to feel the sun within the golden hair. "It is not magic. To help the creature feel but a moment's fright and no pain, you push aside the bird's heart to allow its spirit to go free."

Instead of a fluttering, pitiful commotion of broken legs and necks and ruined feathers, the necessary dispatch of the birds continued methodically until the last was still.

"This is a splendid catch. We have down for pads on the beds and feathers for brooms and meat to store away in the frozen ground for winter," Freyda said. "Your way is much better than ours, is it not?" She turned to the others who seemed amazed at her sudden good will.

"It is getting late. Last night I heard the wind in the grass. The sound was like winter creeping upon us. We need to gather more angelica and herbs to dry," said a woman who sat next to Thornhild.

"We have to see to the eider nests before the cold winds," someone else said.

"What sort of nests?" Sedna asked.

"Eiderdown ducks. We build nests for them with stone cairns piled up in the meadows, making them safe havens so they will lay their eggs and shed their feathers."

"I believe we have birds such as these on rocks near our summer camp. I have never seen nests, They may be too high for us to climb to. Do you catch the ducks to eat?"

"Oh no!" Thornhild drew in a breath. "That is punishable by a severe judgment from the *Althing*. In Norway, it was forbidden to harm an eiderdown duck and we keep the same rules, if we can. There we were forbidden to even gather the eggs, but we do that here, making certain to leave one or two behind for the duck."

"Let us have another outing. Please? Please?" The children jumped up and down, excited at accomplishing so much. Usually they just went along to play.

"I know nothing of herbs, but would like to learn," Sedna said. "My people eat berries if we find any, but there is little of that on the ice. We gather no grass, that is for the deer to eat."

"Good! We can show *you* something then," one of the women said.

"Yes, you have helped us so much. Teaching the men how to make weapons and helping us learn to cure our hides and sew better with furs," several women said simultaneously, their words running into each other's in a shy effort to be heard.

Sedna felt gratitude that these big, open people were willing to accept her. She was happy for Rolv too, for she realized how much his family meant to him—to all Vikings.

It wasn't quite the same with her. The people accepted that, someday, they would separate and go to different villages to live. This was to be expected, since their clans were small and they were forbidden to couple with close relatives.

જીજી

Several mornings later Thornhild came into the bedroom occupied by Rolv and Sedna, paying no attention to Rolv sitting on the side of the bed, naked except for a blanket thrown across his hips and thighs.

"It is time to go herbing, child, and to gather the eiderdown from the duck's nests. Will you go?"

Rolv shook his head. A thin veneer of dark red stubble

nudged his chin and cheeks. Sedna knew he would remove it that day. He scraped his face for her, even though his brothers teased him unmercifully.

He never complained, knowing how she felt about body and facial hair. He refused to shave his mustache though and she had come to like it.

"Sedna must not go. It is too far," he protested. "You wander all over, barely getting home by dark."

"Husband, you shame me," Sedna said lightly. "I do not give you orders and you said you would honor me with the same respect. The women wish to show me something new and I wish to learn."

Thornhild backed out of the room, her hand raised in a gesture of conciliation, her generous mouth spread in a smile. "Settle it as you wish. We will be ready to go soon."

"Ah, lovey, you know I can deny you nothing. It is a miracle how you have changed Thornhild toward me. She used to be so serious and grim."

His words of praise warmed Sedna, but she suspected Rolv too had changed without him realizing it, and he had become friendlier toward his step-mother.

"Is Freyda going?" he asked.

Ever since the falcon's death he never let Sedna stay alone with Freyda, even though Eric strongly maintained the bird probably caught its head between cage bars.

Freyda had been extremely agreeable to everyone since that incident, her good humor extending even toward the two younger brothers to whom she previously never showed a moment's patience.

"I do not think she is going with us, she seldom bothers. Thornhild will stay beside me."

By the time Sedna dressed and stepped outside, the women were impatiently waiting. Aku leaped and capered like a youngster, eager to go.

"Ah, no, my friend. You are a mother now. You must stay home with your family."

Sedna knelt and looked into Aku's yellow eyes. Something within the animal's expression chilled her blood so that it almost stopped running through her body. Aku *had* to go.

To everyone's surprise, Freyda appeared and announced her intention of coming along. For a long moment, the sun seemed to glide under a passing cloud and Sedna felt a spasm in her midsection—something wanted her attention. The day was too beautiful to spend thinking dark thoughts. They had no need of her shamanism. Her powers would return in full after the birth of the baby.

They walked a long way across meadows and up and down gullies, but the walk was not strenuous for any of them, including Sedna who matched their enthusiastic stride, enjoying their singing and laughter. Their graceful long dresses swayed in the breeze, the sparkling white aprons molded to their generous, shapely bodies.

For a change, not a cloud was in sight. The crisp feel of fall had entered the air. As they roamed farther away from the fjord and Brattalid, different trees began to appear: Scrub oak, small, spindly trees that the men hadn't harvested for use in building yet.

"Are you tired?" Freyda asked, walking next to Sedna. Aku stayed close on the other side, never straying far.

"Oh, no. This day is perfect. Sometimes, I wish my people could see that there is another way to live, without the ice, but I fear they would not be easy to teach."

Freyda listened for once without interrupting impatiently.

Encouraged, Sedna asked, "Are they starting to harvest the angelica yet? We'd best hurry and catch up."

"No, they are picking daisies," Freyda said disparagingly. "It will be a while before we get to the herbs and vegetation. That is why I seldom come with them. They dally all over the place and it takes twice as long as it should."

"But they enjoy themselves," Sedna protested. Could she trust Freyda after the falcon?

Thornhild led the pack of women and children and from her vantage point ahead, she waved at Sedna to come along.

Sedna motioned in response and, when the group topped a rise and headed back down over it, Freyda plopped down on the meadow grass.

"Look over there! An eiderdown nest. We will be the first to find one." Freyda leaped to her feet, her voice rich with excitement.

"I don't know." Sedna hesitated, looking at the others, mere dots on the horizon now. "We should all stay together." The first twinge of uneasiness stirred in her breast.

"Nonsense." Freyda laughed, her voice hard around the edges as if she didn't use a laugh much. "Besides, I am tired. I am not used to walking like you and the others."

That made perfect sense. Freyda hardly went anywhere unless she rode horseback. As for water, if Freyda feared nothing else, water terrified her so that she refused all the crowded boat rides the family took during the summer.

Sedna knelt to investigate the cleverly concealed pile of stones filled with soft feathers. She began to gather the eggs into a sack. "It is like a little house, with a flat stone on top and the sides and the back, all for this little bird. Amazing." When she had gathered part of the eggs, leaving several behind for the bird to sit upon, Sedna sat down primly, smoothing out her dress around her ankles. She was still unaccustomed to wearing the soft woolen material but she liked it very much and she knew Rolv liked her in it. He couldn't keep his hands away when he was near and thought no one around.

The long, flowing dress was more comfortable and less confining than the summer furs and leggings worn by her clan. Thornhild had put flowers and birds on the front of her apron with long strands of many colored strings. She called it embroidering when Sedna had asked about it. The apron bib crisscrossed over her shoulders and back and tied behind at her waist. All the women and girls wore the same style, colored with different dyes, some embroidered.

Freyda lay sprawled across the grass with her hands behind her head, looking out through slitted lids. A second tremor of something akin to fear nudged Sedna. Still, it was not a strong sensation—unlike her usual warnings.

"How does the babe feel in your stomach?" Freyda asked abruptly. That was her way of speaking, impatient with small pleasantries that most people used to communicate.

"Feel?" Instinctively, Sedna put her hands across her stomach. It pushed out enough now to be noticeably round in her small frame. "How can I say how it feels? I just know it is there."

"Can I touch you?" Freyda crawled over and reached to put her hand lightly on Sedna's belly.

Aku growled low in her throat, her teeth showing in an open mouth, yellow eyes narrowed with threat.

"No, Aku. Stay." It would never do to have her wolf tear Freyda's beautiful face. Erik would never forgive them.

Sedna felt the first tremor of real misgivings. No one in her tribe would have dared such an intrusion as to touch another without permission.

She willed herself to hold still while Freyda's hand pressed gently around her stomach and, at the last moment before she pulled away, slipped upward as if by accident to brush Sedna's filling breasts. Sedna trembled with outrage, in spite of all she could do to hold still.

Freyda gave her a hard, knowing look. "A pretty little piece, you are. I can see why my brother prizes you. You have charmed even Eric. He is looking forward to this first grandchild. I thought I would be the one to give it to him." Her voice sounded petulant, but she looked away so that Sedna could not read her eyes.

"You might have done so. You are older than your brothers. Pity you have not found a suitable mate."

"Suitable!" Freyda snorted through her nose in a rude copy of her father's expression. "I doubt I will ever find anyone suitable until we leave this forsaken land. They are all geldings. I look for a stallion."

Like your father, Sedna wanted to say. "But this land is home to your family now. They will never leave," Sedna protested. "Your brothers, and Thornhild and even your father."

"Nonsense! They are just settling down like a pack of sheep. Leiv is the only one who will amount to anything. He is going out to look for new lands. Perhaps if he finds a good place, we will leave here and join him."

Sedna had her doubts. Eric told Rolv that he was done exploring, that he had found his place.

"Eric adores Rolv since he came back from Nordrsetur a wealthy man. Wealthy and with a new child—he may become chieftain when the old man dies. That is not right. It should go to me, the oldest."

Sedna sucked in her breath. What a callous, cold-blooded way to think. Fear began to make little furry traces on the backs of Sedna's arms and up her neck. Aku crept closer.

Why should I fear this woman? Am I not Sedna, shaman and Raven Woman of the Inuits? What is Freyda?

An ordinary person, came the answer. Great waves of fear and distrust washed over Sedna's emotions. *She* was the person in command of her own body and mind. Although she had allowed the Raven Mother to help her in times of need, Sedna knew, as a Raven Woman, she had much to prove to earn the right. With great effort, she pushed back the strong emotions and forced her voice to a normal quality.

"I do not think Rolv wishes to become chieftain. You may be mistaken about your father's wishes. Anyway, your father looks very healthy. When it is his time to die, he will choose Leiv, his favorite after you."

"My, my, we are speaking plain today, are we not?" Freyda stared at her with a bold scrutiny that made Sedna want to leap to her feet and rush to join Thornhild and the others. But she would never show Freyda a weakness, never.

Freyda jumped up gracefully, and leaned over to take Sedna's hands. "Come, we must catch up with the group." As soon as Freyda moved toward Sedna this second time, Aku snarled, a terrible wild sound, and threw herself between them.

"Shame!" Sedna scolded. "She is only helping me." She looked up in time to see the fury banked in Freyda's eyes as she glared at the wolf.

Aku backed away, still growling.

They walked upward over the hill where the flock of women had disappeared. They had scattered in the distance like flowers on the mountainside with the colors of their dresses and the sharp white of their aprons shining in the sunlight that dappled the land through fine, shifting clouds.

Freyda shielded her eyes and stared upward. "Those

are clouds that bring cold winds," she predicted. "You spoke of an early winter. You may be right."

A shadow loomed above and Sedna looked up to see a raven circling overhead in an agitated fashion.

"A raven. He is making sweeps above us. Perhaps he belongs to your Raven clan," Freyda suggested with sarcasm.

Sedna ignored the scorn and shielded her eyes to look at the bird above them. As it circled, the sun rays struck the wings, blinding her briefly.

"Look there!" Freyda pointed in a direction off to the side. "I see a plot of angelica. If we pick it now, we will be finished first can rest again and wait for them."

Without waiting to see if Sedna followed, Freyda ran forward and stood looking down.

Her excitement was contagious. Sedna ran to her side. They stood on the edge of a little ravine, the bottom of which looked far away.

"Where is the angelica?" Sedna asked.

Freyda shoved her fingers up under the Raven Belt around Sedna's waist and yanked, pushing forward at the same time. Sedna soared over the edge with the wind whistling past her ears as she plummeted into space. For an instant it felt as if she might fly and she thrust out her arms to slow her speed of descent. Then she screamed and braced herself, fingers instantly clenching the fabric where the belt had circled her waist. Freyda had stolen the Raven belt. To Sedna, the loss of the belt was a worse catastrophe than falling. At the last moment, she turned and curled her body to protect her stomach. The world turned black for an instant. She couldn't breathe. Her bones felt liquid, as if they had turned to water.

Sedna lay without moving, fully conscious. On the ledge high above, Aku emitted fierce grows and snarls. Opening her eyes slightly, Sedna tried to cry out as she saw Freyda on the ledge, trying to push a giant boulder down on top of her. Sedna struggled to move, but her body was in shock and she could not move. She watched in horror as the wolf leaped on Freyda and began ripping her clothing away, slashing at her arms and face.

Freyda shrieked and held up her arms to defend herself. She turned and ran away from the edge.

Sedna's pain came in waves, with nausea beginning from the bottom of her pelvis at the V between her legs and worked upward, choking her. She wanted to go to sleep. It didn't hurt when she slept. But she heard Aku howling and saw the shadow of the raven's wing passing over her. The feeling of something warm, rough, and wet moved across her face. She awoke to feel Aku's tongue licking her face as the wolf nudged against her body gently, trying to coax her to awaken.

"Rolv," Sedna whispered. It hurt to speak, it hurt to breathe. "Rolv."

The last thing she saw through a hazy vision was the tail of the wolf vanishing upward over the ravine to the top. The raven still circled overhead.

એન્ડએન્ડ

Out in the smithy barn, supervising the work being done on a new lance tip, Rolv heard the commotion. He hurried outside just in time to see his sister dashing past on her way to the house. Alarmed by her torn clothes and the blood, he stepped out and shouted to her.

"Freyda! What happened to you? Are you hurt? Where are the others? Where is Sedna?" His heart thumped in his chest, and icy sweat broke out beneath the hair on his arms.

She slowed and then stopped, hanging her head down and panting to catch her breath. "The wolf. It attacked me." She held out her arms to show her tattered, blood-soaked sleeve.

By now the men had poured out of the outbuildings and rushed in from the fields. Eric moved toward his daughter and took hold of her arm to examine her wounds.

"Where are the others?" he asked, repeating Rolv's question.

Before she could answer, Thornhild with the women and children came hurrying up from another direction. When they saw the men gathered, they stopped in confusion, dropped their baskets and bags of herbs and vegetation, and ran toward the men. Chaos and disorder rose in the courtyard and no one could understand anyone.

Eric shouted at them, his great voice breaking into the melee of confused shouting. "Quiet! Listen to Freyda!" he said, with a voice filled with authority that everyone immediately obeyed.

Freyda clung to her father and whimpered pitifully. Rolv wanted to shake her until her teeth rattled. Sedna looked to be the only one missing. He knew he wouldn't find out anything until Freyda finished speaking. She was enjoying the attention.

"I do not know where the *skraeling* is. I thought she was with Thornhild. I was alone, wandering, picking flowers. I found a large growth of angelica and had started to harvest it when the wolf jumped on top of me." She pointed at Aku who stood off to a distance, pacing back and forth and stopping only to let go with a pitiful howl, plainly agitated, wanting to get to Rolv.

Thornhild came forward, to look at the arm Freyda extended for everyone to see.

"The last I saw of your wife and this one, they were wandering off together," Thornhild told Rolv, her worried frown matching his. "I beckoned for Sedna to come back with us, but she waved me away. They were laughing together like old friends."

"There's the wolf! Kill it!" Someone shouted and the men grabbed up their bows and arrows, some had lances.

"No!" Rolv shouted above the men's voices. "Something's happened to Sedna. The wolf knows where she is." Rolv turned to Freyda, grabbing her shoulder, his suspicions so great that it barely surprised him when the Raven Belt fell out of her pocket onto the ground.

Everyone knew it was the magical belt belonging to the Inuit girl and that she was never without it. For a hushed moment the crowd stilled. Rolv felt a fiery rage well up inside his body, which quickly turned to implacable hatred so powerful he thought he might burst apart. If this woman had hurt Sedna, nothing could protect her from his wrath.

He held Freyda by her shoulders and shook her hard. He didn't realize his fury until many hands pulled him away. Eric struck his son with the side of his open hand, half-knocking him to his knees.

"Leave her be! She is covered with her own blood from that wolf's slashing. You do not know what you say. My daughter would never—"

Rolv steadied himself, looking from Freyda to the father who defended her. "I will see to you later. If my woman is harmed by your hand, you will regret it every day you live."

He turned and sprinted after the wolf who, in spite of the angry mob heading her way, refused to move until Rolv did.

"I'll come with you," Leiv shouted, close behind him.

"Us too," the two younger brothers shouted over the melee.

They all set out at a run, following the wolf up the meadow and over the ridge until when they looked back, they could no longer see the house or the outbuildings.

"Something has happened to her, I know it." Rolv panted and did not slow in his pace in the wake of the wolf. "She would never willingly surrender her belt."

"Do not worry, we will find her," Torstein consoled him.

In the distance, they saw a large raven making wide circles against the blue sky. With a sinking feeling, Rolv thought of what this could mean. The wolf, ahead of them, stopped at the lip of a precipice. They ran to the edge and looked down.

"By Thor's breath, there she is!" Leiv said.

Rolv stared down in horror at Sedna lying crumpled at the foot of the cliff. Tiny, fragile, she lay like a broken doll. He cast about for a way down, but the wolf was already showing it to them, and they followed.

Tripping, sliding, not caring how he descended, Rolv scrambled downward, his heart in his throat. He heard the others behind him, but all his thoughts centered on Sedna, lying so pitifully on the valley floor.

By the time he reached her, Aku stood over her prone body, growling low in her throat. Rolv knew it was not meant as a warning for him.

He picked up Sedna and held her close. She weighed no more than a child. Tears streamed down his cheeks. The others arrived and stood by helplessly.

She stirred in his arms and reached up a hand to touch the tears running down his jaw. "My love," she whispered. "You found me. I sent Aku. I need my belt."

Leiv pressed it into Rolv's hand and he placed gently it on her chest.

"Shush. I am here now. Where do you hurt?"

She moaned. "Everywhere." She put her hand to her stomach. "Here. It hurts here."

The child. Rolv's blood stopped in his veins, his

breath congealed so that nothing seemed to come out when he thought of the baby within her. He looked upward as did the three brothers, all thinking the same thing, a long way to fall.

"Let me take you home." It was then he saw the blood, still wet and sticky, saturating the lower part of her dress.

"Mother will know what to do," Leiv said, coming forward and touching a large hand to Sedna's shoulder. "We must hurry before there is too much blood lost."

"What happened? Can you tell us that?" Torvald, the curious, asked.

She pulled closer in Rolv's arms so that her head rested on his broad chest. "It was Freyda," she said unhesitatingly.

This time the woman could not escape without blame. She would have to face her responsibility.

Sedna felt Rolv's arms tremble beneath her body. Did he suppose she lied? Would he defend his kin? One look into his stormy countenance and she knew better.

"She seized the Raven Belt and pushed me. As I lay here, unable to move, she tried to roll that stone on top of me." She pointed upward and the men looked at the huge boulder teetering on the edge of the chasm. It would have squashed Sedna like a bug. "Aku attacked her and she ran away, leaving me here."

Rolv pulled her close, burying his face in her tangled hair, inhaling her essence. He had nearly lost her. He still might lose her. "We must hurry. She needs Thornhild now." He held her gently, easily in his arms, as they climbed up and out of the gorge.

Part way toward home, Leiv put a hand on Rolv's arm to halt his steady progress. "Let me take her. Your arms are tired."

Rolv shook his head. He couldn't bear to release her. He only wished he could transfer some of the energy from his healthy, strong body to hers. She curled her fingers around the nape of his neck. The warmth of fresh blood surged forth again, and wet her legs.

"You cannot die, Sedna. Stay awake and talk to me. It is not your time."

The brothers spoke to her while Rolv carried her along as fast as he dared. He couldn't take a chance of tripping over a rock and throwing her to the ground.

It seemed to him to take forever to get to the rise of the hill above Brattalid.

CHAPTER 17

Word had spread. Neighbors and family gathered in the courtyard when Rolv and the brothers rushed into Brattalid. When Thornhild saw them, she ran forward, her strong face creased with worry. "Is she dead?"

Rolv's face looked almost as old as his father's. "Close to it." He struggled hard to keep away the tears that pushed behind his eyes. A Norseman was not afraid to cry, but this was not the time. He must be strong for his beloved.

"Bring her inside—hurry," Thornhild commanded, heading for the big hall. "Lay her there. I've fixed a place for her."

Rolv hated to release his hold on her, as if he were able to impart some of his own strength. He kissed her cold cheek softly. When he bent to place Sedna on the bench softened with wool blankets, he saw Freyda, at the end of the hall, sitting next to Eric's giant chair, as if seeking protection. "I will not leave my wife in the same room as her!" Rolv's voice rang out in the long hall, bouncing off the walls in the sudden silence.

"Then bring her to your room and hurry!" Thornhild urged.

After Rolv laid Sedna gently on top of the woolen blanket in their room, Thornhild waved the men away impatiently. "Leave us. This is woman's work," she commanded.

She beckoned to the women from the neighboring farms who crowded around, bringing tubs of hot water and soft cloths to bathe Sedna.

Once again in the long hall, Rolv raked his fingers through his hair in agitation. It took courage to confront Freyda in front of Eric, even though the thought of Sedna lying helpless and in pain left him so wild with outrage that he wanted to break his sister's neck as she had the falcon's. His conditioning of obedience, of respect and fear of his father made him hesitate for a moment, angering him even more.

The three brothers standing by the wall moved closer to him. They would back him up in this, even against their father, if need be.

Sunlight entering the open doorway lit Eric's carved chair so that he looked like a giant god—a powerful king on a throne. Eric the Red, or Eric the Terrible, some had called him in his younger years. Right now Rolv would have gladly traded his remarkable father for any other.

Before he could speak, Eric thundered, "Your woman's beast nearly killed Freyda. Something must be done."

The firelight played with his thick red beard and hair. The narrowed glints of ice in his pale blue eyes, and his expression of self-righteous anger would have been enough to send the entire population of Ericsfjord running toward the hills.

Rolv heard the brothers suck in their breaths at the wild accusation. He stepped forward, holding the Raven belt up to Freyda's smirking face. She pretended to cower against her father, but Rolv knew better. Freyda feared nothing unless it was in her best interest to have someone think she did.

"She tried to kill Sedna. My woman spoke the words. Freyda stole her belt when she pushed her. Everyone in the yard witnessed it fall from her clothing."

The three brothers spoke at once. "Yes, he speaks the truth. We heard her say Freyda did it. We saw the belt fall from where Freyda hid it away."

Eric rose to his full height and stood between his son and daughter. "What say you? This is a perilous accusation you make."

"It is true and time she owned up to what she is. She killed your white falcon too." Rolv did not want to say Sedna saw it in a vision. That might not have carried much weight at this moment.

Freyda hid partially behind her father. "What proof have you I harmed the *skraeling*?"

"Show us your hands," Rolv demanded.

"What? I will do no such thing!" Freyda's voice rose to an indignant squeak.

"Sedna said Freyda tried to shove a giant boulder over on top of her as she lay helpless at the bottom of the ravine—where this one had pushed her. That is when the wolf attacked her. Show us your hands, woman!"

Eric sat back down and taking his daughter's hands in his, he turned the palms upward. The brothers surged forward to join Rolv as they all stared.

Freyda's hands were torn and scratched with little punctures and tears where the rough boulder had mangled the delicate skin. Eric pushed them away, his bushy eyebrows lowered so that they almost obscured the slits of his eyes as he stared into his daughter's face.

"Did you do this monstrous evil? I demand the truth from you."

Even Freyda, the spoiled, would not dare lie in the

face of this terrible visage before her. She sighed, as if the whole situation was merely bothersome. "You were all fawning over her. I am weary of hearing her name spoken. Even grown men listen to her prattle about hunting and fishing, as if she is some goddess. She had no right to birth a child before me!"

Eric's face had lost most of its color, and his lips thinned in a straight line, but Freyda, in her tantrum of self-righteousness, did not notice the warning.

"I am the one to give you your first grandchild, I am the eldest. It was my due! The others waited, why could your bastard not wait? It is all your fault!" She pointed an accusing finger at Rolv who clenched his fists in an effort not to spring forward and knock her to the floor.

"And the white falcon?" Eric's voice was deadly quiet. No one in the room dared breathe. He never took his gaze from her face.

"Of what importance is a foolish bird? It was as if she had brought you a crown, a new ship, something glorious and grand. It was only a bird, yet you thanked her over and over. She had you in her apron pocket, too. You paid attention only to the bird and to the one who gave it to you. You forgot me."

Her breath came in short spurts, her anger slowly ebbing in the face of her father's implacable rage, barely held from exploding.

"It was not right that a stranger intrude in our lives." Her voice quivered, as she realized she had told everything without meaning to. "I did not like what she had done. Brattalid is my home, not hers." Her voice had lost its stridency and she finished with a whine, a weak whimper. Tears of self-pity coursed down her cheeks.

"Ah, Freyda, what have I done? What have I done?" the big man groaned. He tore at his hair. No one had ever seen him so agitated, not even in his worst fit of anger.

She knelt at his feet, her fingers plucking the hem of his garment, her eyes overflowing with tears.

"Get out! Get out of my sight!" He kicked her away. "I may never again call you daughter," Eric shouted at her, pointing toward the door.

He waited until she slunk away, out of the room and put his head down on his arms, hiding his face. For the first time, perhaps in his entire life, his shoulders moved, as the stern Viking began to cry.

The four brothers eased out of the room, away from the appalling sight of their father laid so low. Rolv crossed the hall to stand near their bedroom doorway. Inside, he heard Sedna moan like a wounded animal. He could not stand outside any longer. If he could not help, he must be near her, touch her hand at least. He pushed the blanket aside that covered the doorway and entered.

Sedna's eyes were closed but tears oozed from under her lids. Even now her training of reserve was with her, strengthening her. Rolv knelt at her side and laid his head next to hers, gently smoothing away her tears.

"My husband, he is gone from us and it is my fault."

Thornhild stood at the foot of the bed, holding a tiny bundle wrapped tightly. She lowered the baby to let Sedna hold it one last time. "I am sorry, Rolv. Sedna. I— I could do nothing to save him. The babe died when Sedna struck the ground at the bottom of the ravine. It is—it was a man child." Tears streaked Thornhild's usually stoic face. She beckoned to the neighbor women to follow her. "We will have a funeral later, when Sedna is able to attend."

"Thank you for what you have done for her, Mother."

It was the first time Rolv had ever called her that and Thornhild looked stunned for a moment before her face folded in on itself with sorrow and pain. She turned to hurry out of the room.

Rolv laid down carefully on the bed and put the wrapped bundle between himself and Sedna. The three lay touching for a long time in silence.

"Are you in pain, my love?" he asked.

Sedna touched her now flat stomach and nodded. Her skin was ashen from the loss of blood. "We still have each other and nothing can change that," she murmured. "If this tears us apart, then Freyda will have won."

"We will never say her name again in our room." He kissed her forehead. "And she cannot come between us, nor anything or anyone else."

"If only I had listened to you and to Thornhild and even to my own spirit within me."

"Never say it is your fault, my beloved, my heart and soul. You trusted that woman. She can be very beguiling. Get well. You will bear other children. I love you so, words cannot be enough."

Sedna reached to touch Rolv's cheek. "Love. A beautiful word. You have taught me much, my husband, my love."

He took her hand and, turning it, kissed her palm and the faintly beating pulse near her wrist. The bones of her wrist were like the rest of her, fine and delicate. In spite of that exquisite fragility, her heart was as stout and powerful as any Viking, a spirit as brave and loyal as any warrior, and, he hoped, a body strong enough to survive because her inner spirit would not give up.

She pulled her hand away from his face and wrapped her arms around the baby. "I must say a chant to speed his return to this Earth."

"Do you wish me to leave you?"

"No, stay. Only move me to the window so that I may look out. And bring Aku inside. She is my helper spirit, I need her."

When Rolv brought in the wolf, waiting just outside

the hall door, he eased Sedna up into his arms and took
her and the baby to the small window overlooking the
back meadow. He placed her carefully on the bench and
sat at her feet, to be sure she didn't fall. The wolf lay
down beside him, her chin touching the hem of Sedna's
gown.

Sedna held the bundle close and laid her cheek on the
soft wrapping. Her voice started weak and hollow, but as
she continued with the chant, words came stronger and
stronger, as if energy come back to her body in a gradual
flow.

"Child of the moon and sun,
you who will never know the kiss
of snow upon your cheek
or the caress of rain upon your soul.
Your father mourns your passing,
you who left him without knowing
how much you would be loved.
Your mother mourns your passing, you who left
her without knowing the bond between you
which will never pass away.
We will mourn for you together. We will cry out
at the flight of birds overhead,
And see you always in the
soaring wings of the white falcon and in the North Star.
Though you are not of this Earth,
you will not leave us,
for we will never forget you."

Rolv eased her up and cradled her close in his arms.
"My love, my precious one, forgive me for not watching
you more closely. I want to kill her with my bare hands,
twist her neck, like she did the falcon." After pressing his
face to the bundle, he rose, took it gently away from

Sedna's arms, and handed it through the doorway to the waiting Thornhild who would prepare the funeral.

Sedna sighed. "Bring me my belt. And a sharp knife."

Rolv frowned, his mouth tight. "You would harm yourself? I will never permit that."

She smiled at his concern, tears dried on her cheeks. "No, my love. But a mother must make a small sacrifice for our child, to let him know he was loved. To lead him back to this world again."

He understood that. There were times back in the old Norway when Vikings sent entire households of servants, wives, and beloved horses to Valhalla with a dead chieftain. Yet he could not permit her to disfigure herself. He loved her face too well.

Rolv set her back down on the bed and in two strides retrieved the belt and the knife, placing them together in her outstretched palms. His trust showed in his gray eyes and Sedna was moved beyond any words he might have said.

Bringing the belt close to her cheek, she held it for a moment.

"What kind of magic do you possess that will not protect you?" His voice was harsh, his words angry.

She took his hand and placed it on her breast. "Feel the beat of my heart, love? I am still alive. She could not slay me. It is as you said. We will have other children. I am left to give birth to the next Raven Woman. It is not the end for us. I had a raven, a wolf, and my own power to protect me. That is why I am here and did not follow our babe into the land of the departed."

He understood. This was not the time to offer anger when what she needed was comfort.

Sedna slipped the belt around her waist. Slice, slice went the knife until her long black tresses lay in disarray on the floor.

He drew in a breath, forcing himself to stop his hand that reached out to stay hers. He loved her glorious hair! It was her decision to observe the loss of her child in the way that would best serve her.

When she had finished, she leaned her head back against his chest. He moved his fingers in gentle rapid movements across her face, as he had seen Inuit mothers do with their children, touching the drying tears on her cheeks. When she stopped crying, he leaned her forward and felt the ends of her hair, which now turned under toward her neck in a delicate curve.

"Does your father know what she has done?" Sedna asked.

"Yes. She must be punished. It went hard on him, for he loves her. All her life, he—nay, all of us—spoiled her, and now she has made our child her victim and you are forced to suffer for it."

"She is evil. Perhaps her mother was evil, I do not know. But her cruelty comes from more than being spoiled by your father, you, and your brothers. Her blood is tainted."

"If he does not punish her properly, we will return to Nordrsetur. We can live there alone. You have taught me much about how to hunt the Inuit way."

Sedna shook her head. "We cannot go. This coming cold season will be the worst the land has ever seen. We would not survive alone and neither will your family. We must stay together, combine our knowledge so that all may survive."

Poor little thing, he thought sadly. She still imagined that trance she went into showed the truth. The family had lived at Brattalid for years, and each winter had been the same. Some winters were as good or even better than summer. The seals, the great white bears, the reindeer stayed to eat the grass of the valleys. Plenty of game roamed the land and always would. They had cows and animals in the barns to eat. What could go wrong? Though he believed her prediction was amiss, he said nothing to her, because he did not want to give her more distress.

Rolv held her, caressing, kissing her eyelids, her cheeks, her lips, but with passion banked, offering his devotion with gentle affection.

He, too, mourned for his son. Their lives were at the lowest point and he did not know how to reassure her.

CHAPTER 18

The next morning, Eric called everyone for a meeting in the long hall. Rolv carried Sedna out in his arms, where she had slept all night, cuddled into the curve of his body.

Eric stood at the end of the room in front of his great chair, a giant among giants.

Sedna held her breath at the power emanating in the room. All neighboring farmers and their wives had been called in to witness the punishment meted out to Freyda.

Without waiting for her elders to begin, Freyda, who for the first time had not seated herself next to her father, pushed back her chair at the long table, her chin defiantly in the air. "This is not a proper *Althing*. It is only a judgment of a daughter by her father. I need not accept his decree."

Eric slammed his fist on the great trestle table, causing timbers overhead, holding the ceiling, to rattle. "*You will accept it*," He bellowed into the hall. "You are not worthy of going before the *Althing*. They would put you to death—a life for a life."

Sedna didn't look at Eric, not wanting him to see the pity in her eyes. She had the urge to grab up a lance among those that always lay against the wall near the door and run it through Freyda's black heart. That would be expected in her village, to avenge her child so he would be free to return a whole person to dwell in the body of another. She was glad Rolv held her.

Would their son come back as one of the people or a Viking? The thought was so unsettling, so puzzling, that she blocked the speech outside her head for a moment, until she saw the shocked look on everyone's face.

She looked up at Rolv and whispered in his neck. "I am sorry, dear one, I did not hear what your father said."

Rolv put his fingers lightly over her mouth, to hush her. "Wait, let me listen now and I will tell you everything."

She felt his comforting heartbeat next to her skin and knew she should be paying more attention, but she had no room for anything but sorrow for her lost child, lost in two ways. First lost because it was killed without being born and then lost because it was a male, forbidden to Raven Women. She would never know what decision she might have had to make.

"Since it is Rolv's woman who was aggrieved, it is for her to decide Freyda's punishment," Eric decreed. "Does this meet with your approval?" he directed his speech at Rolv.

"Yes, that is just, if she chooses to do it."

Sedna stood to face the assembly. Her legs felt shaky, but Rolv's big hand pressing firmly against the middle of her back helped hold her steady. She touched her fingers to her Raven belt for the wisdom this moment called for.

If she asked for the woman's death, Eric would always be her enemy. If she asked that they banish her to Nordrsetur, Freyda would die also. The room was as still as the land after the first heavy snowfall.

"I am not the person she has injured beyond recompense, but our unborn child who now must seek entrance again in another lifetime. It has been said they cannot always find their way and may exist between worlds, which makes me very sad."

She felt the pressure of Rolv's hand to steady her and his warm, sweet breath against her neck. "I have an emptiness where once there was life." She touched her palms to her stomach. She turned to face Freyda. "You have done harm to me but also to your brother and to your father who wished for a grandchild. It is fitting that you find a void also, so you can know the anguish of loss." Sedna wanted to get it said and over with now, the eyes upon her had begun to sap what little strength she had left. This time she spoke directly to Eric. "It is my decision that she go with your son, Leiv, if he will have her. To sail upon the water, to enter a land of strangers, not as punishment, but so she will have time to consider the damage she has done. If that is acceptable to all, that is my wish."

The wise words came from Sedna and she realized that the Raven Mother did not need to help her this time. Rolv had told her Freyda feared the water above all else. She hated sailing, was sick near to dying for most of their journey to Greenland. It would be a far worse punishment for her than the sudden release of death.

"I will not go," Freyda screamed, pounding the table with her fist, much the same way her father had done moments before. "You cannot force me. This is my home. I would sooner die." She stripped away her tunic, leaving her breasts bare for all to see. "Someone, anyone who is a man, shoot an arrow into me here!" She struck her chest with her fist.

"Enough! You are displaying yourself like a whore for all to see your shame. The mate of my son has spoken with a wise judgment that is fair, and I agree." Eric turned to the others sitting near. "What say you?"

They all nodded, speaking their "Ayes."

"Leiv will take you with him on his journey. Since he will be gone many years, that will give you time to consider your base behavior."

Rolv had enfolded Sedna in his arms again, holding her next to the warmth of his body.

Eric brushed past his daughter, without looking at her, and knelt in front of Sedna, turning her gently to face him, looking into her eyes. For the first time she saw his hidden gentleness, his strength, his intense sense of honor. It was easy to understand why all of these people followed him blindly to a new home in Greenland just because he led them here. "Forgive us, little one. We meant you no harm. I offer you Freyda's dowry in compensation and anything else at Brattalid that you wish for."

Sedna pushed away from Rolv to sit up straight. It was hard to be dignified, cuddled in your lover's arms in front of everyone. She had no idea what dowry meant. "Thank you. That is generous of you, but I want nothing from her." Sedna folded her arms across her chest and made the short little nod that was her people's gesture of finality.

She must accept part of the blame, for not paying attention to the signs that day in the meadow. The Raven tried to warn her; Aku tried to warn her. She was so besotted by Freyda's offer of friendship, wanting so desperately to fit in with her new family, that she had ignored the warnings.

Leiv scraped back his bench and stood to face his father. "We will be ready to sail soon. We must leave before the pack ice enters the channel. If neighboring farmers and their families wish to make the journey back to Iceland for a visit I can take them, too."

☙❧

Later, in their room, Sedna and Rolv lay talking.

He nuzzled against her ear, touching his hand to the short curve of her hair. "That was a wise decision you made."

"I did not understand your justice at first," Sedna said. "My people would have taken her out on the ice alone to die. Or perhaps the shaman, Analusha, would have commanded a hunter to put a knife into her heart."

"Ah, but in spite of it, she is our kin and Eric still loves her. This will be fitting punishment, sweeting. She will hate every moment of her journey. She was sick nearly to death on the ship here. She must obey Leiv. She cannot have her way on board the ship. And best of all, you will be safe. By the time she returns—if she does— she will have learned to behave."

"What did your father mean, 'dowry'?"

Rolv laughed, a deep delighted laugh that cheered her for the first time in hours. "You refused something when you did not even know what it was he offered? You are more stubborn than we are. A dowry is the small treasure that some women have set by over the years for the day they marry. This helps begin a woman's home if she does not marry well. Freyda was always determined to marry well, or not at all, to capture a man of substance, but she owns a fine dowry too."

"I do not accept anything from her."

"True, my little dove, we have no use for her possessions. We have traded for nearly everything we need to start our own home. Eric offers me land adjoining his."

She shook her head. "It is not the time to build our home. I have looked into the future often, to be certain. We must all stay together now for warmth and comfort in the coming time of famine."

He pulled her close, laying her head against his chest in order to kiss the top of her hair. "Those dour thoughts still possess you. You have spoken of them and I counsel you not to speak again or you will turn everyone against you. They will think you a witch."

❦❦❦

The morning came when Leiv pronounced it a good day to sail. The Vikings never said ahead of time when they would depart for fear of evil spirits noticing. The entire village turned out to see them go. Eric, Thornhild, and the sons, along with Sedna stood on the banks as close to the shore as they could get at high tide. Leiv's ship was a mighty vessel, much larger and finer than the one Rolv sailed on to Nordsetur. Many of the men from the surrounding farms would go with him, eager to find new worlds to explore and to get away from boring farm life. They were Vikings, after all, not farmers.

Freyda appeared finally, just as Eric commanded someone to go find her. She was dressed all in black, with a cowl covering her head and face. Sedna wondered if it was truly her and not a woman she had bullied into taking her place. Eric must have had the same misgivings for he beckoned her forward to stand in front of him. He lifted the thick lace covering over her head and face and everyone peered close to see if it was truly her.

Her face was puckered in an unlovely scowl and before her father could speak to her, she turned and, without a farewell to anyone, made her way up the plank.

Sedna almost felt sorry for the solitary figure who walked with a straight back and head high up to the ship's deck. '*This is the last we will see of her,*' a voice from within said to her in a whisper.

Until then Sedna hadn't realized she'd been holding her breath, as if waiting for someone to say, "Stop, Freyda. Come back."

Leiv came around to hug everyone. He knelt before his father to receive his blessing and kissed Thornhild tenderly on her cheek, rubbing away the tears streaming down the usually stoic face. When he came to Sedna, he lifted her off the ground and held her up like a doll a child might have held.

"You have brought us many blessings with your coming to Brattalid. If my brother ever mistreats you, he has me to answer to." He hugged her close and set her back down next to Rolv.

ᏋᏁᏋᏁ

After their departure, life in Brattalid calmed down.

The neighbors and family gathered around the burial ground behind the house, up on the meadow overlooking the inlet. Thornhild had prepared the tiny bundle by wrapping it in a soft velvet material the color of the sky.

It fell to Eric as a leader to lay the babe in the open grave. He knelt and put the bundle down gently, adding his gold and jewel-encrusted cup he drank from each day. It was one of his prized possessions, a cup he had considered his talisman and brought from Norway.

When he stood back, Sedna came and knelt. She scattered her cut hair over the blanket and had carved some small weapons and animals to accompany him on his journey. When it was Rolv's turn, Sedna gasped and wanted to stay his hand, but it was his decision. He placed his sword, Gramr, at the side of the babe.

One by one, those who wished, put a special possession inside the grave. Thornhild had woven a tiny blanket so delicate it seemed to float as she folded it and placed it on top of everything when they had finished with their gifts.

Sedna felt the sympathy, the sorrow, shared among

them and knew she and Rolv were not alone in their grief. This was her family, this was her place to be.

∽∾∽

During the ensuing days, Rolv and Sedna took long walks together. The pups romped through the dying grassland, following their staid, dignified wolf-mother.

"The pups remind me of your brothers." She laughed. "So big and handsome, yet so like children—clumsy and filled with spirit."

"The pups are beautiful, are they not?"

They admired the thick gray coats, the ruff around their necks and the long, black eyes.

"They are like Aku but for the color of their eyes."

"They have Legbiter's dark eyes," she agreed. "Except for the shape. They are not round like his but slanted like the wolf's. They will be the beginning of a new breed for the Northland," she predicted.

She stopped speaking, afraid she would talk about the forbidden subject of starvation and want. She had not mentioned it again since he asked her not to.

Rolv pulled her to him and held her in front of him, facing outward so she could look, his muscular arms surrounding her protectively. They stood on the edge of the bluff, overlooking the bay. The wind swept across the prairie behind them, rippling the grass to a golden splendor, swaying her long dress gracefully, whipping it around his legs. He turned her to face him and looked deep into her eyes.

"Ah, woman-child, do you have any notion of how besotted I am with you? How fearful I was that you were dead at the bottom of that canyon? I feel sorrow that we lost the child, but *you* are my North Star—the most important person in my life and I wish you to always be so."

He cleared his throat as if the next words were hard to say. "If you hate us all now, I would understand. We are rough and loud and not at all like your people. I will take you back if you wish it, although it would tear my heart out."

It was the first time they had talked about the babe since the funeral.

Sedna reached to touch his face. "I can think of no place I would rather be than here at your side, my love. You give me great happiness. I feel sorrow at losing our child but he is blessed to come back and may have a choice. He could be a Viking or one of my people. Is that not a miracle?"

"I had not thought of that. And we will have other children, you will see."

Would they? Aku had not bred again and Sedna wondered if the wolf would have any more litters. Was the wolf's destiny also hers? She shivered, fearing the end of the Raven Woman line.

Rolv pointed to the sky. "Look how the big white birds fly away for the winter."

The sky filled with silent movement, the setting sun reached out and struck fire to their wings and backs as they swept across the heavens.

One could not say if it was a portent of good or bad. The old shaman in Sedna's village would have known for certain, but since her fall, she had lost confidence in her ability to see the future. Everyone here became impatient when she quietly counseled them to lay away for a harsh winter. Even Rolv lost his wondrous patience when she spoke of it.

Perhaps she was wrong. For all their sakes, she hoped so.

❧❧❧

The first disaster struck at the time of the earliest winter storms, bringing the heavy rains that preceded snow. The roofs of the barn and outbuildings collapsed one night and, when the residents awoke, they were shocked at the devastation.

"This is a dire misfortune," Eric proclaimed at the morning table. "We have examined the damage and it is formidable. All the winter fodder for the animals will be ruined. Unless we see sunny days sufficient to dry it out, it will mold and not even serve as straw for the floor of the outbuildings."

"The animals cannot eat it, then?" Sedna whispered to Rolv.

"No, they would not try to eat it unless they were starving and then it would bloat and kill them."

A week later a pack of wolves broke into the sheep pen, slaughtered at least half of the herd, wounding and scattering the others out into the drifted snow. By the time they found them, most had frozen in the cold night, standing like carved ice statues.

In the meantime, the men gathered in the long hall during the short days and long nights while Sedna continued to show them how to make the ivory swivels on the ends of harpoons and the bear weapon.

She carefully wrapped the light sinew around the sharp piece of metal, which was bent in half at the middle and could spring open if not tied in place.

This one was even better than the ivory double-edged knife her people used, for her people had no metal. She molded seal fat around the entire package and froze it outdoors.

"Lay this outside where you think the bear will come and when he swallows it down, as bears do, it will spring open inside his gut when it thaws. He will bleed to death. We track him by the blood then. Keep the killing bait away from your dogs," she warned. "It will do the same to them."

"Can we also use this for wolves?" Torvald wanted to know.

"Sometimes, we use it for wolves. But you must promise me, no matter how hungry we get, we must not partake of wolf flesh, else we will surely all be doomed."

She received no sense of satisfaction that now they listened to her with great respect, for all of her predictions gradually came true.

The intense cold without snow caused the cod and the other fish to migrate. No matter how many hours they spent in the frigid air, trying to net or hook a fish in the bay, they never saw the silver flash of one. The pack ice drifted into the mouth of the fjord, closer than it had ever come in previous winters.

Wolverines dug up the fish and birds they had buried in shallow pits behind the house and, what they didn't eat or carry off, they urinated on. It completely ruined their reserve, making it barely fit for animal food.

As winter deepened, Eric posted guards at night around the buildings, but they couldn't be everywhere at once. One night they awoke to the barking, growling, and howling of Aku and the dogs, along with the shouting of men.

They all rushed outside, to see a giant grizzly. Sedna stood next to Rolv and watched the creature rear on its hind legs, challenging them, while the dogs leapt in to attack.

"Legbiter! Away!" Eric called out. For once the dog did not obey his master but darted in toward the huge bear's legs.

"By Odin's breath, that is the biggest bear I've ever seen," Rolv said.

"I, too, have never seen one this size. He must have

journeyed from far away, drawn by the smell of the animals."

Thornhild and the women huddled together, freezing in the cold but not wanting to leave. "Should he be denned up in a cave somewhere?"

"Yes, this is their time to go to the bear caves, but sometimes there are bears who do not go by their instincts. These have no fear and are the most dangerous of all beasts." Sedna held to Rolv's arm, knowing he wanted to run forward to stop the dogs from challenging the beast.

"The lances and harpoon! Get the bows! We will slay him," Torstein shouted, his high pitched voice filled with excitement without a trace of fear.

"No! You will need his fur. Throw him a bear bait," Sedna answered.

"The dogs are in the way. It would never reach him or one of them might make off with it," Eric said.

At his bidding, several men ran back into the house and brought out weapons, handing them around. Eric selected his broad sword and hefted it in the air.

"Come, men. We will see how brave the creature is."

"Wait!" Rolv stepped forward. "Sedna reminded us, we need his pelt undamaged. We need his body for meat. Let us try the people's way first. If he does not take the bait, then it is time to put him to the lances." Rolv picked the bait out of the pack he carried and carefully threw it at the bear.

Sedna closed her eyes, creating a magic circle around the bear, one that he could not leave and the dogs could not enter.

Brother Bear—in this time of ice and snow—
why are you not sleeping?
We must slay you now. We have need of

your coat and flesh.
Take no offense at mere men
daring to touch you.
What we do is with great admiration
for your powerful spirit.
When you return to another life,
you must tell your brothers and sisters
we treated you with respect.

She opened her eyes to the sound of a dog's squeal of pain as the bear lashed out. His curved black claws were as long as a child's forearm, his teeth gnashed and terrible growls and roars issued from his mouth. The men stood back, lances at the ready, waiting for the giant to consume the packet that Rolv had thrown at his feet. It was clear the men hesitated to mar the pelt by slicing up the bear.

For a long moment time stood still. Sedna held her breath, her will sustaining the magic circle to keep the bear inside.

The bear, with gestures jerky and nervous, at last gave one loud roar that shook the snow off the edges of the outbuildings. He scooped up the bait and swallowed it, turned, and ran off up the slope toward the meadow and freedom.

The men started to rush after him.

"No!" Sedna held up her hand. "Let him have a lead, but press on behind him so he never has time to stop. Soon there will be a blood trail to follow. When you have slain him, remove his head and bury it under rocks and tell him that you thank him."

The men nodded. Sedna's eyes met Rolv's and she knew he would see to it.

☙❧❧

While the men tracked the bear, Sedna, with Aku at her side, wandered out on the ice. Farther and farther, she roamed over the frozen fjord in the direction of the glacier that both beckoned and repelled her more and more with the passing time.

On the ice, so far from Brattalid that she could no longer see the towering pile of stones on top of the cliff above Ericksfjord, she stopped to look around. She had no need of her sun goggles, carved of ivory, narrow slits for eyes, fastened with sinew around her head. The day was as dismal as those preceding, for no sun had appeared for a long time nor would, until the end of winter. Only a faint light from the sky reflected on the pristine white snow made it possible to see.

Sedna turned to look in another direction, feeling a presence. A small line of black dots appeared on the horizon. For a moment she tightened her fist on the lance she carried and then relaxed her mittened fingers, as she recognized her people.

She plodded toward them. They stopped. She felt the accumulation of their black eyes looking in her direction. They waited for her to come to them. Joyous to see them, Sedna ran forward, forgetting the dignity that befitted a woman with a husband.

"Analusha! Nagatok!" She named all of the others, one by one, to respectfully show her memory of them.

They touched mittened hands, each one in a quiet gesture of recollection. How different her people seemed to her now. If this had been a crowd of rowdy, boisterous Norsemen who suddenly came upon kin, there would have been back-slapping, shouts of glee, and what she had come to know as profane words meant as endearments.

She loved her new people, but sometimes missed the old, calm ways.

"You are at peace with the white giants." It was not a question so much as a statement from Nagatok.

"I miss my mother and father. I miss the old ways, sometimes, but I have found harmony with my new family."

"In a vision, I have seen you acquire much respect and strength from your husband and his family," Analusha commented. "Also much sorrow has come into your life. Even though you warned the giants, they did not heed." The Inuit owned no words for love or the promise of continued devotion that Rolv had given her. She understood the shaman came as close to the idea as he was able.

Sedna was grateful for his dreams and visions and that she did not have to explain. "My mother and father, they are well?"

"Your father hunted one season after you left. He was as brave as any man in our village, young or old. He lost the kayak sickness, but the pain has settled in his leg so he cannot move it much. He can no longer hunt, but we provide. Nagatok took a mate and his wife has a big belly," the shaman said.

Nagatok beamed back at her, his eyes narrow slits in his dark face, his middle teeth missing. She wondered how she could ever have thought him handsome.

"I am happy for you," she told him.

Analusha closed his eyes and spoke in the deep sepulchral voice of the shaman. "You have gained a family and lost a son. Your new people angered the animal spirits by caging their brothers and sisters and sending them far away for the entertainment of strangers. They refused to lay away provisions as you counseled, therefore you hunger. Your men search in vain for game that has moved past this place, beyond our village, and toward the land of the trees."

She, who had always been in awe of this shaman, was

deeply moved by his visions, for each of them was correct.

He held out a sealskin sack, which she knew contained frozen fish. The other men laid down harpoons, carved sun goggles, a bear bait weapon, and a pile of sinew.

She knew she was not to touch the weapons in their presence. "Sedna is grateful," she said, uncertain how to express her feelings. It was so easy in her new world, everyone hugged and kissed and shouted at each other.

The shaman held up his hand. Sedna closed her eyes, nodding acknowledgment. When she opened them, the snow was swept clear of their presence even as the wind had swept away their footprints.

She gathered up the treasures and made her way home across the ice.

By the time she reached the bottom of the fjord, the men from Brattalid had formed a hunting party to come looking for her. She saw them approach. The women in a huddled group stood at the edge of the ice bank above the fjord.

"By Thor's great beard, we worried about you, lass." Rolv ran the last few feet between them and, picking her up, swung her around and around. She heard the women clapping and laughing from the bank and the men crowded in to see what she brought.

"Do not leave alone, Sedna." It was the first time Eric spoke her name. "Even if you are shaman and at home in this land more than we, it is dangerous. You carry only the knife in your belt and a lance. You would be no match for a bear or a pack of wolves. You might fall into an ice crack and we could walk by without knowing where you were. You are of our family now, and we do not wish to lose you."

Eric put his giant hand on her shoulder and squeezed. She felt his powerful fingers clear through the layers of her coat. She looked up into his face, unafraid of meeting his eyes, for she knew his secret. He was a human being, not a god.

"I promise to stay close by her side," Rolv said, bending to kiss her cheek.

It still felt strange to have Rolv declare his feelings for her so openly, but over their time in Brattalid, she had learned to cherish his honest affection.

"I met my people. They gave us food and more weapons."

Eric looked at Rolv. "What if they had taken her away? Have you thought of that?"

She stood between father and son, looking up into their earnest faces, unwilling to intrude.

Rolv shook his head and she recognized the stubborn set to his shoulders. "She is a woman in her own right. I cannot and will not command her to obey me."

"What if her people took her against her will?"

Sedna pushed gently against both their chests and stepped away to give herself breathing space. "The people understand this is where I have chosen to live. They have no wish to intrude, only to help when we need help."

"How did they know we needed help?" This from Thornhild who stepped away from the group of women and walked toward the men.

"The shaman, Analusha, has dreams more powerful than mine. He knew everything that has happened," she said simply.

As they walked homeward, Sedna felt surrounded by love. In spite of their adversity, Eric's family joked and laughed and teased each other.

Rolv and Sedna fell back a little, separate.

"I have something to tell you. I don't know how to start," he said.

"Did you slay the bear?" she asked.

"Yes, just as you said it would happen. But I've heard the others talking. They have not said anything to you about it yet, but they regret not listening to you when you warned them about this time of cold. We have never seen the like since we came here. I am certain they—we—will believe you next time."

Sedna smiled, hoping there would be no next time. Often extreme cold years fell upon the land, but those were usually separated by many other years.

"There is something else I must tell you. I begin to understand how it is you place in little regard the gathering of possessions—wealth, as we call it. It isn't important, is it? What has always been truly important is honor, truth, family. This is something any Viking should know."

She stopped him from walking by putting her hand on his arm and turning him to face her. He stood, tall as a tree, and her heart swelled inside her breast until she thought it would burst like the tiny bird hearts.

"Yes. When a man seeks possessions, more than he can use, it changes him. I am pleased you have understood, husband."

He lifted her up by her elbows, her booted feet dangling in the air. "I love you, my North Star. You are free to go where you will, but promise that you will not go without me again."

If it made him feel happy, it was a promise she could easily give.

For now. Sooner or later her destiny lay with the glacier. She knew that when the time came, she would have to go alone, for she might not return.

CHAPTER 19

In the deepest winter, Sedna wondered when the old, the infirm, and the youngest children would be put out to die to save the rest of the clan, but it never happened. She learned a valuable lesson from the Vikings—in that, either all perished or none, but they did not detach themselves from their families. They saved most of the best and fattest foods for the children and old people. Thankfully they had a huge pile of driftwood and cut trees for the fireplace. They had long since stopped using the seal oil lamps that Sedna had taught them to use and instead poured the fat on boiled vegetation they had gathered and dried in the summer. To get the children to eat more, the women poured the seal oil on clean snow, stirred a little honey in, and offered it to them as a treat.

During the long nights, Rolv recounted sagas or poems to pass the time. Several of the young people sang songs. The oldest man in Greenland told many tales about going a-viking from Norway and capturing entire cities in the name of their king. Torvald and Torstein's amazingly clear, mellow voices lifted nightly in song. Everyone loved to listen to them sing.

Thornhild sat at her loom, constantly working, The need for clothing was never ending. They had salvaged the wool from the sheep that had frozen to death when the wolves tore into the shed.

Sedna, part of all the winter life, felt she had truly come home. Though these people had empty bellies, they refused to grow morose and introspective as her clan tended to do in hard times. And still no old people or babies were put out on the ice.

ᑫᑐᑫᑐ

One morning Sedna awoke cradled in Rolv's arms and shook him, pushing back that unruly shock of thick hair that swept across his forehead.

He still remained beardless as a favor to her, a gift he knew she treasured and the others had finally learned to accept.

"Husband, I must visit the people on the ice again. Will you accompany me?" She did not refer to them as "my people" any longer, which she knew brought pleasure to his heart. He kissed her tenderly and touched his hand gently to her now flat stomach. He groaned as she in turn caressed him in places where she had learned it pleased him.

They made love, lingering and long, and, when it was finished, he held her close in his arms and they slept again.

"Sometimes the strength of my love for you terrifies me," he whispered in her ear when they awoke. "I have looked death in the face many times without a trace of fear, yet I open my eyes each morning with the fear of losing you, now that the specter of starvation is among us."

"Do not think such thoughts. I will be with you always. Am I not your North Star?"

"Aye. But I regret we did not listen to you when you

warned us not to trade off all our meat." He nuzzled his chin into the side of her neck, tickling her.

"I was a stranger to your people then. How could a stranger expect to be believed? It is no one's fault."

"They will certainly believe you now."

She hoped it wasn't too late. The adults were strong. They would make it through to spring, but perhaps many of the children and old ones would not.

When they dressed and went out into the hall, everyone sat inside working at chores or playing chess or games.

No one wanted to brave the icy wind. Without the comfort of soft snow, the winter dragged on with inexorable harshness, the temperatures staying low in unremitting monotony.

No children played outside with their skates and sleds. They had to bring in the dogs. Aku preferred to stay outdoors, in the shelter made for her just outside the window where she could hear human voices.

They approached Eric who sat in his usual big chair in the front of the long room.

"Father, Sedna wishes to visit her tribesmen. I do not understand how she knows when they will appear, but she always does."

"Daughter," Eric said, beckoning her to come closer.

It never failed to thrill Sedna that the great chieftain gave her the name so beloved and coveted by Freyda. "Yes?"

She couldn't bring herself to call him father and perhaps never would.

"I want you to give the trolls two of the pups, a male and a female. That leaves us with one female. But your people have been generous with us. I have no desire to continue accepting gifts without giving something in return."

Even though Legbiter and Aku never mated again, the descendants of that first litter continued to look just like them.

"That is generous," Sedna said. "I know what importance you set by the pups, training them as you have for pulling the sleds. I will explain their purpose to the shaman. They will prove a great help to the people."

Sedna and Rolv set off for the ice as soon as they partook of weak boiled tea and a small piece of what remained of the fish the tribe had given Sedna. Eric and the men took a different direction. They left at the first pale streak of light, which they had been doing each morning to hunt beyond the meadows. After weeks of hunting from daybreak to day's end, they had brought home nothing more than an occasional rabbit or fox.

Rolv deliberately slowed his long stride to match hers. "It does not set well with us that we must accept provisioning from strangers."

"I know. You are proud, but the people do not wish us to starve. There may be a time when you can provide for them."

"Will I see them too?" Rolv asked. "Sometimes I think they might be part of your strong imagination or magic, except for the fish and weapons they leave with you. None of us have seen any of the people."

"That is because when you first landed you captured men and took them away in ships. They will not forgive this or forget it unless you brought the men home again."

"We cannot do that. I have been told the king has given them every comfort they could wish for."

"Except their freedom." She doubted the men were still alive, so long away from their families and the land they understood. "You may see them, but you must stay back. They do not wish to speak with you." The Raven Mother gave her the sense that the two peoples must be kept separated or war would damage both sides. A bridge had to be made first, between the two cultures. The new Raven Woman would serve as that bridge.

"I understand. The Norsemen have no desire for contact with the little men either."

They walked for a long time. Finally Rolv stopped, taking hold of her shoulder. "How do you know they will appear? Perhaps we should save our strength for hunting."

She shook her head. "I conjured Analusha last night. He will answer."

Rolv frowned. His smoky eyes, sharp and assessing, regarded her. "Your magic makes me uneasy sometimes. You are not my soft little woman when you become a shaman."

"But that is who I am. You knew that when you captured me."

"Who captured who?" Rolv teased.

They smiled at each other, remembering.

Suddenly a line of tiny black dots appeared on the sheer white of the horizon. They walked a little closer.

"I must go. Wait here for me."

"Yes. Be careful." He held her chin to give her a gentle kiss that deepened until they were both breathless. Then he settled down on a fur they had brought on their sled.

She moved forward slowly, with deliberation, Aku at her side. Her energy slowly waned as did that of the others in the Viking compound. A steady diet of boiled tea, dried greens, and fish were not enough to sustain them for long. Sooner or later the Vikings would begin thinking about eating the horses and then the dogs. She shuddered.

The animal's souls would be endlessly offended since they trusted the community to care for them. Long ago, when the dogs might have been wolves like Aku, they surrendered the ability to take care of themselves in exchange for mutual affection. If they were forced to eat their dogs, with this dreadful offense on their hands, the Norse might never regain the animal's trust so that game returned to the land.

When Sedna reached the men, she touched mittens in greeting with each one and they sat on the hard packed snow. They gave her a piece of musk-ox jerky which she broke in half and, eating her share, put the other away for Rolv. She handed Analusha the bag with the wriggling pups. When they tumbled out, Aku disdained looking at them. She was finished with mothering.

The men picked up the puppies, holding them out for inspection. She knew they were pleased, especially when she told them how strong they would be when grown and explained that the Vikings used them to pull sleds. She showed them how to tether them with sinew and already the pups stopped playing and stood patiently waiting to be sent off with the sled.

She could see the people were impressed.

"Thank you for the gift. You come seeking. You come to ask a favor that troubles you. Speak, daughter," Analusha commanded.

"We are starving. Soon winter will be finished, but not soon enough to help us. I wish you to tell me where *nunavit*, the water of magic lies, so that we too may partake of the animals there."

Analusha leapt to his feet, while the others inhaled shocked breaths. "You speak like someone with kayak sickness," he exploded. "You know we may not reveal that secret to outsiders, lest the animals become disgusted and leave forever. Then *we* will starve."

Sedna rose to her feet and stood facing him, no longer fearing his power, sure of her own. "We are not separate any longer. The Norsemen and the people are bound together by the new Raven Woman who grows in my belly." She had not realized the truth of this until this moment when something put words into her mouth.

The old shaman came closer and reached out toward her. She pulled aside her furs and let him put his bird claw of a hand against her stomach.

He cocked his head sideways, listening. She felt intense heat from his hand. His narrow black eyes, his front teeth sharpened to short fangs, his headdress of wolf fur, all made him intimidating beyond anything she had remembered. Even the formidable Eric paled beside this ferocious magic man.

Before Sedna met her beloved and learned the power of true love, before she suffered the loss of a child, and had learned to live among the Vikings, she would have been devastated by the savage power emanating from the shaman. She would have fallen down prone before him in a faint of pure terror.

Now she pulled her furs back in place and whipped off the Raven Belt to hold in front of their astonished faces.

"I believe in your powers, old man. I do not dispute your prowess as a shaman and your experience, which I lack. But I too am shaman, come into my own right. "

Analusha looked at her wide-eyed, in awe of her boldness. His dark stare told her she was right, that he accepted that.

"We must survive the winter, and we can only survive if you guide me to the secret place. I promise to make a strong charm that will prevent anyone with me from ever remembering."

She sat down again, folding her arms across her chest and nodding her head once sharply in a sign that she had finished speaking.

All the men began talking at once, so astounded were

they at her speech and her dangerous challenge of Analusha's control.

"Silence!" His voice rang out harshly, knocking against their jumbled words like rocks thrown against a cliff of nesting birds. Their voices scattered with shock momentarily and then stilled to hushed quiet.

"The people's blood will join with the Norsemen from the time of your daughter's birth to the death of the last of all of us then," Analusha said softly. "I see it happening." He had that far-away look that said he was gone from their presence.

Everyone waited for him to return.

When at last he shifted positions and gave a great shuddering sigh, Sedna spoke again. "Did you see the new Raven Woman who comes after me?"

He stared at her, a look so unsettling, she wanted to call out for Rolv to come to her. "I have seen this one who you will bring forth and she will be strong and wise beyond her years."

Sedna was so relieved that he understood, she could venture nothing else to say.

"I have said your new people are wasteful and careless with that which has been put in our care. They waste meat, they barter food and pelts away for useless possessions, which now you cannot eat. They cut trees for houses rather than live underground as we, so that they have no wood to burn for fuel to keep warm."

Sedna listened in silence, knowing he spoke the truth as he had told her before when they met.

"We were here first," he said when she didn't answer. "On this side of the water. You were but a child, do you not remember?"

"I remember. When we saw the giants and their huge boats, we left our homes behind and moved across the ice, away from them."

Analusha gestured with a sweep of his arm. "As far as we could see across the water where you now live with these pale skinned people, trees covered the land. Now it is barren. The wind sweeps away the soil until not even the wild grass grows. That is why they have to journey farther and farther to find the reindeer and muskox."

Sedna knew the Vikings cleared the land to put green plants in the ground to feed their animals and used trees to burn in their fireplaces and to build with. What answer could she give? Could they have lived any other way? She looked down at her boots, saying nothing.

"Now they are faced with starvation, possibly for offending the animals or the trees or the grass they disturbed with their ugly houses of stone."

His meaning was clear. Her people had lived on the ice from the beginning of time without disturbing anything. These giants used up everything in their path. She searched for words to justify their behavior.

"It may be because they are so big. They are strangers to our land, but they will learn. I am teaching them."

"If you wish to live with them, if you wish your children and your children's children to live here and across the ice with us, it is your duty to teach them how to live on this land properly. If you do not, the Raven line will surely die."

His words began to sing in her heart and she knew that he spoke the truth.

"Sit and we will journey to Brother Moon. He is up there, even if we cannot see him. After that, I will tell you how to find the secret place. You may take your new people there to save them, load up your sleds, but they can never remember how to return to it." He sat down, crossing his legs at the ankles, and began to beat softly on the drum he had removed from his pack.

Sedna obeyed, sitting in front of him, facing the line of

hunters. She hoped Rolv would stay where he was, otherwise it would go badly for her and for the Norse villagers. They would surely starve if the shaman left here, outraged at an unwanted presence.

Everyone closed their eyes, Sedna closed hers and surrendered herself to the magic, trusting Analusha as never before.

She felt herself lifting off the ice, holding on to his outstretched hand, swept through the sky—up—up—until she mixed with the wispy white clouds. At first, she felt an intense cold wrap around her body, which soon turned to numbness and the pain disappeared, leaving behind a soft sense of movement and empty space.

Suddenly Analusha left her and Sedna was alone. She felt a sharp stab of panic that was replaced just as quickly by a soothing pleasure. It was so peaceful here, floating along above the clouds.

Sedna opened her eyes and looked down on Brattalid, but it was not as she knew it. She sensed it was far into the future. Very little had changed on the landscape except the people dressed differently and there were many more buildings. Soaring closer, she could see the people were not well. The workers looked frail and thin. There was an air of decay about the place.

She saw a large building out back in the meadow with a cross in the front and men with long red robes attending people in the graveyard. There were many graves. She saw the rocks surrounding them, in the shape of boats.

Tears fell from her eyes as she watched helplessly. One by one the men, women, and children died.

Then she saw a mother take her child wrapped in many blankets and set out alone, across the ice. The woman had a feathered headband and, even without seeing the belt around her waist, Sedna knew she was watching a future Raven Woman.

Sedna soared above, wishing she could help her, but they did not abide in the same place or time. The woman moved painfully, slowly, but with purpose and what remaining strength she must have possessed.

Finally, the woman stopped, her legs no longer holding her up, and she sat, waiting.

Time passed. The woman's head tilted back, her eyes closed, her tormented expression changed to peaceful resignation. She held the child with stiffened arms.

Over the rise, Sedna watched the approach of men along with dogs looking like Aku, pulling a sled. Small, dark men of the people. They came slowly, as if mistrusting what they saw. When they arrived at the woman's side, they stood for a long time, staring, until the child started a muffled bleating from within the blanket.

One of the men walked forward, unafraid. From the look of his attire he was a shaman, the only one daring to act so boldly.

He touched the woman. Sedna could feel the cold of her skin through his fingers. Her spirit had gone. In her hands, she held the Raven Belt.

The shaman gently unfolded her arms and disentangled the baby. He turned to the others and held the child toward them, asking what he should do.

Should he leave it by the mother, to die peacefully with the cold surrounding them?

One of the men eased up, gently removed the headband from the woman, and put it in the blanket with the baby, then he took the belt from her stiffened fingers and put it inside the blanket, too.

Sedna had looked into the bittersweet future and knew a Raven Woman would live on, mixing again with Inuit blood. One day would be the finish of the Vikings on this land but the people would continue, for they would always be a part of the ice, the snow, and the land.

Above the scene, Sedna soared toward the glacier, un-afraid now. She would live to watch over a Raven Woman, and so it would go until the last one. When she returned to Rolv, they would journey home together, just the two of them and the child she carried. She knew they would be for each other from this day forward. Always there, like the North Star.

THE END

GLOSSARY OF INUIT AND
NORSE WORDS OR PHRASES

Aaliq, aaluq: Inuit for seal's blow, a hole in the ice.

Aaxlu: Inuit for killer whale

Althing: Norse for judgment assembly or jury

Amawk: Inuit for the wolf.

Angokok: Inuit for shaman

Ayvuq: Inuit for walrus.

Baleen: Inuit/English for the springy material from a whale's mouth.

Bibrau: "Maiden who sits in the blue," the Norse equivalent to Inuit Sednah

Brattalid: Norse, Eric the Red's home in Greenland

Ericksfjord: Norse, water entrance to land on Greenland where Eric the Red made his home

Iglu, Igloo: Inuit for snow house.

Ikikak: Inuit for magical Raven feather

Ikirrak: Inuit for the drying racks for game

Ilitkosiq: Inuit for the "ordinary dead," those who haven't come back to haunt the living.

Inua: Inuit for the spirit or soul residing in all of nature

Inuit: Inuit for the Men, or People, as they called themselves. Eskimo.

Itiqiktoq: Inuit term applied to Indians because of their more aggressive nature.

Ituk: Inuit for an old man, past his prime

Kablunaet: Norse for a stranger

Karigi: Inuit meeting place for villagers

Kayak: Inuit/English for a one-person skin-covered boat.

Kilivaciaq: Inuit for the wooly mammoth.

Knarr: Norse for a trading ship or merchant vessel

Kunik: Inuit for an Eskimo kiss, rubbing noses

Kvad: Norse for an epic poem

Lanskibe: Norse for warship

Makaraaq: Inuit for fighting, dissension, trouble making.

Mukluks: Inuit for fur snow boots

Naanuk: Inuit for polar bear.

Napaktuk: Inuit for trees

Nordsetur: Norse for Elismere Island, the place where Rolv was banished

Nunavit: Inuit for the place where a body of water never freezes, due to currents. Fish and game are plentiful.

Rune Stone: Norse/English for the ancient stones the Norse carved poems and epic words on

Sastrugi: Inuit for the tall ice structures formed by the wind

Sednah: Inuit for goddess of the sea, provider of food from the water.

Sermisiraq: Inuit for glaciers—a place to avoid because of evil spirits

Shaman: Inuit for male or female wizard who serves as buffer between the people and the supernatural.

Siksik: Inuit for ground squirrel.

Sisuaq: Inuit for whale

Skalde: Norse for the high priestess who goes to war with warriors and sings and recites poems to lift spirits

Skaldes: Norse for old songs and stories

Thrall: Norse for a captive used as a slave

Tulugaak: Inuit for the raven—believed by aboriginal people to have created the Earth.

Tulunixiraq: Inuit for someone who can change forms from a person to a raven and back again. In this book the name refers to the Raven Mother, living around 2,000 BC

Tunarak: Inuit for the shaman's helping power—usually, an animal, but sometimes ancestral spirits

Tununirn: Inuit for the country beyond the back of something—probably where the *Wiivaskaat* stay

Ulu: Inuit for a woman's curved, circular shaped knife, usually of bone or slate

Umiak: Inuit for a large skin-covered boat used in hunting or for journeys

Ukpic: Inuit for tree, another name for a tree

Wiivaisaat: Inuit for those who come around again, or strangers in the sky (dead people)

Wittiki: Inuit for crazy acting, sometimes from "kayak sickness"

About the Author

Born in Phoenix, Arizona, Pinkie Paranya traveled all over the US, Alaska, and most of Mexico with her late husband. Ever since she can remember, writing has been her passion. After completing her fifteenth novel, trying to discover the genre she loved most, she still hasn't decided.

Paranya enjoys romances with their intrigue and uplifting happy endings, but she has also published two paranormal psychological suspenses, a cozy mystery, and an Early American Alaskan trilogy. To date, she has fourteen published novels.

Visit her website, www.pinkieparanya.com.

63802032R00171

Made in the USA
Charleston, SC
13 November 2016